HER BEST FRIEND'S HUSBAND

ALISON IRVING

First published in 2024 by Bloodhound Books.

www.bloodhoundbooks.com

Print ISBN: 978-1-917214-19-3

For Andy

CHAPTER ONE

We buried my friend Laura's husband today.

It had been a terrible shock when she had found James lying collapsed on the floor following a bike ride. By the time the ambulance had arrived, he was gone.

It was beyond me how Laura had managed to meet and greet all the mourners at the church door before the service. Tall and willowy, she had been dry-eyed and composed in her black dress, while their son Robbie had shaken hands with everyone, his eyes red rimmed, his face ashen. He was tall and handsome, the image of his father.

I sobbed like a baby as the coffin was lowered into the ground, the rain falling like lead on the gathered crowd, dripping from the floral wreaths onto the sodden grass.

It was bewildering that I had cried so much, as I had disliked James immensely. I had found him overbearing, full of his own self-importance and he had a vile tendency to treat Laura as though he was better than her. It was futile to imagine what happened behind their front door, but it was clear he had an inflated opinion of himself, and I'm sure he wasn't always the easiest to live with.

After the committal, my husband Will had driven us to the hotel where I'd hosted my recent fiftieth birthday party. James's obnoxious father was, for once, subdued, disbelieving that his fit and healthy son's heart had simply stopped. His mother was shell-shocked, surrounded by her family, while two badly behaved children – James's niece and nephew – ran unchallenged around the room.

The air in the function room was heavy and oppressive. Heartbroken faces and dark funeral clothes, the smell of lilies pervasive. Restrained voices broken by a brash laugh, hastily muffled.

We ate the finger buffet and drank our weak tea, the eight of us sombre for a change. One of our own had died, and my friends and their husbands felt it keenly. I surveyed the function room, bare today of banners and balloons, and spotted Laura engrossed in conversation with a strikingly attractive man with silver hair and little round glasses. They were so comfortable in each other's company, I presumed he was a work colleague. I went over to speak to her and the good-looking man politely made his excuses before leaving. Her eyes drifted after him as he threaded his way through the emptying tables.

'How are you holding up?' I asked her solicitously.

'I'm fine, glad today is nearly over, Claire.' She smiled tiredly at me, brushing her red hair out of her eyes. 'Thank you for coming.'

'If you need anything at all, let me know. Casseroles. Soup. Lasagne.' I offered it perfunctorily, at a loss what else to say to a new widow.

Her face broke into a grin, no longer tired but teasing. 'I'd much rather have Book Club and several glasses of Pinot Gris if you don't mind.'

Reassured she was the same Laura, I grinned back. 'Happy to oblige. Name the date and I'll say to the girls.'

She hugged me tight, turning to say goodbye to some other mourners, so I made my way back to our table, taking a seat beside Will. He had loosened his black tie, hung his jacket haphazardly over the back of the chair and was scrolling through his phone. I cringed inwardly at how dishevelled he was, and gazed around the table where our group sat quietly chatting.

These were my friends, the girls I was closest to, the ones I could tell anything to without judgement. We had no secrets.

Except, I was sleeping with one of their husbands.

I did feel some degree of shame about it, occasionally questioning how I had found myself in this position. Superficially, I had been flattered by the attention of an attractive man who showed a bewildering interest in me when at my most vulnerable. Circumstance had presented itself, I had grabbed it with both hands and now almost a year had passed with my reprehensible secret intact.

Most surprisingly, I had a happy marriage to a man who adored me and two adult daughters who were my pride and joy. Irrefutably I loved Will, for he was a beacon of goodness, generosity and kindness. Privately I conceded he could sometimes be overly serious and straightlaced. Nevertheless he earned good money and lavished it on me, Eva and Poppy. So why would I do what I was doing? For myriad reasons, convoluted and complex.

I glanced towards my part-time lover, Mr Ford, sitting beside his wife, arm slung casually over her shoulders, and my heart missed a beat as I caught his eye. Try as I might to remain uninvolved, from time to time my resolve faltered. It was bound to, when after a lifetime of craving something, it was then offered on a plate. Cocking one eyebrow, he directed an intimate smile at me.

Unwittingly my husband tapped on his phone beside me as the rest of us turned to face Laura, who had reached our table.

'How are you?' asked Matt, Annie's husband. Unlike Will, he was still wearing his jacket and was as neat as a pin, brown hair tidily brushed back from his face, no sign of even one grey hair.

'I'm all right,' she replied, taking a vacant seat beside me. 'Poor Robbie has found it hard, having to talk to everyone and putting a brave face on it all.' She was all eyes and freckles and worry lines.

'What about you?' asked Vicky, a concerned expression on her face. She had pulled her long, brunette hair back into a neat bun today, accentuating her razor-sharp cheekbones. She should be gracing the cover of a magazine, not burying a friend. Her husband Tom gave Laura a sad smile.

'Oh, I'm fine thanks. It will be strange to be in the house on my own now. I've told Robbie it's imperative he goes back to his life in the city. He shouldn't think he needs to move back to the village to keep me company.' Irritation niggled at Laura's constant references to her son, however I gave her some leeway. After all, her husband had just been lowered into the earth.

'We're right beside you, so please let us know if you need anything at all,' commented Kate. Her husband David squeezed Laura's hand in a show of solidarity.

'We hope to have Book Club soon,' I interjected. 'At Laura's request,' I briskly clarified as Will gaped at me in shock. Did he think I was crass enough to mention it otherwise?

'As long as you're sure, Laura.' Annie smiled pensively at her.

I knew they meant well, but in reality none of us had been especially fond of James. Everyone had long faces and forlorn eyes as though he had been universally adored. Of course I remained silent and struggled not to roll my eyes at the melancholy expressions.

We were interrupted as a tall, weather-beaten man in an ill-fitting black suit came over to our table.

'Laura, Uncle Leo is about to leave, you need to come and say goodbye.' He said it kindly, face creased with worry.

'I'll come over now, Dad.' She smiled wearily at him as she rose, again thanked us all for coming and we hurriedly arranged Book Club for the following weekend.

At last we could make our excuses to leave and we gathered up our belongings. As a group we exited the function room and Will held open the door as we traipsed towards the porch. Incessantly the rain fell, the car park now a mass of puddles, a thick blanket of grey clouds overhead. Our white Land Rover Discovery was parked in a far corner and my husband, ever the gentleman, offered to get the car so I wouldn't get my sleek, blonde bob wet.

Huddled in the shelter of the hotel doorway, a hand fleetingly caressed the curve of my butt as our friends said goodbye. I leant forward for a farewell hug, lightly pressing against Ford's chest as I chastely gave him and everyone else a kiss on the cheek. His wife smiled and said she'd see me soon. Dispassionately I studied them as they walked together to their car, and I absentmindedly speculated how she would react if she knew her husband had strayed. Not only strayed, but with one of her best friends. Earnestly, he had disclosed their marriage was basically over, they were now nothing more than platonic friends. Anyone would think he was credible. If they didn't know better. Undoubtedly he took me for a fool.

Will and I dissected the day on the short drive home. We had informed Eva and Poppy they shouldn't feel obliged to attend the funeral, and, with obvious relief, they hadn't. To compensate for their absence, we had spent a small fortune on an ostentatious wreath of white lilies, pink roses and gyp, which now lay beside the grave and before long would be shrivelled and drooping.

My thoughts wandered as we drove through Castlebrook village, onto the ever narrowing country lanes, which climbed above the valley into the Antrim Hills. The girls had remained in Belfast at their uni digs, so it would only be the two of us at home. I missed them, although they drove me crazy with their untidiness and ability to change outfits three times a day. Mostly I missed the sheer, undiluted joy of them both and their uncanny ability to lift my mood with their nonsense chatter.

By the time we reached our white bungalow with its vast windows situated a few miles outside the village, the rain had eased. Unasked, Will jumped out of the car, unlocked the front door, then returned to hold an umbrella over me, to protect me from the rain as we dashed indoors. We hung our black coats in the cloakroom and walked through into the open-plan kitchen.

'Do you want a drink, darling?' he asked, already reaching into the freezer for ice.

'Yes, please. A G&T,' I called over my shoulder, kicking off my high heels and going into the conservatory, my favourite room in the house.

Our bungalow nestled into the side of the hills, high above the valley, with open fields behind and a spectacular view below. From the conservatory we could see all the way to Cave Hill in one direction and a thin sliver of Irish Sea in the other. The red roofed houses of the village huddled together far below, the steeples of the two churches rising out of the low-lying cloud.

I sank onto the long oatmeal sofa, swung my feet onto a leather footstool and accepted the gin with thanks. Will threw his jacket and tie over a stool at the breakfast bar then joined me on the sofa with a beer, nudging his feet onto the footstool beside mine.

'I can't believe James is dead,' he began. He'd said the same thing numerous times since we'd heard the news and it was becoming tedious.

'Well, he is,' I shot back. 'You weren't particularly fond of him when he was alive, so you won't miss him much now he's dead.'

Will's kind face fell as he immediately looked uncomfortable, and a pang of self-reproach twisted my gut. 'I'm sorry, Will. It's been a difficult day,' I said in my most conciliatory tone, knowing it wasn't Will I was aggravated with. I reached over and laid my hand gently on his forearm. Regrettably he took it as an invitation to resume his monologue.

'It's been such a terrible shock. A young, fit man with his whole life ahead of him, and leaving Laura and Robbie on their own. How will she ever cope? He took such good care of her. He told me once that he had to as she's useless with money. Though don't tell her I told you, I'd hate her to think he'd confided in me how much she relied on him.'

I was barely listening as he rambled on, hardly drawing breath. All I had to do was mutter or nod once in a while and he was satisfied.

Meanwhile, I absorbed the view, pondering my choices and what I was going to do about my friend's husband. We'd all been friends for years and for so many of them I'd been content to be a spectator to Ford and his wife, excluded from their party of two. Then by a fortunate stroke of luck, he made me a proposal I was incapable of refusing.

And the opportunity arose to right the wrongs of my past.

CHAPTER TWO

Will's gentle snoring beside me on the sofa distracted me from my contemplation, and I eyed him fondly. From time to time he reminded me of when the girls were toddlers and I had loved them dearly, but mostly when they fell asleep at the end of a gruelling day and I could watch them lying peacefully in their cots. He grunted in his sleep and I tenderly pulled a blanket over him.

He was unaware of my scrutiny and I studied him as his head drooped, shirt untucked, mouth open. Sadly, the years had not been kind to him. His once cute face had slipped into flabby jowls, curly brown hair long gone, replaced with a bald top and wispy greying sides. Only the gentle smile and adoration remained.

He spoke in vague terms of retiring from air traffic control at fifty-five, which alarmed me as he was already fifty-two. Aside from playing golf and watching his favourite football team, he had no hobbies. Apart from spending time with me.

It was vaguely terrifying he relied so much on me, and unfortunately it was stifling being the focus of his all-encompassing affection. Will was dependable, but somewhere along the line, despite the love I still felt for him, our marriage had grown stale.

It wasn't helped by the fact that, deep down, I believed I was undeserving of somebody so fundamentally decent as Will. I had always believed I too was a moral person, but when the chips were down, I discovered I was lacking in that department. I was always lacking in one department or another. No matter how hard I tried, I was a disappointment. To me, my shortcomings far outweighed my strengths.

Unwilling to brood any longer on those demoralising feelings, I finished my gin and instead ruminated about Laura and the circumstances she'd found herself in through no fault of her own. I had no idea what her financial state was now James was gone, but I'd long suspected he had a pot of gold stashed somewhere. He'd frequently treated himself to designer clothes, recently bought himself a new Range Rover and I knew his parents lived on the most exclusive street in Belfast. His family were affluent, and unlike me, he would not have had to worry about what the future held. Now he had no future and I suffered the faint stirrings of grief.

In my stockinged feet, I walked into the kitchen and poured another G&T. Adding ice to the glass, I recalled the handsome man Laura had been speaking to at the hotel. There was something vaguely familiar about him, though I couldn't place him. Laura had not introduced us, but it niggled at me. Possibly I had sold him a house through my job at the estate agents.

I dismissed it and wandered down the hall to run a bath, adding several drops of scented oil. Our bathroom had a floor-to-ceiling window, with a freestanding jacuzzi bath, so when I lay back I could relish the scenery. I stripped off my funeral dress in front of the strategically placed full-length mirror, and examined my reflection.

Green eyes stared back at me from a slim, tanned face. My

gaze slid downwards to appraise my gym honed physique with two overly pert breasts, courtesy of my big-hearted husband after carrying his children. Not an ounce of surplus fat: strict self-discipline and conscientious daily exercise ensured it. I could not see beyond the fine lines, slightly sagging jawline and scattering of cellulite on my thighs.

My crippling lack of self-confidence guaranteed I rarely recognised my good points, instead I dwelt on my flaws.

For my glossy façade hid a multitude of sins, both old and new. Externally, I may have seemed polished and elegant, but beneath it I was damaged. Over the years I had perfected the illusion. I concealed my modest beginnings as Clare Hefton, revealing only my reinvention as Mrs Claire Collingswood. The day Will married me was the happiest of my life, allowing me to discard my detested identity and replacing it with a promising alternate. My husband had unknowingly provided a haven which shaved off the sharp edges of my angst.

Tiring of my introspection, I sank into the tub and skimmed the messages on my mobile. Nothing from my daughters, loath to discuss the funeral. I had no friends other than the Book Club, and the WhatsApp was quiet today. No one sent the customary memes or messages in case it offended the widow.

What a sobering fact. Laura was a widow. My stomach jolted in dismay for her. For widows shouldn't be young and pretty. It wasn't fair. They were supposed to be old and lined, equipped for the loss of their life partner. The natural order of things had got mixed up.

Perhaps one day in the future I would urge her to sign up for a dating app, but I'd ensure she avoided married men. For seeing a married man, even on a casual basis, was stressful. Remorse could creep up on me so acutely, it would take the breath from me. Laura was too fragile to be exposed to such excesses of emotion. The subterfuge, the lying, the sheer seediness of it all.

As I reclined in the cooling water, I mused about Ford. The most astonishing thing was how it had begun in the first place. For years I'd been content to be a bystander to their marriage, purely observing, never interfering.

Then last October at a charity dinner dance at the Melville Hotel, everything had changed. Annie worked for a cancer charity, and they'd held a fundraiser. The Book Club plus husbands attended.

I had spent the day at the hairdressers and getting my beautician to do my make-up. The dress I'd bought cost Will £500, but standing in the ladies' loo with my friends before the meal, I had a powerful sensation of déjà vu. I was transported back to my school days and the feeling of never being good enough threatened to overpower me. I'd struggled through the dinner and the dancing, as the noise in my head vibrated loud and incessant, my chest tight with anxiety.

Unable to tolerate it any longer I had sought solace in the foyer, and secreted myself behind a pillar on a wide sofa. Concealed far from the laughter and music, I had sat alone, waiting for my breath to steady and my pulse to slow. I was so consumed with my whirling thoughts, I had not realised I had company until a short time later, once the echoes of the past had stilled, the memories of a time gone by flickering but mercifully now silent.

Ford rounded the corner out of nowhere, talking into his mobile phone, and spotted me. As he hung up, he gave a small wave before walking over to me. My red dress had a split up the side and it had fallen open. I was about to modestly pull it over when I caught him staring at my legs, where the top of my stockings were on display. He swallowed once and rather than close the split, I imperceptibly moved so it revealed more.

He didn't move. Instead he lifted his eyes to mine, the first glimmer of a smile and the detonator was pressed.

It became apparent what I should do.

It was decided for me.

All thoughts of my husband and children were dismissed as I had embarked on an affair which was in turns frustrating and sordid and exhilarating. Over time, I learned how to split my life in two. Wife and mother on one hand. Cheat on the other.

The word lay dense within me that wet September evening. The ease with which I had undertaken this deception had shocked me. Usually I could rationalise it, compartmentalising my life into tiny parts and perfecting both roles convincingly.

Sighing deeply, I got out of the bath and briskly dried off. Then my phone bleeped with a message as I dressed, following my painstaking self-care routine.

Ford and his uncanny ability to message me when I least wanted it. I had to answer, for if I disregarded it, the messages would be unrelenting.

You looked very cosy with Will today

Without hesitation, I responded, though I was not particularly in the mood for him after the funeral and my contemplations. I was never sure what mood he would be in, as he could in turns be needy, then distant, demanding then contrite. Like a spoilt child who believed the world revolved around them, used to getting their own way, astonished if they were not immediately granted everything they desired. Nevertheless, he could also be amusing and attentive, and when you became the centre of his attention, it felt you were the most important person in the world. He was a walking cliché.

Sighing with frustration, I went in search of Will, and found him lying full length on the sofa, asleep. He worked long hours, barely exercised and was plunging so firmly into middle age it was disconcerting. I slumped onto the armchair beside the window and left him to sleep on undisturbed, unaware of what I was doing nearby.

I replied to Ford's insistent texts and then his wife put a message in the Book Club WhatsApp, so I found myself replying to them both simultaneously. I pictured them sitting together in their living room, blind to what was playing out, ignorant their marriage was teetering on the verge. Then I hardened my heart, suppressing my guilt. Will stretched and I signed off for the night.

Ford and I had not arranged to meet up again, but it was not uncommon. I rarely suggested getting together, instead I allowed him to propose our next liaison. Doubtless it piqued his interest and kept him returning for more. We met sporadically and it was regularly a couple of weeks between meet-ups. I'd been careful not to become too invested, for while I had made my choice spontaneously the night of the dinner dance, nothing had been spontaneous since then.

I had planned and plotted. Crafted and contrived.

I rose from my chair and moved over to the sofa, where I moulded my body around my husband's soft one. Without opening his eyes, he reached out, murmuring endearments. My breathing steadied as I relaxed.

What he didn't know wouldn't hurt him.

The only thing I was assured of, he was the innocent in all of this.

He was awake now and I gently scolded him he was working too hard. His response was a groan as I reprimanded him for working too much overtime and encouraged him to take more exercise. He simply smiled good-naturedly and said he would think about it. Which meant he was a workaholic with no intention of listening to me.

Later, I lay beside him in our dim bedroom and mentally locked my worries into a box, then visualised throwing the key into a fast-flowing river. Sleep ultimately claimed me, yet despite my best attempts to thwart them before dozing off, my dreams were bad and I woke slick with sweat, anxious and afraid. Their menace clung to me, the sounds ringing in my ears.

Whack. Slap. Thump.

Pictures persistently flashed behind my eyelids. A lifetime ago and yet only a sleep away.

Distressed, I rolled over onto my side, my back to Will. He typically woke me from my nightmares, mumbling platitudes and soothing me. Tonight I had to deal with them on my own as he slept on.

And I was terrified they were an omen of things to come.

CHAPTER THREE

We had arranged the Book Club meeting at Vicky's for the Friday evening after the funeral. Tom was a pilot and was away overnight with work. Vicky claimed she never knew where his latest route had taken him and over the years, we had stopped asking. This would be the first time, apart from the funeral, we would all be together since we learned about James, so it was certain to be difficult. Maybe Laura would wail and cry, confiding how much she missed him. Part of me was dreading it and the possibility of fresh mourning on display.

Ford had insisted we meet, and we had met late on Thursday afternoon. Finding a place to meet was sometimes problematic, and although I had a lot of time on my hands, we were constrained by his job. I only worked two days a week at a local estate agents, and from time to time we would meet at the houses I was showing, but only if they were remote and far from prying eyes. With his job, we could never guarantee he could sneak away on my work days.

Will worked shifts, which afforded me no end of free time when he couldn't check up on me, but Ford's commitments curtailed us somewhat.

It was dark as I drove down the wet country roads to Vicky's house. Hard rain pounded the windscreen as I entered the village, the wipers sloshing as they ineffectually beat back and forth. I turned into the cul-de-sac my friends lived in, passing Laura's house on the corner, the outside light shining bright, windows blank. No sign of James's Range Rover outside, only Laura's Mini. Vicky's two-storey house was at the end of the street and I pulled alongside the kerb.

As I got out of the car, I briefly glanced at each of my friend's houses. They were either in darkness, or insipid light peeped out from closed curtains. I shivered despite the mild September air, and hurried down the path to ring the doorbell, my umbrella barely saving me from getting wet.

Vicky answered the door with a welcoming smile as I presented a bottle of wine with a flourish. I said a quick hello to everyone in the living room, then followed her into her kitchen.

'How's Laura?' I whispered, as Vicky poured me a glass of white and handed it to me.

'Surprisingly good,' she answered, with a slight shrug and a grimace.

'Has she mentioned James?'

Vicky shook her head, then led me back through to our friends. I greeted them all and tightly hugged Laura who sat on her own on a corner armchair. The four of us spread out on the squishy velvet sofas facing her, sipping our drinks apprehensively, uncertain of Laura's mood. Clusters of candles flickered on the shelves and marble mantelpiece, the scent of jasmine wafting throughout the room. We had spent many Book Club nights in this room over the years, and yet I still admired its stylish, elegant décor.

Laura immediately declared she couldn't discuss James anymore, and requested we act normally and keep her glass topped up. Laura and Pinot went together like strawberries and cream.

The atmosphere was strained to begin with, as we chatted loudly, eager to avoid any lulls in the conversation. I covertly studied Laura, expecting her cheerful exterior to splinter and her sorrow to spew out. Soon though, we had drunk enough alcohol to ease the anxiety of saying or doing the wrong thing, and the evening unfolded as it had so many times before.

Secretly I watched Ford's wife, wholly unsuspecting it was me who had chosen his latest aftershave. Nor did she suspect he had rung me last minute so we could have a rendezvous after work. I swallowed my integrity as the five of us gossiped together. All the while, my phone buzzed beside me and I knew without checking it was her husband.

Kate got merry in no time, and kept us regaled with stories about her three children, who sounded like hard work. She also mentioned how busy David's job in an architect's firm was, now he had to travel more with business again. Her lovely face twisted with dissatisfaction, and I had to bite my tongue to prevent myself from snapping at her to stop complaining about her husband in front of Laura. She had grown silent and was gazing intently at her wedding band. Kate's insensitivity toward Laura set my teeth on edge, though I knew I was overprotective about her.

In an effort to deflect from the subject of husbands, Annie mentioned a Christmas party night. It was incongruous, but she was subtly trying to change the subject. Unexpectedly Laura was the most vocal about it, feasibly because she needed something to look forward to. Seemingly grief could do strange things to the brain, because she asked if we would consider a night in a hotel rather than our traditional festive meal out in Belfast.

'What a great idea!' Vicky and I exclaimed together, and we grinned at each other. Anything to please Laura.

We bandied about various suggestions until someone mentioned the Averie Hotel. I quickly dissuaded them, while my stomach lurched at the idea. The Averie was where I occasionally stayed with Ford on the pretext of going with my mum. I'd made the mistake of extolling its virtues following our first night there, and my palms became sticky at the mere notion of the five of us there. What if a staff member recognised me and asked about my 'husband'? I would have to find a better alternative, and vowed to give it serious attention over the next few days.

The subject of New Year's Eve was raised by Vicky. I shut it down immediately, heedful we would never again go to Laura's house for James's overcooked ham. Nor would she flap round like a mother hen topping up glasses and serving up delicious canapés while pretending she and James had not quarrelled before we arrived.

Annie once again deftly changed topic by updating us on her much younger sister Iona and her various boyfriends, who all seemed to be a progressively more appalling version of each other. Darth had been replaced by an older man called Mervyn, who sold handcrafted wooden genitals on the internet. She said this with a straight face, then broke into fits of giggles as she informed us Iona had become especially adept at judging girth and length with a mere glance.

As was normal for the Book Club, the discussion unsurprisingly turned to menopause and specifically the MAAF – Middle Aged and Fantastic – app, which was a source of much hilarity amongst us. It purported to be inspiring, full of tips and quotes to 'live your best mid-life.' I had yet to see any inspirational quotes about sleeping with your friend's husband, but I was tempted to devise one and submit it to them.

'Did you see the article on the MAAF app yesterday about the kale and bean soup diet? You can lose up to five pounds a week on it,' announced Kate, who groused incessantly about her middle-aged spread, though seemed incapable of doing anything about it.

'Yes, but it will make a fool of you behind your back!' sniggered Vicky.

By midnight I was tiring and messaged Will to ask him to come and collect me. He always volunteered to bring me home, no matter how late or how tired he was, and I was so spoiled by him, I automatically expected it.

'Have you decided whether to return to work, Laura?' Vicky asked, as she replenished our glasses one final time.

'I'm hoping to in a few weeks, after I've sorted out all the paperwork,' she replied, studiously avoiding eye contact with any of us. 'This is the first time I've had to contend with anything like this before, so it's a steep learning curve.'

'If you need any help with it, let me know,' offered Kate, who didn't know one end of a spreadsheet from the other.

'Laura, do you want to go yogalates on Tuesday with me and Vicky?' I asked offhandedly, as I was hunting for my handbag, which I'd set down somewhere and forgotten.

Vicky gawped at me in astonishment and I blushed at my faux pas.

'Yes, I'd like to,' Laura replied, eyes lighting up at the thought of a yoga/Pilates fusion class. Though it may have been as a result of the multiple glasses of Pinot she had consumed as though parched.

'Great, I'll see you there,' I smiled at her, thankful she'd not been offended by my mistake.

After a quick search, I found my handbag lying on the worktop in the kitchen, where I eyed the spacious room with a trace of envy. Nothing was out of place in the impeccable kitchen; cookery books were neatly stacked on floating shelves, saucepans suspended from a chrome ceiling rack and the granite worktop of the island reflected the muted lighting from three dome pendants. Perfect Vicky and her perfect house. Suddenly I caught sight of her cat Keiko, who observed me balefully from her basket by the door, startling me with her amber eyes.

Unnerved, I retrieved my jacket and umbrella from the coat stand in the hall and returned to the living room. The rest of the girls were also leaving and after the mandatory group hug, we stepped out into the peaceful street, dimly lit by murky yellow lampposts. The rain had stopped though a damp smell lingered. No sign of life except for a cat skittering soundlessly from behind a shrub into the gloom, making me jump.

Will was waiting in the car and as I climbed in beside him, we watched Laura unlock her door and let herself into her still, dim house. Her stark silhouette in the hall evoked a pathos in me I fought to suppress. My poor, poor friend.

I pulled my coat tightly around me as I shivered, although Will had the car toasty warm.

'I love you,' I said, and I meant it. I reached over to rest my hand on his thigh. 'I can't imagine how awful it would be to be in Laura's position and going home to an empty house. If you weren't waiting for me. If you were never coming home again.'

Easy tears sprang into my eyes, and I blinked them away impatiently. Though I was uncertain if the tears were for me, for him or for us.

'I'm going nowhere, darling,' Will replied gently. 'I love you too.' His worn, tender face curved into a smile and the world righted itself on its axis. This man anchored me when I was adrift.

As we drove through the jet-black night up into the hills, I refused to mope about the dishonesties and the cheating, concentrating only on Will. For I truly didn't want my husband to be a casualty of this war I was waging.

I should have known it would be inevitable.

CHAPTER FOUR

On Monday morning, once Will had left for work, I fretted about him as I ate muesli and Greek yogurt at the breakfast bar. I'd been wrestling with the knowledge he'd been letting himself go, not taking care of himself as he should. He was piling on the pounds and had started buying clothes only middle-aged men wear. Trousers with the creases pressed down the front of them. Extra elastic bits at the sides which are available only for the under-fives and the over-fifties.

Uneasily I wondered if he could be depressed. Then a sharp slice of terror; possibly I wasn't as skilled at deception as I supposed. Cold fingers of dismay crawled over me, as I faced the potential ramifications if it were true.

For Will completed me.

As much as anyone could complete me.

Possibly I was so profoundly broken I could not be made whole. Compassionate, benevolent Will who supposed he knew me so well, in fact knew only the surface of me.

Forcing myself to finish my breakfast, I purposely set my worries about him aside before dressing with care in a bottle green jumpsuit. We were holding an impromptu Book Club meeting behind Laura's back to discuss the upcoming charity dinner dance in October. Checking my watch I saw I was too early, so wandered through into the conservatory and sank onto the armchair by the window. Curling my legs under me, I opened the MAAF app. It was like having a best friend whose job it was to buoy me up every morning and never criticise.

There's only one ME in phenomenal

MID-LIFE is Marvellous, Incredible, Daring, Lovely, Inspiring, Fabulous, Extraordinary

Double chins need binned.

While averse to admitting I was indeed middle-aged, I readily accepted its positivity and encouragement at face value, even on days when my own positivity was at rock bottom.

With a start, I realised I'd become so enrapt with the app I was now running late, so I sped down into the village. The one downside of living so far out was I needed to drive everywhere rather than walk.

On that early autumn morning, I parked my black Audi convertible beside the coffee shop, under the old oak trees. Dappled sunlight threw dancing shadows on the car as a gentle breeze stirred the leaves. I inhaled deeply, exhaled my tension and dropped my shoulders. Crisp leaves crunched underfoot as I walked into the café.

Kate, Vicky and Annie were already seated at our usual table by the window. They'd ordered coffees and a selection of scones, and I waved cheerfully to them, stopping only to order a skinny latte at the counter. Our dilemma today was, should we cancel attending the dinner dance so Laura was under no duress, or should we support her to come along on her own.

I joined them with a smile and allowed them to all chatter on, listening more than I contributed. Back and forward the arguments for and against. Simmering viewpoints were tempered only by the close proximity of other customers. I felt strangely detached from it all, as if I watched the disagreements from a distance.

Kate was strongly of the opinion we should cancel, observing us gravely with her rather bloodshot blue eyes and pronouncing, 'Poor Laura doesn't need the stress on top of,' here she dropped her voice a notch, 'being a widow.'

Twirling one of her rich chestnut curls around her finger Annie retorted sharply, 'My charity would lose a table they might not be able to fill, so let's not make any quick decisions.'

Vicky leaned back in her chair, then delivered her words of wisdom. 'Why don't we ask Laura what she wants?' It was said glibly, as though it was obvious. As ever, she was distracted, only half concentrating. She was dressed for her work as a GP in a silk coral blouse and black palazzo trousers, her envy inducing hair neatly pulled back in a high ponytail. Her mobile phone lay face up on the table between us and the screen illuminated constantly with messages she pretended not to notice.

'I agree with Vicky.' I smiled pleasantly at my friend. 'We should ask Laura outright what she wants to do.'

'It's only been a couple of weeks! It's too soon for her to decide yet,' protested Kate, hands wrapped around her mug of black coffee.

'She's doing amazingly well so far,' I fired back, probably too harshly. However it was true. Laura seemingly was doing better than I would have ever imagined. Nevertheless I relented, mumbling some gibberish about how well she was holding up.

After a time, we agreed to say nothing for now, we'd wait and see how Laura was closer to the date. My leg bounced up and down under the table, relieved we had reached a decision of sorts, though I was nervous about a night where we would all be together. I stopped it jiggling with effort, conscious one of them might notice and comment. Music thrummed from the speakers as Dolly plaintively begged Jolene not to steal her man.

Our decision made, Annie complained about how obsessed Matt had become with rowing. Methodically she ripped at her paper napkin, discontent creasing between her eyebrows. His work as a headteacher kept him busy and she plainly resented the time he spent training during his time off. Seemingly he had another regatta coming up next month, this time in Cork.

'Why don't you go with him?' asked Kate with a puzzled expression.

'I can't think of anything more boring than him and his teammates eating, sleeping and breathing rowing,' retorted Annie. I was taken aback, for I'd jump at the chance to go on a trip with buff men in skimpy kits.

However we all sympathised with her, telling her what she needed to hear. After we paid the bill, Vicky was first to leave, explaining she had to go into work early. Annie needed to complete online training in the office, leaving only Kate and me. I asked if she'd like to go for a walk but she declined, grumbling she wasn't feeling well and wanted to lie down. Possibly she was coming down with something.

It's called a hangover, I thought uncharitably, as her unsteady hands and pale face hadn't escaped me.

On the spur of the moment, I decided to drop in unannounced to Laura's and offered Kate a lift back to their street, which she accepted at once. She carped on about 'poor Laura' to such an extent I had to suppress the impulse to pull over and deposit her on the footpath, leaving her to walk back.

Fortunately for her, she lived only a couple of minutes' drive away. I slowly drove up her street and inched around a large yellow skip which was half blocking the road outside Laura's.

Bits and pieces of furniture were sticking out the top of it and curiosity got the better of me. I pulled up outside Kate's and walked over, wanting to check if Laura was all right.

She came out of the house carrying a brown, leather swivel chair and wearing her customary jeans. No striped top today, instead she was pretty in an aqua sweatshirt. She smiled when she saw us and called a greeting.

'I'm getting rid of some old rubbish,' she clarified, throwing the chair forcefully into the skip. It didn't appear to be some old rubbish, and neither did the solid oak desk with the leather inlay it landed on. Broken pictures in black frames, records and hardbacked books lay scattered in the skip. Potentially she was having some sort of breakdown, throwing out good quality stuff.

Then I noticed the expression in her eyes and said nothing. They were shining, her smile warm, content and at ease. It seemed like the proverbial weight had been lifted off her shoulders.

A tall, handsome redheaded man exited the front door carrying a cardboard box, and I smiled warmly at him.

'Thanks, Harry,' Laura said. He threw the box into the skip as yet another tall, attractive redhaired man exited the house carrying a bag of Lycra clothing. It was chucked into the skip as well.

'These are my brothers, Harry and Charlie,' Laura introduced us. 'You may have met them at the funeral?'

I'd noticed them, but straight away forgotten about them as I had been too preoccupied with my own deliberations.

'Nice to meet you,' I shook their hands, thinking they could be the Pontipees in *Seven Brides for Seven Brothers*. I'd loved the film when I was growing up, imagining I would be captured by a gorgeous man and taken to a log cabin in the wilderness. I was so eager to leave my real life back then, even living in a wooden hut with no running water was preferable to my existence.

'I wanted to check you're all right and if you needed anything,' I explained to Laura.

'I'm fine thanks,' she said. 'If it suited, we could meet for a walk and a coffee later this week? I don't think I'm up to yogalates on Tuesday evening.'

'Sounds good,' Kate replied. 'Would Thursday suit?'

'Fine by me,' I answered with a smile. I only worked Tuesdays and Wednesdays, though I did toy with the idea of upping my hours when this was over and done with.

We confirmed our plans to walk on a local beach on Thursday, then I got into the car and drove off with a last glimpse in the mirror of Laura and her brothers. The three of them were so comfortable standing together, like normal people who came from a large and supportive family. Normal people with no deplorable secrets.

I envied her then, which was despicable. Imagine envying a woman who had lost the great love of her life.

As ever, I was overcome with guilt, and my rocky self-assurance took another battering.

CHAPTER FIVE

As soon as I arrived home after seeing Laura, I made a cup of green tea and nursed it in the armchair in the conservatory. Disinclined to be on my own, I texted my mum to see if she was free for a visit later in the day. Generally the solitude of our house invigorated me, though occasionally it sapped me. I could lose hours to mindless introspection, usually resulting in my mood dipping. Luckily when the first pangs of dejection lapped at my heels, I knew better than to sit and languish alone.

A short time later, I stripped off and pulled on my gym kit. Although I had foregone scones, unlike my friends, the urge to do a workout was overpowering. I grabbed my exercise mat and put a HIIT workout onto the television in the living room. Then I repeated it for good measure. Sweaty and panting, I heard my phone ping as I finished my crunches.

Ford was demanding we meet up. Giving it minimal thought, I suggested Saturday morning, when Will would be playing in a golf tournament on the North Coast. He swiftly replied and suggested he come to my house. I knew his penchant for the underhand was matched only by his thirst for taking risks, so carelessly I agreed.

As I stood under the pounding water in the shower, I thought about Ford and our planned night away in October. We rarely spent a night together as it was too onerous to both arrange and to lie about. However Will would be in England for a football match with his brothers in the middle of the month, meaning I didn't need to formulate a reason for staying away overnight. Ford would make his own excuses to his wife. Spontaneously I considered an Airbnb rather than a hotel, wanting a change and the opportunities it would afford.

Filled with sudden energy, I stepped out of the shower, checked my phone and saw Mum had replied to say she would love to see me. I dressed casually in jeans and a jumper, arranging my visit for later in the day and ate a salad at the breakfast bar while searching through the available properties on Airbnb. The late September sun plunged down behind the trees as I favourited a few cottages which ticked all my boxes. I'd make the final decision soon, for time was running out.

Pleased with myself, I drove to Mum's. Like me, she had moved out of Belfast years ago and lived about twenty minutes' drive from me. Her bungalow sat proud on a hill with a superb view of Belfast Lough. Tubs of early autumn colour clustered together at the edge of the precisely trimmed lawn, and far below the lough shimmered silver as a ferry sedately glided towards Scotland. I got out of the car and waved to my stepfather Philip, who was painting the garden fence a fresh sage green.

'Hi, Phil,' I called over my shoulder towards his wide, congenial frame.

'Your mum's in the kitchen, watching the terrible game show she hates to miss,' he shouted back, with an unmistakable fondness in this voice. I loved how cherished he made my mum feel. Every day he made her former life recede further away.

As I entered through the back door, Mum groaned loudly when a contestant lost a fortune by incorrectly answering that the smallest habitable island in the UK was Sark. Apparently it's Oronsay.

Disgusted at his ineptitude, she switched the television off and offered me a cup of coffee. Their kitchen was light and airy, with tall windows facing the lough. The log-burner in a far corner of the L-shaped room burned cheerfully, and I made myself comfortable on one of the armchairs. Mum nattered companionably as she searched for the chocolate biscuits I only indulged in when I was there. The security of a home where I could shed my polished Mrs Collingswood exterior and revert to being plain Clare.

Mum was one of the few people I trusted absolutely. Whereas my faith in most people had proven to be misplaced, my mum knew me and loved me unconditionally, regardless of my faults. She took a seat opposite me and we caught up on each other's gossip, yet I sensed she was preoccupied.

Sure enough after the smallest hesitation, she asked in a relaxed manner, 'Have you spoken to Liz recently?' The words were as surprising as they were unwelcome.

Mum knew I'd had no contact with my sister for many years, so it came out of left field and my hackles rose. There was too much bad blood, recriminations and regrets.

'You know I haven't,' I replied firmly, and waited for her to continue. I clutched the mug with such force my fingers ached, and consciously I loosened my hold before Mum noticed.

'She wanted me to tell you she's been contacted about a school reunion. They couldn't find you on social media, but they found Liz. You know she'd never give out your details unless you consented.'

Promptly my stomach clenched and I couldn't speak, the words wedged within the pressure of my chest. Instead I focused on my breathing, like I'd been taught by my counsellor. Mum continued in a soft voice, 'It was all so long ago, you're a different person now.'

Dumbly I shook my head at her, concentrating; in for four, hold for seven, out for eight. I set the mug down on the coffee table and leaned forward to rest my forearms on my thighs, aware of nothing beyond dragging air into my lungs. Spots of light danced before my eyes at the connotations.

'You don't have to decide anything now.' Her tone was measured and there was the briefest pause before she rushed on, words tumbling over each other in her haste. 'Liz would like to meet up with you. To see if you can make your peace.'

Helplessly I raised my eyes to hers. So different from mine and Liz's, hers were a washed-out blue, whereas we had both inherited our green ones from our father. The only thing I would admit I had inherited from a man I had despised.

'I can't, Mum, I simply can't,' I managed, when my breathing had settled. I sank back against the chair, my mind spinning chaotically, while lethargy pulled me down. The after-effects of anxiety.

'You're both as stubborn as each other.' Her lips compressed sadly. 'Think about the reunion. Possibly it's time to leave it all in the past where it belongs.' Her expression was optimistic, her gaze too penetrating for me to respond to.

I dismissed it with a shake of the head, suspecting I was too much of a coward to step back in time. Astoundingly then the beginnings of an idea whispered appealingly in my ear; possibly this was not coincidental.

Wouldn't it be perfect if everything came together at the same time.

There was no time to consider it further as Phil arrived in

the kitchen with a clatter. Happily it also put paid to any further talk about Liz or the reunion. Mum offered me another coffee and I remained for a while. Phil was easy company and he and Mum bickered affectionately together about a holiday in January. She preferred Lanzarote. He fancied Tenerife. It contrasted so vividly with my childhood, when we never holidayed abroad but visited the North Coast on the train for day trips.

Before long, I needed to leave and gave them both a quick hug. Will would be back soon and I wanted to cook him an elaborate dinner, to compensate for my treachery. Though of course, he knew nothing of it.

When I pulled onto our driveway, his car wasn't there and the empty house greeted me as the light faded, leaving me no distractions from what Mum had said. Persistently it replayed on a loop.

Liz wants to meet up with me.

It had been nearly six years since I had last seen her, when voices had been raised and doors had slammed. My throat tightened as I recalled it, and I poured a large gin to ease it. Even thinking about my sister invoked an involuntary reaction. I perched on a stool in the kitchen, sipping my drink and fighting the recollections swarming within my head, bellowing their presence.

Not even Will knew exactly what my life before him had been like. We had lived in a two-up, two-down house in inner city Belfast, with my dad's job as labourer bringing in regular and decent wages. For a time during The Troubles, when this wee island had viciously fought within itself, he had worked with a company which was employed to rebuild bombed police stations. The not so hidden threat on the workmen's lives meant he couldn't cope with it for long. Subsequently he drank too much and most of his wages were spent in the pub before he staggered home late on a Friday night. He would hand my poor mother a fraction of his pay, then hit her a slap across the face when she dared complain.

Dad drank himself to death the spring before I got married, and a nasty, bitter part of me thanked the heavens he wasn't there to walk me down the aisle, afraid of his volatility and fists.

Thankfully I heard the rev of a car engine before I could sink further down the rabbit hole, and I blinked rapidly to dislodge my memories. Will was home and he would break the silence and consign the undesirable memories to the recesses of my mind. Swiftly I downed the remainder of the gin and moved my face into the vestige of a smile. I greeted my unsuspecting husband with a quick peck and the instruction to watch television while I cooked dinner.

He disappeared into the living room while I extracted food from the fridge. I could hear the muted sound of the television as my father's presence fluttered about the periphery of my imagination. I did what I had become expert at over the decades. I blocked him out. Deliberately and ruthlessly buried all thoughts of him, but it was harder and it took longer than usual. Mechanically, I refilled my glass, discarding the measure and splashing in more gin than was sensible.

Finally my father was gone, his last remnants a mere shadow and I heaved a sigh of relief. Although many years had passed, I knew the reunion was a gateway to a time I was petrified to return to. While I had discarded Clare Hefton long ago, the reunion might invite that poor, sad child back to bother me. What I yearned for was peace. I craved it, but it remained elusive.

Suddenly furious, I shouted at Alexa to play The Killers and prepared the food, singing along to 'Mr Brightside', refusing to allow the pain of a bygone age to intrude on the present.

In the brightness of the kitchen, with music drowning out

the incessant internal noise, and the reassurance of my husband in the next room, I believed I could defy it all.

For I was resilient, I was strong.

I just had to repeat it often enough and it would be true.

CHAPTER SIX

I had no time to consider the reunion as I had work the next day, followed by yogalates with Vicky in the evening. We always celebrated with a frothy coffee after we had planked, stretched and relaxed, though that evening I would have been happy to forgo it. The two of us sat next to the extensive windows of the leisure centre café beside the Irish Sea. The moon shone pale on the tranquil water, a glimmering white stripe slicing the blackness. The sea was flat calm, inviting in an icy, freezing kind of way.

Vicky was in talkative form, chatting about Tom and their two daughters, remarking how strange it was now they were both at university and the house was empty without them. I empathised with her, feeling the absence of my own daughters deeply. I encouraged her to chitter on as we drank our lattes, content to let her do most of the talking when it became clear she needed a sounding board.

Generally, I preferred at least three of us to get together, as sometimes I found seeing my friends on a one-to-one basis challenging. If someone else was there, I could leave them to steer the conversation, and I could add as much or as little as I wanted. Friendship hadn't come naturally to me, as every friend I'd had before failed me in one way or another. Even those I had trusted, ultimately betrayed me.

All those years ago when Laura moved into the village and was frantically scouting out potential friends, she had approached me with the idea for a book club when I was pleasant to her at the school gates. It had been so long since anyone had extended the hand of friendship, I had been paranoid about her reasons. When I got to know her better and truly liked her, I was pathetically grateful she had chosen me. My inherent suspicion of female friendship had been superseded by the desire to be included. I had been an outsider for so long, I was terrified of rejection, but amazingly the four women readily welcomed me. Initially I didn't know who else would be in the Book Club, and when I found out, it was too late and I was an integral part of the group.

The Book Club had its advantages, and once we stopped pretending to read more than the wine labels, I enjoyed it better. Although we still called ourselves a book club, we had become so much more. Our husbands had become friends, and the ten of us had socialised together routinely over the years. Our children had grown together into adulthood, causing us worries and fears we shared openly, knowing no one would gossip or judge. We trusted each other.

And from a place of distrust, I had learned acceptance.

With our coffee cups drained, the conversation was beginning to stall. I missed Laura's easy chat and ability to make us laugh. The café staff were shooting us daggers, obviously ready to close up, so we said our goodbyes with a friendly wave in the leisure centre car park. I hurried to the car, which I had cautiously parked under a streetlight. A thick band of cloud had blocked out the moon and it was pitch-black as I manoeuvred my way along the country lanes towards home. I kept the radio on for company and idly contemplated what mood Laura would be in during our walk on Thursday. Surely grief would hit her hard at some point, though she was proving to be tougher than I would ever have expected.

Wednesday evening was spent selecting an Airbnb for my night with Ford. I preferred somewhere no further than an hour's drive. And it needed private parking and an out-of-the-way setting. Also, a small kitchen where we could heat food, so we didn't run the risk of being spotted while eating out.

I browsed through the cottages I'd favourited earlier, while Will watched golf on the widescreen television in the living room. Frustratingly as I'd left booking late, I had limited choice. In the end I selected a quaint stone cottage on the North Coast. It would be roughly an hour from the village and we could park both cars safe from curious eyes. Crofters Cottage itself looked blissful, tucked into the sweeping curve of a sandy strand, its white gated fence edging the beach. On a whim, I booked it for both the Friday and Saturday nights Will would be in England. When Ford left on the Saturday, I could remain there on my own until Sunday.

Satisfied with finding the perfect hideaway, I then scoured the internet for a decent hotel the Book Club could stay in for our Christmas night away. Much to my delight, I stumbled across the Mourne View Hotel in County Down, which was offering party night packages at a reasonable rate. Enthusiastically, I posted the link on the WhatsApp chat, and waited for the obligatory disagreements to start about dates. I'd ignore the discussions as long as possible, for once they accepted the venue, the dates were irrelevant to me.

On Thursday afternoon, I collected Kate and Laura from their houses, before driving them to the coast. It was a beautiful early autumn day with a mild balminess in the air as we zipped along the uncommonly quiet coastal road with the top down.

The road tended to be snarled up with day-trippers, but remarkably we weren't hindered by campervans dawdling at thirty miles an hour, instead only the occasional motorcyclist gamely overtook us.

Laura had suggested a popular beach, renowned as a surfers paradise, which to me implied angry breakers and a strong wind. We pulled into the car park and I put the top up in the car, then we strolled towards the shore, where white tipped waves played chase. There were few robust surfers and body boarders today, leaving long stretches unoccupied. The sun was high in the sky with wisps of white cloud, however the air was cooler on the shore and I shivered, glad of my gloves, feet sinking into the damp sand.

To begin with, we chatted light-heartedly as we ambled along. Then Laura's face changed as her lower lip wobbled and her eyes brimmed with tears. One by one they rolled down her cheeks as she wrapped her arms around herself, staring out to the horizon like a sailor's wife waiting for her husband's ship to reappear. Kate stood closely by, rubbing Laura's back and murmuring words of comfort. I handed her a hankie to wipe her nose, uncomfortable in the face of such palpable suffering, and at a loss about what I could say or do to support her.

Cold gusts whipped us as we huddled in a group, when from nowhere, a fierce stab of sorrow threatened to floor me. These girls thought they knew me inside and out, but they didn't. For they knew nothing of the emptiness inside and the deception I was intent on.

Unable to help myself, I began to weep too. Great ugly sobs anyone watching would assume were in sympathy with my bereaved friend, but in reality were because I was ashamed of my true self, and frightened they would dislike me if they uncovered it.

It seemed Kate couldn't be outdone and began blubbing too,

and soon the three of us were wailing like we were possessed. I envisaged the men in white coats appearing and popping the three of us menopausal women into the back of a van, before locking us up somewhere secure.

I'd forgotten how cathartic a good cry is and once I'd dried my tears, I temporarily felt optimistic. When Laura regained her composure, she suggested we get a takeaway coffee from the van in the car park, which we could drink in the fresh air. We sat together at a wooden picnic table at the verge of the car park, the hot drinks warming us. Seagulls hovered above us, then lunged low, scrounging for food, their shrieks mournful. I raised my face to the sun, unforeseen contentment washing over me.

'How are you feeling now?' asked Kate apprehensively, brow knitted.

I hesitated briefly, considering my answer. Which was fortuitous when I realised she was directing it to Laura.

'I'm so sorry for crying,' she replied. 'I was thinking back to the last time I was here, when I was so unhappy Robbie was at university in Scotland.'

She lifted her eyes to us and it seemed she was about to say more, but her gaze was drawn back out to sea and she fell silent. Emotions chased across her face; dejection, sadness and a hint of regret. It was on the tip of my tongue to ask if this stretch of coastline reminded her of James, but I didn't want to upset her further by mentioning him, so held my tongue.

'Does this stretch of coastline remind you of James?' Kate queried, instantly infuriating me.

'No, James didn't like coming here even though I love it. We rarely walked by the sea. In fact,' Laura smiled sadly, 'he never once walked with me on this particular beach at all. This place was mine, all mine.'

There was something so poignant and sad about how she said it, I was genuinely moved. Imagine having a no one to walk on the beach with. Hot tears pricked my eyes again. Try as I might, it was impossible to be unaffected by her obvious pain. Sensing my dismay, she grasped my hand firmly between her own cold ones.

'I don't know what I'd do without you girls,' she said, her voice thick with tears. I somehow smiled back, my throat constricting at the maelstrom of feelings.

To make matters worse, Kate joined in and the three of us sat with our hands built in a pyramid for what seemed like an hour. Doing nothing but peer forlornly out to sea, as Laura wiped her wet eyes, Kate sobbing noisily beside her. I found myself staring at our hands, fingers intertwined and an unaccustomed sensation spread within me.

This is what inclusion felt like.

It had been many years since the walls I had built to protect my heart had been erected, and just as long since I had chipped away at them. As we sat beside the benign Irish Sea, fracture lines appeared, and I basked in the unexpected glow of friendship for a short time.

However peace was transient. For I imagined when they discovered my secret, they would desert me in exactly the same way I had been deserted before. Therefore I withdrew my hand from theirs, and the cracks in my defences sealed over as I hid my face and swallowed my pain.

Soon I would be alone again.

It was inevitable.

CHAPTER SEVEN

Because I had agreed to Ford's suggestion we meet at my house on Saturday morning, it was imperative neither of my daughters would arrive unannounced and disturb us. I'd messaged first Eva, then Poppy, and bribed them to meet me in Belfast for an all-expenses paid lunch on Friday.

I found a parking space easily at Victoria Square, an exclusive city centre shopping centre, and walked briskly through it, barely pausing to scan the shop windows. There were a couple of expensive lingerie shops in the complex which caught my attention, and I considered treating myself to something new. Luckily I realised it would be inappropriate to be seen by my daughters carrying racy underwear from Boudoir Confidential, so hurried past the scraps of lace and satin.

The city centre streets were bustling, packed with shoppers and tourists who had been discharged from a massive cruise ship docked at Stormont Wharf. I inhaled the fumes, the racket and smells of the city before I sank onto a free seat in the chic French bistro beside City Hall. There I ordered a glass of mineral water while I waited patiently, for I knew my daughters would be late. It seemed arriving at the prearranged time was old-fashioned, but I had learned patience over the years and rarely reprimanded them for it. Will was forever rebuking me, certain we should teach them a lesson, but my heart was soft where they were concerned.

To pass the time, I relaxed back on the plush seat and glanced around at the other customers. A group of middle-aged women gossiped and shared a bottle of Prosecco. A curmudgeonly looking elderly man threw infuriated glances at them as the volume grew. The pretty young waitress was too busy flirting with the floppy haired barman to notice.

Bored, I retrieved my phone from my bag and scrolled through the MAAF app, reading its daily quotes.

> I don't need you to like me, because I like me

Which was so flagrantly untrue I nearly laughed out loud. I moved on to the next one.

> Do not be afraid to show the real you to the world. For you are perfect in every way.

Now it was simply teasing me and inexplicably I was so incensed, I deleted the app on the spot. I didn't need my make-believe friend pretending to bolster me while actually exposing my failings.

My reflections were rudely interrupted by the commotion which accompanies my daughters everywhere. Their vivacity was infectious, and instinctively I grinned at them, happiness rising within me as they hugged me tight. They both resembled Will, with warm brown eyes and wide smiles. Eva had piled her hair into a messy bun, while Poppy's dark curls almost reached her waist. Today they were dressed alike in wide legged jeans and black leather biker jackets. They were my Irish twins, with only eleven months between them, and were each other's best friend.

For the next couple of hours, they blethered constantly, filling me in on city dwelling. They were both in their last year of studies, and were hoping to get jobs in Belfast when they graduated. They had outgrown the village and the countryside, and I knew neither of them would choose to live permanently with us again. The knowledge saddened me occasionally, when the remoteness of our home made me regret not buying a house in the village. However, at the time I had been determined to live far from intrusive neighbours and the seclusion had appealed.

I hauled my attention back to the girls as we finished our lunch and listened to them, chattering happily, squabbling in the manner only siblings can.

A small part of me envied their youth and exuberance. Their whole lives spread before them, they could do whatever they wanted, whenever they wanted with whomever they wanted. Because they had been protected, coming from a secure homelife, I knew they wouldn't suffer the insecurities I had been forced to face. I was proud of them both and the success we had made of parenting. Primarily, they gave my life meaning.

'Why don't we go shopping, Mum?' said Poppy innocuously, brushing her curls back from her clear, creamy brow.

'What a lovely idea!' exclaimed Eva, the wide-eyed ingenue, playing along nicely.

I knew this was code for 'We'd like you to spend a fortune on all the pretty things we want.' As I had not come up the Lagan in a bubble, I cut them off at the pass, gave them both fifty pounds, and told them to treat themselves as I had a hairdresser's appointment. I excused myself, paid the bill and hugged them again before saying goodbye outside the café. They disappeared into the crowd, heads together, Eva a fraction taller, and I turned back towards the car park, my mind having already jumped onto other things.

My attention was once again taken by the window of Boudoir Confidential, so I gave in and spent a satisfying half hour selecting new, skimpy French navy lingerie before returning to the car. Tucking the bag into the footwell of the passenger seat, I exited the underground car park onto the busy city streets.

I was only half concentrating on my driving, thinking about how proficient I had become at separating my two lives. My marriage which represented so much, could seemingly be thrown aside, discarded as if it were insignificant. Which was absurd as without Will, I was nothing. It was him who helped heal the trauma of long-ago and who gave me everything I had ever desired.

Practically everything.

There was the crux of it.

Our marriage hadn't fulfilled my every need, and conceivably I was destined to always pursue the unattainable.

Sat in the hairdressers a short time later, I barely made small talk, lost in reflection. I was oblivious to the apprentice washing my hair and offering me coffee. I blocked out the hum of voices around me as I remembered when I had crossed the line from content wife to devious liar.

It had happened less than a fortnight after the dinner dance, when Will was working late. Ford had come to my house 'to chat.' I'd worn a fuchsia jersey dress, far too smart for a casual evening at home, but I was fraught with nerves and it gave me the guise of confidence. I was split down the middle; on one hand despising what I was on the precipice of doing, on the other coolly anticipating what was certain to happen.

It had taken me by surprise, how speedily Ford had forgotten his wife and how passionate he had been. I questioned if this was his first time straying, or if it was habitual. The ease with which he requested another meeting. A facetious comment about unoccupied houses and a wealth of opportunity. I doubted he was a novice cheater, it came so naturally to him.

Afterwards I had stripped off my clothes and thrown them into the washing machine with an aching heart. Alone in the bathroom I ran a bath, and stared at my reflection in the mirror. I half expected to see a different face observing me, as though my actions would be seared across my cheeks. Impossibly, I was physically unchanged.

The same features. A different person.

'It will be worth it in the end.' I had reassured myself. *'Will knows me and will forgive me when I explain it all.'*

Each time it happened, it became easier to convince myself the end justified the means. However the flashbacks and the dreams told another story.

I gave my hairdresser an extra-large tip to compensate for my coolness, and on my return to the car, I rashly decided to pay Ford and his wife a visit. I rarely made a reckless decision, but the urge to see them both grew as I reached the village. It was nearly six o'clock and everyone would have finished work. Cars were parked in driveways, children kicked a ball about and a sullen teenager walked a yappy dog while riveted to his phone. There was a beat-up Focus outside Laura's house on the corner, though no sign of life.

My excuse at the ready, I pulled up to the Fords' driveway. I'd found one of his wife's earrings down the side of my sofa after the last Book Club I'd hosted. It had been quite a while ago, and I hadn't returned it until now. Ford liked to be in control about how often and when we met. He disliked it when I showed initiative and I knew he would not appreciate me turning up unannounced on his doorstep. There was a small chance it pricked his conscience.

I rang the doorbell and a few moments later he answered the door barefoot, dressed in jeans and a tight black T-shirt. His smile vanished when he realised who it was, and he shiftily glanced over his shoulder towards their kitchen.

'Hello, Claire, what are you doing here?' His voice was light, but his expression darkened. He was as attractive as ever, having matured into his looks like a fine wine.

'I found this down the side of the sofa and wanted to return it.' I smiled blandly, as his wife emerged from the kitchen behind him, wearing jeans and a black T-shirt. Matching. How sweet.

'Hi, Claire, do you want to come in?' she asked brightly, stepping around him.

He gave an almost imperceptible shake of the head, warning me not to push my luck.

'Sorry, I can't stop,' I replied with an insincere smile. 'I wanted to return your earring, I found it at last!' I passed the earring over and as she reached her hand out, he circled her waist, pulling her hard against him.

Marking his territory and subtly warning me of my apparent mistake.

No doubt he deemed this show of solidarity would rattle me. However, I was fascinated by his discomfiture at his wife and lover standing together. She chatted cordially with me, and he wordlessly stood behind her. I could tell by his pinched face he was not best pleased with me.

It wasn't long until I said goodbye to them both, blithely commenting I should get home to Will. As I shut the car door, I lifted my hand in a cursory wave. It was then I noticed Ford hadn't waited for me to leave. My friend was standing alone in the doorway, smile in place.

A ripple of guilt spread within me. Sometimes I didn't understand myself or my motivation behind another bad choice.

All I knew was I was risking everything for what could amount to very little.

CHAPTER EIGHT

After my visit to the Fords, I reached home before Will arrived in from work. Since my conversation with Mum, I had refused to dwell on the school reunion, though it was never far from my thoughts. I could ignore it no longer.

With some consternation, I trudged through into my dressing room and stared at the bottom drawer of the shelving unit. Taking my courage in both hands, I knelt on the carpet and tugged it open. Obscured at the back under some neatly folded T-shirts, was a bland manilla envelope. Although it had been years since I'd removed it from its hiding place, its contents were burned into my consciousness. Nevertheless, I knew if I was to contemplate attending the reunion, I would have to unveil its secrets. Even without opening it, my body responded, my pulse quickening, mouth dry. With quaking hands, I pulled out the envelope, turned it upside-down and allowed everything to tumble to the floor in a small heap.

Photographs. Scrawled lines on a page ripped from a school jotter. A single newspaper cutting.

Mementos from my past. Lying on top was a first-year school photograph of a round faced innocent, with mousey long hair, big glasses and protruding teeth. The smile was gentle, the eyes filled with pride at wearing the grammar school uniform. It was irrelevant the rough woollen blazer was second-hand and the skirt too short from a sudden growth spurt. The eleven-year-old me, thrilled at the anticipation of new adventures. I now abhorred the naivety, so unsuspecting of future hurt. I felt the usual sting of tears, but refused to let them fall.

Brusquely I set the photo down on the carpet alongside the newspaper cutting and torn page, before I selected another photo. My maths class, taken at the end of fifth year, a few days before we broke up for GCSEs. Thirty faces stared unseeingly out of the photo. Frizzy eighties perms, skinny ties, gawky boys. I slouched at the end of the front row, slightly apart from the class, or it was possible I was simply projecting, conscious of what had occurred in the weeks before the photo was taken. Still the thick glasses, face skinny now with a rash of spots on my forehead and chin. Braces on my teeth in an era when they were a source of ridicule. Hair cropped short. Conspicuous by the fact mine was the only face unsmiling. A deep-seated pain gripped me as I studied my classmates.

I could recollect most names. I never forgot the important ones.

My eyes were inexorably drawn to the back row. The original mean girls, or the Coven as I had labelled them.

Five friends who were convinced they were untouchable. Superior to the rest of us. They spat their venom with breathtaking abandon, though saved their worst for the softest targets.

Elodie. Tori. Michaela. Kathy. Anya.

When I first heard it, I thought Elodie to be the most beautiful name in the world, invoking exotic suggestions of a mystical being. In reality she was the ringleader, the instigator of all things despicable. However, with her cloud of blonde hair and sparkling blue eyes, the teachers refused to condemn her, compounded by the fact Daddy was an influential barrister. They had their choice of any boy in the school, such was their appeal. Arrogant smiles, blemish free skin, shiny hair. One by one I studied their faces for the longest time.

My eyes moved to the boys standing either side of them, one of them laughing, mouth open, hand gesturing towards something unknown behind the camera. He was devastatingly handsome, tall, well-built and the object of my youthful fantasies. I had nicknamed him the Hunk, confiding only in my friends Mandy and Shirley. Such a childish nickname, but it had suited him well. For five years I had pined after him, envisaging he would notice me, select me above all others to be his girlfriend. Hours were wasted daydreaming he would see beyond the plain features, Deidre Barlow glasses and acne. Somehow against all odds, he would fall for me, and the Coven would be livid with jealousy.

Lastly my gaze moved on to Mandy and Shirley, standing on the far side of the photo from me. We'd been smart enough to pass the 11-plus exam and had bonded in first year. The reality of life with classmates whose parents had seemingly bottomless wallets and who thrived on maliciousness, had been unforgiving at times. We were not included in their extra-curricular activities and as I had not been musical, or sporty or terribly clever, I was a complete nonentity. However, while Mandy and Shirley were on my side, I was able to tolerate their spite. Most of the time.

I was so stricken at the photo, I had dug the fingernails of my right hand hard into my palm, leaving angry pink crescents and a sharp smarting in the delicate flesh.

I dropped the photo as though it had singed me. It was unhealthy to see in technicolour the tormentors of my youth. Glancing at the remainder of the pile, I knew it was the wrong time to delve further, so stuffed everything back into the envelope, my eyes deliberately unfocused.

One discoloured Polaroid remained on the carpet. In some respects, the most unbearable relic of the past.

A man, woman and two young girls sat on a sea wall, holding ice cream cones. Their eyes were screwed up against the brightness of the sun's glare, smiles broad at the novelty of eating ice cream. The girls were wearing homemade matching floral pinafores, one blue, one pink. The man had his arm slung over the woman's shoulders, fingers curled protectively around her broderie anglaise blouse.

Dad. Mum. Liz. Me.

I surmised the photo had been taken on a summer's day in Portrush. A day so hot the tar melted on the roads, and we had taken a stuffy, overcrowded train from Belfast to the seaside. There we had paddled in the sea and eaten egg and onion sandwiches while sitting on an old tartan blanket. When I closed my eyes I could almost feel the golden sand under my toes and taste the salty tang. I recalled girlish giggles as Liz and I ran elatedly in and out of the sea after Dad disappeared, having declared he was thirsty and was going to buy water. Mum had remained on her own on the blanket, a grim smile in place.

Hours seemed to pass before he returned, no water, eyes suspiciously bright. He had played horses with us on his back, bucking us into the welcoming sand. Mum's silence was prolonged and heated, her pupils sharp pinpricks of controlled fury.

Once we arrived back at our house in the city, it hadn't taken long before the shouting started. Liz and I clasped hands as we crept upstairs into our bedroom, where we shut the door and cowered nervously under the bedcovers. We were accustomed to our parents' rows, and had learned to remain hidden until the door slammed behind Dad as he headed to the pub.

However, my memory was unreliable after years of suppressing unwelcome thoughts. There was a chance the photo had been taken on a different seaside trip, and the two days had become entangled. The gaps in my memory irked me, but I couldn't discuss them with anyone, especially Mum. I shied away from making her relive the episodes which haunted my dreams.

I set the photo down in front of me and stared at it impassively, until I became conscious of Will calling my name down the hall. I had no idea of how much time had passed, but with one final glare at the despised photograph, I shoved it back into the envelope and thrust it into the drawer, concealing it for another day.

I shouted I would be out in a minute, and rose on aching legs. When I blinked, pictures of wide smiles and ice cream cones goaded me. Eventually they subsided, and I was able to raise my eyes, and studied my face in the mirror.

Smooth skin, shiny hair, straight white teeth and thanks to the generosity of my lovely husband, laser eye surgery had corrected the need for glasses. I was unrecognisable as the child in the photographs. No one would ever identify me as Clare Hefton. She no longer existed except in the crannies of my mind, where she dwelt on, thriving on the knowledge she had survived. But never, ever forgetting. Or forgiving.

Frowning at the closed drawer, my determination stiffened.

I strode out of my dressing room and found Will in the conservatory, lying on the sofa and flicking through the television channels. I tucked myself in beside him on the wide cushions, kissed his rough cheek, and reached my arms round his generous waist.

'Hello, darling,' he said, as he pulled me close, stroking my hair.

'I love you, Will,' I whispered into his ear. 'Thank you for loving me.' I breathed in his familiar scent, my erratic heartbeat slowing as I returned to the present.

'Well you're very lovable.' I felt his mouth lift into a smile.

If only he knew.

We ordered a takeaway for dinner and ate it together in the kitchen, while he talked animatedly about his swing, his driver and putting. I knew next to nothing about golf, but he was inevitably nervous before a tournament, though he was quite good. His brown eyes lit up with excitement, and there was an unusual energy about him. I was happy for him and for a short time was able to think of nothing except his tournament in the morning.

After dinner, I ran myself a bath as he tidied the kitchen. I sank under the bubbles and he handed me a G&T, then sat on the wooden stool beside the tub, while expounding about something enthralling. Like how much damage potholes were doing to the environment. Mildly irritated, I drained my glass in one vast gulp, held it out and sweetly asked him to top it up with plenty of ice and some fresh berries from the fridge. I knew it would keep him occupied for a short time, and as I soaked, I peered at one of the recessed lights glinting in the white ceiling.

The same obdurate question over and over, triggered by my musings earlier.

Can anyone ever escape their past?

There was no straightforward answer. You could run from it but you couldn't hide. Everyone knew that. The illogical had perversely become logical to me, and I hoped to reclaim my past, to rewrite it. My quest for justice superseded everything else.

My ruminations were cut short as Will re-emerged at the bathroom door and handed me a second G&T. I accepted it with a smile of thanks, and swirled it around my mouth, savouring it this time. He vanished into the bedroom to sort out his golf bag and by the time I had finished the gin, I was calmer, no longer ruminating on the unfathomable question.

Almost inevitably, I was woken in the blackest hours of the night by Will, who shook me gently by the shoulder. It was the recurrent theme; yelling, thrashing, slamming. He held me close and reassured me everything would be all right. His soothing words coursed over me and I consoled myself this was the present, those desolate days were long gone and I had everything I ever aspired to.

Almost everything.

What I truly coveted was close, just tantalisingly out of reach.

But possible.

CHAPTER NINE

Will slid noiselessly out of bed in the early hours to leave for his golf tournament. I barely woke and simply wished him 'Good luck,' before I dozed off again. Ford wasn't due until ten, leaving me plenty of time to claw back some of the lost sleep following my bad dream. While I lay awake for hours at night, my mind jumped about frenetically. Contrarily when dawn broke, I habitually struggled to wake, my head feeling like it was submerged under water.

Eventually fully awake, the brightness of the new day chased the remnants of the nightmare away. Languidly I stretched in bed before going into the kitchen, where I prepared a small bowl of muesli and a cup of green tea. I had no appetite, but forced myself to eat breakfast as I sat in the conservatory and immersed myself in the view. It was early October and the morning mist hung low in the valley. The peaks of the hills rose above it, fields assorted shades of green, sheep pale white dots in the streaky morning light.

Then I registered the time. I would have preferred to sit awhile longer, captivated by the peace and quiet of a country day, but needed to get ready. An hour of prep, then I dressed in the miniscule satin and lace lingerie I had purchased at Boudoir Confidential. I hid it under a royal blue wrap dress. One final check in the mirror to ensure I would present glossy, groomed Claire, before I rested on a stool by the breakfast bar. The giant metal clock on the wall above the table ticked down the minutes until he was due.

Half an hour later I was still at the breakfast bar, watching as the hands of the clock moved inexorably round. I resisted the urge to rip at the skin beside my thumbnail, a nervous habit I submitted to at my most anxious.

By eleven o'clock Ford still hadn't arrived and I fought the attraction of a G&T.

As half past eleven came and went, I eased off my stilettos and poured myself a drink. He wasn't coming. Part of me was relieved, the other part irritated. A day like every other. Always on his terms. I had to show no fragility, or how vulnerable he could make me with a throwaway comment or action.

As the clock struck twelve, I heard the purr of a car engine. My heart rate increased as I strained to hear footsteps. It could be the postie. Or a neighbouring farmer scouring the countryside for an escaped sheep.

Or it could be Ford.

The doorbell rang and I pushed my feet back into the stilettos and readied myself as I walked into the hall. One last check in the oval mirror on the wall, and a sharp tug on my dress to reveal more cleavage. It could do no harm to tantalise whoever was behind the solid wooden front door.

Either Ford or the ancient farmer next door would get an eyeful.

I opened the door to find Ford standing on the step, a wry expression on his face, hands on hips, in another tight T-shirt and jeans. Luckily we had never got around to installing a Ring doorbell.

'What were you thinking yesterday?' he asked in a low voice. 'Why would you come unannounced to the house? You know I don't like you to do that.'

Which was precisely why I had. In response I lifted my chin and leaned provocatively against the doorframe, the image of insouciance. 'Did you enjoy embracing your wife while your lover watched?' I replied softly.

He didn't answer, but his eyes dropped to the V of my dress, and I knew in spite of his posturing, the outcome was unambiguous. We barely made it inside the house as he untied my dress and we christened the rug in the hallway.

Predictable as ever.

Later we went through into the living room and stretched out side by side on the long sofa. Threading my fingers through his, I informed him I'd booked a cottage for our night together. Immediately he tensed and withdrew his hand from mine.

'A cottage? Why would you book us a cottage and not a hotel? It seems very domesticated.' In one fast movement he pulled away and stared aghast at me. His voice was cold and I felt a twinge of alarm. He probably thought I was trying to move our relationship onto a different level.

As casually as I could, I replied, 'I booked a cottage because variety is the spice of life. If you don't want spice, then I'll cancel. No big deal.' I shrugged indifferently, eyes locked on his to see what he would say or do next.

The silence was so lengthy I anticipated the instruction to cancel it and cancel us. I could practically see the cogs in his head turning as he worked through all the implications. After an interminable wait, he nodded, and confirmed it was a good idea.

A pause, then, 'Claire, things have changed at home, so we'll have to see less of each other for a while. I think she's becoming suspicious.'

He attempted this from time to time. Feigning culpability. I doubted his wife was suspicious, otherwise she would have confided in the Book Club. However, I participated in the charade.

'What do you mean?' I made a show of my furrowed brow.

'She's made a few comments, such as wondering why I've been so busy lately. I've tried to make excuses, but I don't think she's buying them.' His eyes slid to the side, a sure sign this was an elaborate lie.

I sat up, swung my legs over the side of the sofa and ran my fingers through my hair. When I turned, he was staring hard at me. The very image of decency.

'There's no problem. If we need to cool things then of course we should.' My tone was sweet.

He nodded, ostensibly satisfied, then pulled me back into the crook of his arm. We lay for a short time together and I thought about how he never called me any terms of endearment, nor bought me gifts, except garish red lace lingerie for Valentine's Day. It seemed this was purely physical for him; no ties, no expectations and evidently no guilt.

We parted then with no firm plans to meet. Shoeless, I stood with my arms folded on the outside steps, watching as he drove off without a backwards glance. I shut the door with a bang, then went straight into the utility room. There I stripped off the dress and put it directly into the washing machine. The lingerie would follow.

Naked now, I walked down the hall into my bathroom to run a bath. I added pomegranate noir bath oil, anxious to cleanse his scent from my skin. I might enjoy our trysts, but had no desire to replay them once they were over. Slipping under the water, I meticulously scrubbed every last remaining particle of him off me. It was a ritual of mine.

Soak. Scrub. Erase.

The innermost part of me hated how my body responded to

him and shards of shame pierced me. I had never planned for it to last this long, on so many levels it was unnecessary. Once would have been enough, yet I had discovered it wasn't. I excused my weakness by telling myself it gave me ample occasions to accumulate all the evidence I required for my scheming.

I snorted when I considered Ford and his apparent newfound morality. If someone had always been attractive and used to having women admiring them, was it possible to become immune to other people's feelings? On the contrary, if they had to work hard to improve their looks or lot in life, would they be more empathetic towards others? My thoughts meandered as I soaked. Once again I wondered if I was the first person he had cheated with, or if was I simply the latest in a long line. Surely he was too adept to be a novice. One thing I was certain of, this was the last time we would use my home.

The rest of the day stretched out before me, no friends I wanted to spend time with, no family commitments. I could drive into Belfast, browse the shops and buy Will something nice for tolerating me. He deserved a lot more, however a new shirt may suffice. On the spur of the moment, I got out of the bath, dried myself off and decided to go for a drive along the coast.

I was going to have a sneak peek at Crofters Cottage.

If it was as perfect as it promised, I'd book Will and me a couple of nights there for his birthday in November. Ordinarily I chose a hotel, but hankered for some downtime with him, when I didn't have to make an effort to dress up or wear make-up, and he would love me anyway. We could take long walks along the shore, light the wood burner and close the curtains against the outside world. The two of us cocooned together.

First however, I removed the dress from the washing machine and hung it in the sanctuary of my dressing room, where I knew Will wouldn't stumble across it. Next I washed the lingerie on a short cycle before hanging it alongside the dress. The flimsy material seemed cheap and tawdry hanging there, taunting me. A small pit of humiliation solidified in my stomach.

In a concerted effort to feel better about myself, I messaged Laura. An image of her sitting alone had worried me, and I presumed she would be lonely today. How would she fill her time when she was on her own, day after day, week after week? I offered to go for coffee with her if she felt up to it. Or shopping. Whatever she fancied. I wanted to be a good friend to her, despite my preoccupation with Ford and his wife.

She messaged back, thanking me and explained she had planned to go for a walk near her parents with a friend. We would do something together soon and my conscience was salved.

I texted Will, asking him how his tournament was going. I received no answer. He was simply too busy, I told myself, as I pushed my phone into my bag. He'd be full of it when he returned home later.

I slammed the door behind me and took a deep breath before getting into the car. The valley spread out beneath me, and there was a chill wind. Autumn was well under way and soon everything would be over.

With a final glance at the green fields below, I sped off in search of our perfect hideaway, forgetting for a time I would be staying there first with another man.

CHAPTER TEN

I found Crofters Cottage despite a couple of wrong turns. As I drove through Ballydunn, the neighbouring seaside village, I passed a row of squat stone cottages, one single shop and a thatched pub, The Stile and Donkey. The tantalising smell of turf hung in the air, puffs of smoke lazily curling heavenwards. Rounding a sharp corner as I exited the village, I caught a quick glimpse of the whitewashed cottage nestled at the far end of the headland. It was obscured from the road, the drive a mere slit in the hedges, and I was past it before I realised. Secluded as guaranteed. I carried out a nifty U-turn on the deserted country road and returned to the village, where I parked in one of the car park's dozen spaces. Fishing boats bobbed in the sheltered harbour, and a young couple held hands as they sauntered towards the lighthouse. I pulled on my woolly hat and gloves, gasping as a fresh sea breeze blasted when I opened the door. Swiftly I zipped up my black padded jacket against the crisp autumn day and walked towards the headland.

Gulls squawked desolately above me as I stepped onto the sand, and I roamed along, skirting clumps of wet seaweed. The tide was out and I was alone save for a single set of footprints leading the way along the water's edge. As I inhaled the salty air while listening to the thunderous waves, the tension ebbed from me. Laura may have been right about the seaside being therapeutic after all.

Even at my slow pace, it only took a few minutes to reach the cottage, and I could make out glints of movement behind the windows. True to the website, the garden ran down to the sand, the parking area hidden by the cottage. There was no way to tell who was inside. Not wanting to get caught snooping, I walked on towards the end of the cove, where smooth black boulders clustered together at the foot of a vertical cliff face. Taking a seat on the largest one, I surveyed the cottage and snapped a quick photo to confirm how private it was. I'd send it later.

Then I did what I had sworn not to do earlier. I stared out towards the horizon. Unbelievable. Smiling, I resolutely thought about anything other than my current state.

About how I'd never been abroad before I met Will. I recalled our first holiday together to Barcelona, where we drank sangria from an enormous jug on Las Ramblas, charmed by the human statues and the burble of an unfamiliar language around us.

About the times the four of us had gone on holiday and Will had patiently built sandcastles with the girls, while I topped up my tan in a bikini nearby. The giggles of my daughters as they buried him in sand up to his neck, and my patient husband had played along with them, allowing me time to unwind.

Blissful times with my family.

Soon I became stiff as the damp chilled me through my coat, so I leisurely retraced my steps. A single muted light shone from one of the windows in the cottage, casting pale shadows. It was perfect. I continued towards the car park, and passed a couple entwined on a wooden bench, eyes only for each other. They were young, barely out of their teens and I felt ancient as I almost instructed them to get a room.

When I reached the car, my phone vibrated and I read a message from Will.

Had a great round, 3 under par. At the nineteenth hole now. Should be back by six. Love you x

Well done! See you later. Love you too x

I was pleased for him, delighted he had had a successful day. As I drove back along the winding coast road, I appreciated the scenery; craggy hills on one side, the sparkling sea reflecting the last of the day's rays on the other. I felt an unaccustomed bubble of pleasure as I hummed along to the radio.

Daylight was fading as I reached the house, and I'd neglected to leave the exterior lights on. An involuntary shiver passed through me as I climbed out of the car and hurried over to the door. I securely shut it behind me and reached immediately for the switch. Brilliant light flooded the hall and my heart's uneven thumping slowed. Although I'd lived in the country for many years, the speed at which darkness fell and the resulting inky nights left me off-balance.

I poured a double gin to settle my nerves and began to prepare supper. I'd not eaten since breakfast, but that was not unusual. Often if I was on my own I'd not eat much, the telltale ache in my stomach as common now as the sound of my breathing. It wasn't conscious, but it was a regular occurrence. I planned to heat a tasty dinner of chicken forestière with potato dauphinoise from Marks and Spencer, followed by chocolate melt-in-the-middle puddings. I'd worry about Will's waistline another time.

Upbeat music blared from the sound system as I pottered in

the kitchen, downing another gin. It wasn't long until Will was dropped off by one of his golfing friends, his grin jubilant. He was merry after spending time in the golf club bar and his good mood was infectious. Holding his face in my hands, I kissed him tenderly, congratulating him on his round.

He plonked himself down at the breakfast bar as I finished cooking, chatting about everyday things. Then he said, 'I was thinking about Laura today and how hard it must be for her to be on her own.'

'I messaged her earlier to see if she wanted to go for a coffee, but she said she was going up near her parents for a walk,' I replied, smiling at his thoughtfulness.

'What if we had an end of season barbeque in the hut? We usually have one in September, but with James and everything, we didn't this year.' He took a slug of his beer, careless of my response.

Warily I turned my back to him, afraid to see the innocence in his eyes; or of him seeing the flush on my cheeks at his words. I didn't want Ford here again; nor did I want all of us cramped together in the wooden hut. Nine people would be a squeeze and I could do without the stress of my worlds colliding.

'How about we invite Laura over by herself some evening?' I intentionally kept my tone even.

'It might be a bit strained with only the three of us.' Will finished his beer and helped himself to another one from the fridge. 'Better to have everyone here to keep the conversation flowing.'

I bit my lip and nodded dejectedly. Once Will got a notion for something, he rarely changed his mind. I couldn't think of even one good reason why we shouldn't hold a barbeque. I had to agree with him about this idea, one he was harmlessly proposing for all the right reasons.

'Will you message everyone and get a date sorted? You

know how hard it can be to suit all of us,' he asked, resuming his place on the high stool once he had topped up my gin.

Forcing a smile, I put a message in the Book Club WhatsApp.

Anyone free over the next couple of weekends for a barbeque in the hut, before we shut it up for the season?

One by one the replies appeared on my screen -

Possibly. I need to check if we're free next Saturday. We've got plans for the following weekend.

Yes if Laura's all right with it?

We're free next Saturday night if it suits everyone? Busy the Saturday night after.

Laura gave it her blessing, texting to say she would love to come, and I replied it would be great to see her. And I meant it. For a Book Club night without Laura would be like summer without the sun. Or gin without tonic.

It will be fine, I thought, as I served up the food. *I can get through one night without my life imploding.*

Later Will and I lay together on the sofa, listening to music, the lamps turned down low. It seemed like it was the two of us against the world, my head resting on his chest, listening to the regular beat of his heart. I experienced a momentary spark of distaste at the image of me and Ford lying in exactly the same place earlier in the day, but I erased it as quickly as possible.

'I've been thinking about your birthday in November,' I said, in an effort to feel better about myself. 'How would you like to go to a cottage on the North Coast for a change?'

Will beamed as he answered, 'Are you sure you wouldn't

prefer a hotel?' Continually putting me first. 'I know how much you love a spa break.'

'Not this time. I think it would be lovely if we could go somewhere cosy and quaint. We could go for long walks by the sea, have a drink in a country pub and make love by the sound of the ocean.' I smiled wistfully at him, fully indulging my fantasy.

'Is that why you've been searching for an Airbnb?' The words so inoffensively uttered caused something sharp to jam at the back of my throat. How stupid I had been to think he was blind to everything. Did he suspect?

Keeping my face still, I raised my head and unblinking held his gaze, before asking, 'How do you know I've been searching for an Airbnb?' as my heart leapt within me.

'You're not very good at deceit, darling!' He was so naïve, eyes dancing with a mixture of booze and joviality.

'I saw you looking at the website the other night. I didn't know it was for us though, I thought it was for you and your other man.' He laughed uproariously, the idea so absurd he supposed it was hilarious.

I forced a feeble laugh too, sickened with myself.

Swallowing my anxiety, I voiced a half-truth. I'd found somewhere perfect for a weekend break. 'Leave all the booking and such like to me,' I managed as I buried my head in his chest, a sour taste in my mouth. It would be my treat, paid for by my separate bank account which Will never checked nor monitored.

For he trusted me absolutely.

Bad decisions, poor choices.

One after the other.

CHAPTER ELEVEN

In the small hours of the night Will slumbered beside me while I tossed and turned, unable to sleep. The past had crashed into my present, horn blasting, lights flashing. Impossible to ignore.

Since I had liberated the photos from the envelope, I had a nagging compulsion to pick at the sore of my past. Finally, at around 2am, I discarded the notion of sleep and padded through into the living room. I flicked on a lamp beside the sofa and wrapped a warm throw around me.

I had struggled with insomnia periodically over the years, and mostly prevented its effects from dragging me down. I'd tried everything from lavender spray on my pillow, to creating a relaxing bedtime routine. No napping during the day, however appealing. Cutting out alcohol and caffeine late at night. Truthfully, cutting out alcohol was the one thing I refused to try.

With the spectre of the reunion, it seemed I was to have no respite. I had still not fully decided whether to contact Liz or not, one minute tempted, the next too afraid. I had to make the final decision soon, but it felt insurmountable.

The wind whistled a furious tune outside the windows as I lay snug beneath the throw, while hazy recollections clouded my vision. Unable to resist, I apprehensively unlocked the door to long-ago. Before I eased it open, I reassured myself I was no longer Clare Hefton. *I am Claire Collingswood now.* However it gave scant reassurance. Clare was to be pitied. Claire was pitiless.

I had been a shy teenager, with bad skin and mousey hair. Glasses and braces. No redeeming features at all, meaning I was the perfect target for a callous nickname. Hefton had become *Hefty Lump.* I had been called it every day for years by everyone except my two friends, Mandy and Shirley. The nickname had only been a small part of it all, everything else had made the deepest cuts, leaving the most extensive scars. I had such a good heart, but they never bothered to find out. They had eroded my confidence and permanently tarnished that period of my life.

Like all schools, there had been the cliques. The popular ones. The sporty ones. The musical ones. The misfits. I fell squarely into the last group. While I had Mandy and Shirley, someone to sit with at break and lunch, I was able to make it through each school day, never aspiring to get above my allotted station in life. We saw each other out of school too, however I never invited them to our house, afraid what state Dad would be in. Sober and charming or drunk and abusive.

I had confided in them about my secret crush on the Hunk. Almost superstitiously, we only ever called him by his moniker. Even in first year, he was gorgeous. Slightly cocky, witty and, I mistakenly believed, good-natured. No gawky stage for him, no gangly arms and legs. Only enticing eyes and a wicked smile.

Almost inevitably, he and his friends gravitated towards the Coven. They were the popular girls, sticking together like glue, tittering and preening. It seemed they had it all and were not afraid to flaunt it.

In reality, they had been vicious and bitchy, displaying a ruthless indifference for other people's feelings. They were sweetness and light in front of adults, but their darkness was never far from the surface. Mandy, Shirley and I envied them and feared them equally. Woefully, while I was now fifty, married and attractive, even the idea of them made my heart thump and my jaw ache from clenching it so tightly. I exhaled slowly, working my jaw from side to side, counting my breaths, angry at my automatic response.

'They will not win,' I thought to myself, *'I am not the person I used to be.'*

My pulse slowed and the ache in my jaw eased. I rose from the sofa, and crept back into the bedroom. Will slept on, unconscious of my middle of the night ruminations. I grabbed my phone from beside the bed and returned to the living room, intent on discovering some of those faces which were hounding me from yesteryear. Soon I had been sucked into the vortex of social media, as I examined the profiles of people I had almost purged from memory. Boys I had fancied who had snubbed me. Girls who had vindictively called me names and shunned me. Then I found the person I had been subconsciously seeking.

Elodie Brooks.

An insipid blonde women smiled tiredly out of my phone at me. She looked every day of her fifty years, with a thick waist and badly fitting clothes. Her profile was private, but I could deduce from her photos she was single, painted bad seascapes and had a fondness for Corona. Her favourite pose was in front of a rusting Land Rover in the same old wax jacket. My nemesis was a nothing. The person who had plagued me for years was a mediocrity. It was inconceivable she was so ordinary, as I had long believed she would have made a great success of her life, lording it over everyone she considered inferior.

I laughed to myself, shaking my head in disbelief. Much happier, I searched further, unearthing her Coven.

I had spent my formative years hating them, therefore it was a shock to see their adult faces. With families of their own, to whom they doubtless preached that hackneyed phrase 'Be kind', while hiding their own cruelties from long ago. Time had not been gentle on them; wrinkle ravaged faces, stodgy bodies and bad haircuts.

How could I still be afraid of these people?

Now I was grown-up and a mother myself, I could appreciate in a way I couldn't when young that they had been bullies. They had stuck together because that's how bullies worked. Victimising the weak to inflate themselves.

My phone lay in my lap, my brain swimming. In all likelihood the reunion was a bad idea, for although their photos were innocuous, meeting them in the flesh may be more difficult. There was a very real chance it wouldn't matter how well I looked, or how successful my life was, I would never shake off the past and the emotions it provoked.

The wind was blowing a ferocious gale outside the house, the rain hammering on the windows so hard it seemed gravel was being thrown at them. I listened to it, reminding myself I was safe, nothing could hurt me now.

Nevertheless my search through social media unearthed memories I had banished to the no-go area of my mind. Still fully awake, I recalled my last year at school, fifth year, the year of my GCSEs. I had aspired to pass my exams and continue on to sixth form to do A-Levels. I aimed to be the first generation of Heftons to go to university, where I hoped to become a primary school teacher.

It had seemed everything was on track when I passed my

mocks with decent marks, and got a Saturday job at Woolworths. Money of my own to spend on frivolous things. Mandy, Shirley and I continued to be thick as thieves, although they weren't interested in studying and neither wanted to return for A-Levels. They were obsessed with finding a boyfriend, something none of us had been lucky enough to do yet. They permed their hair and spent their money on *Just Seventeen* magazine and bubble-gum flavoured lip gloss. We had fantastic fun and as sleep evaded me, I remembered some of our escapades.

We had such fun until it all went so devastatingly wrong.

I could uncover no more that night. It was nearly four o'clock and the need to sleep took hold of me, soothing my tattered edges. Something toughened within me. Bruises stained my heart and my mind, but I was no longer helpless. For too long I had been defeated by the past, but slowly and surely, I was seizing back control.

I weighed up my options.

Vindicating the worst choice of all with reasons which were in reality flimsy as gauze.

I crept back into bed beside Will, and when I closed my eyes, the darkness was welcome. No images circling, no memories tyrannising me. I listened to the roar of the wind which now comforted me, blocking out the moans of anguish and distress in my mind. Sleep came, and I willingly succumbed.

Next morning, I stood in the kitchen with Will and wound my arms around him. I was exhausted after my disturbed night and wearily rested my head on his broad chest. We didn't speak for a time, his reassuring presence soothing me. I was torn. Part of me wanted to confide in him, to share some of my load. The other sensible part knew it ludicrous, and admonished me: *your husband is the last person you should unburden yourself to.* To share this problem would not halve it. It would multiply it a hundredfold.

In the end, I raised my gaze, stared into those tender brown eyes and asked, 'What did I do to deserve you?' Common sense had won.

'It's me who is lucky to have you,' he replied, smoothing my hair back with his hand. 'Every day I thank God you chose me.'

He was unaware I had originally chosen him for the security he offered. Over time, it had grown into love, and a reliance on him which was unshakeable. He was my rock, the stabilising influence when everything else was badly askew.

He gave me a kiss and went outside to retrieve the bin which had blown across the garden overnight. I leant against the units, clutching my green tea and watching ominous grey rainclouds scudding across the sky, my mind careering around unfettered.

Though exhausted from lost sleep, I sought the oblivion of exercise, the craving too great to ignore. A short time later, Will watched football on the television in the conservatory and I worked out in the living room. Only when I achieved my aim of numbing the pain in my heart did I stop, replacing it with the good ache of tired muscles.

As I showered after, I recited my new mantra – *It will all be over soon.*

If I said it often enough, surely I would start to believe it. Then we could move on with our lives intact, the past paid for and the future rosy.

Foolishly I discounted the most glaringly obvious thing of all.

When this was over, would my husband still want me?

Or would my obsession with retaliation have taken a wrecking ball to my marriage, shattering it so absolutely it might never be repaired?

CHAPTER TWELVE

The week leading up to the barbeque was busy with exercise, work and indeed anything to fill the hours.

I spent Monday morning at the gym, working out until my muscles burned, I gasped for breath and my skin glistened with sweat. I had exercised until the endorphin rush made it worthwhile.

On my return home I made a list of everything I needed to do before the barbeque. A list which grew and grew, until it included insignificant things like *'Trim the candle wicks.'* I laughed to myself. This list confirmed I had too much time on my hands.

That afternoon I visited Mum again, with a vague plan to discuss Liz and the reunion. She'd been patient with me, not wanting to push me into a decision before I was ready. I pulled into their driveway, still unsure what I was going to do. I hoped talking it through would clarify it.

I got out of the car and looked admiringly around the garden, noting the freshly painted fence and newly turned over flowerbeds. Phil had started the laborious task of tidying the garden in preparation for the cold winter months. The sage green garden shed was tucked down the side of the house, and I peeped inside the open door. Rows of spotless tools, boxes of bird feed and even a stray Christmas gnome made me smile. Phil was a fastidious gardener and loved nothing better than the hard labour of digging out a flowerbed.

I called a cheery hello as I walked into their kitchen and found him and Mum standing side by side at the sink. They were doing the dishes together, she barely reaching his shoulder. She tilted her head towards his and they shared a private smile.

'The garden's looking great, Phil,' I complimented him, knowing the hours of back-breaking work he put into it. His genial face creased with pleasure, and he muttered his thanks before making his excuses and disappearing out of the kitchen. I heard the subdued rumble of racing cars through the wall from the sitting room. Mum and I sat together with a cuppa either side of the log-burner, and caught up with each other's news. Ultimately though, she asked her expected question. I was primed for it this time.

'Have you given any more thought to the reunion?' Her gaze was intense, emotions running high. 'Or meeting your sister.' She couldn't disguise her enthusiasm at the possibility of her two warring daughters definitively burying the hatchet. Preferably not in each other's backs.

'Yes I have,' I answered, astounding myself. 'I'm more or less certain I'm going to go to the reunion, if I can find out who's definitely attending. And Liz can contact me so she can set it up.' I held my hand up as Mum's face broke into a dazzling smile. 'I'm not promising anything is going to come of this, so please don't get your hopes up. I need to move on once and for all, and making my peace with Liz is central to it.'

Mum tried unsuccessfully to wipe the grin off her face. Smiling ruefully back at her, I dropped my eyes. It had burst from me spontaneously, but once it was out of the ether, I didn't want to unsay it. It was time to face my demons. She probed no further, though I could tell by the set of her face she was ecstatic I was open to communicating with Liz. Whether she was as ecstatic about me attending the reunion was less certain.

We gossiped together for another while. I filled her in on Eva and Poppy's latest news and she astounded me by divulging Liz was going to become a granny. Her only child Max, aged twenty-one, was going to be a dad. I was shocked, as I couldn't imagine Liz being a gran, nor Max being a responsible father. Of course I hadn't seen him for six years, so presumably he had matured since then.

'She wants to be called Glammy,' my mum continued with a straight face. I found myself laughing at the idea of my sister being called Glammy. Mum giggled irreverently with me, and I asked her what she wanted the new baby to call her.

'I was thinking Mimi,' she nearly choked on her own joke. Her name was Millicent Mildred, known as Millie to her nearest and dearest, though she had always aspired to the more exotic Mimi.

As the afternoon stretched towards dusk, I made my excuses, explaining Will would be ravenous when he got home from work and I wanted to have dinner ready for him.

Mum enveloped me in a hug at the door, and whispered into my ear, 'I'm glad you're starting to move on, love. Never forget, you're so much better than them, and it was such a long time ago.'

Unexpected tears welled in my eyes as I waved and got into the car. Mum's loving face was still wreathed in smiles at the hope of her fractured family reuniting. On the drive home, sorrow at the wasted years jabbed me, and by the time I had opened my front door, determination to heal the rift swept through me. I simply needed to summon my nerve and swallow my pride. Soon I would reach out to my sister.

Friday was spent preparing for the barbeque. I'd spent ages at M&S selecting all the tasty side dishes to accompany the meat Will would buy in the village butchers on Saturday morning. Zingy slaw, slow-cooked caramelised red onions, salad and baby potatoes, my trolley was brimming with excess food and drink. Afterwards, I treated myself to a skinny latte in the first-floor coffee shop, which had an unbroken view of Belfast Lough. I watched the ferry sail placidly down the calm waters on its return from Scotland, but it failed to relax me.

For my nerves were on high alert at the prospect of us all together. What if I said or did the wrong thing, or Ford tried something out of order. An errant comment or an inappropriate touch. It wouldn't be the first time he'd found the deceit an aphrodisiac. Last New Year's Eve at Laura and James's, he'd sat beside me as we ate dinner, fingers wandering over my thigh out of sight under the table, while his wife unwittingly discussed their planned holiday. Then at my fiftieth birthday party we'd spent a frantic few minutes together in the cloakroom of the hotel. My cheeks burned at the memory.

My mouth was dry with apprehension and I swallowed the coffee with difficulty. Occasionally it seemed I was no longer thinking straight, and had gone along with this get-together against my better judgement. However, Will was stubborn and would not have relinquished the idea once it popped into his head. Aggravated, I gave up the pretence of drinking the coffee and headed for home.

Once I had unpacked the groceries, I retreated to the conservatory when my phone beeped with a notification. My sister Liz had sent me a text. Curt and to the point:

> Hilary Smith from youre yr mssgd me on FB. Theirs a school reunion the 1st wk of Dec in the City Chic Hotel. Do u want to go? Says shell send a mssge if u accept her friend requst

It took a minute to decipher it. For all her grammar school education, she couldn't spell to save her life. Liz had not waited for me to extend the olive branch; instead she had taken the initiative.

Delight uncurled within me, and hurriedly I messaged back:

> Yes, please give her my contact details.
> Congrats on the new baby BTW

Uncertain how she would respond, I watched the three rolling dots while barely breathing. It didn't take long before her next message arrived:

> Tnks. Cant believe the stupid eejit is going to
> be a dad

I couldn't help myself, she had succeeded in making me laugh. Liz was blunt, forthright and called a spade a bloody shovel. Part of me grieved for the lost years and I knew she was not the only one to blame. No one but the three of us knew exactly what had happened behind the closed door of our home.

I messaged her back and whilst neither of us suggested meeting up, I was happier about our relationship than I had been in years. Possibly it wasn't too late for a rapprochement between us.

All evening I was on tenterhooks, waiting for a friend request on Facebook. Will and I watched a complicated film about Cold War spies. Rather he watched it, while I barely lifted my eyes from my phone, anticipating Hilary's message.

My Facebook page was private and my profile photo of an anonymous golden retriever. My cover photo was an arty shot of Cave Hill, the sheer basalt drop of Napoleon's Nose brutal against a striking blue sky. A single figure had been captured alone at the top, facing the Lough and the city, tiny on its vast bulk. I had made the account when the girls were younger, insisting I had access to their Facebook, apprehensive they would get bullied online and I wasn't there to prevent it. It was under the phoney name 'CWood' so there was minimal chance anyone would find me.

I had very few Facebook friends and none were people I'd gone to school with. However I enjoyed lurking on social media sometimes, and it never ceased to amaze me how many naïve people had their accounts public, allowing anyone to monitor what they posted. I presumed that's how people lost their jobs – rogue photos, questionable politics and unsavoury beliefs expounded to the masses. It was ominous how easily people could be cancelled for expressing unpopular opinions.

It was nearly ten o'clock before Hilary's friend request came through, and I accepted it with some trepidation. She followed immediately with a message:

> Hi Clare, Liz gave me your contact details. We are having a school reunion at 7 o'clock on December 9th at the City Chic Hotel. Can you believe the time has passed so quickly and we're all 50 now! It will only be our year from school. Please let me know if you can attend for food etc. Hilary

A trivial, harmless invite. As though my school days had been a bundle of laughs. I didn't care we would now be fifty, when it was impossible to move past sixteen.

Absentmindedly I ripped at the skin beside my thumbnail, then cautiously replied. It was vital to uncover who exactly would be attending, as only then could I make my decision.

Will shifted on the sofa beside me, breaking into my reverie by asking, 'Claire, is everything all right? You sound like you've run a marathon!'

I was so engrossed in my phone, I was oblivious to my rapid, shallow breaths. Such was my involuntary response to anything school related. Adrenaline pumped through my veins at the very thought of it.

'Sorry yes, I'm fine,' I replied, and on the spur of the moment, confided in him. 'Liz messaged me earlier today and I've been invited to a school reunion.' It exploded out of me, my head dizzy with the effort.

He stared at me in amazement before asking gently, 'Are you okay?'

He didn't even question Liz's reason for contacting me, or what I was going to do about the reunion. All he was concerned about was me and my welfare. My adorable, loving, unsuspecting husband.

'Yes, I am. I think it's time for me to lay these ghosts to rest.' My voice was barely above a whisper, yet I knew it to be true.

He reached out and gently squeezed my hand. 'I'll go with you and sit out in the car if you want.' Solemn eyes beseeched me, trepidation written over his face.

I had never loved him as much as I did then.

'I think I need to do this alone.' I smiled feebly, unwilling to involve him in my convoluted plans.

Reckoning and revenge.

My savage bedfellows.

CHAPTER THIRTEEN

I thought of the barbeque hut in the back garden as our hobbit house, with its wooden walls and twinkling fairy lights, homey and welcoming, irrespective of the weather. Will had laid paving stones into the grass leading out to it, and I'd furnished it with cushions and throws in shades of blue, scented candles and a beer cooler in the corner.

It would be a snug fit for the ten – well nine – of us, but it would be all right.

Saturday dawned crisp and sunny, resulting in a glorious autumn day. The dry weather meant we wouldn't get wet going between the house and the hut. Our back garden caught the evening light and as the sun bathed the surrounding trees, the russet and red leaves flamed bright. The scent of autumn hung in the air as our closest neighbour's bonfire wafted over to us.

Our friends were due at seven, and by half past six I'd sunk my first G&T. The meat was marinading, the side dishes were prepped and I drifted through the house ensuring it was spotless. I'd spent the day scrubbing and tidying while Will watched golf on the television. I said nothing, self-reproach drubbing through my veins, as I cleaned and he languished.

They arrived together in two cars and had pre-booked taxis home, intending to leave their cars here and collect them the next morning. Will flung open the door to greet them, and I was showered with kisses and hugs, compliments and gifts. The men all kissed my cheek, my friends gave me tight hugs. Ford asked if we'd got a new rug for the hall floor with a loaded smile. A cold chill ran down my spine as my face simultaneously grew hot. He was never usually so crass as to allude to where we had been together. Abruptly I turned on my heel and shakily went through to the kitchen.

Before long, our house was a hive of activity, though restrained compared to our standard get-togethers. Before they arrived Will had doggedly reminded me James had only recently died, so it couldn't be as raucous as normal. As if I could have forgotten and suggested we party like it was 1999. I nodded each time he said it, chewing the inside of my lip to stop myself snapping back at him. His preaching got tiresome after a while.

I poured beers for the men and popped the cork on a bottle of Prosecco for the Book Club. Laura seemed relaxed, chatting with David and Matt, while Vicky muttered to me she had found her a wee bit preoccupied over the past few days, staying with either family or friends, her house empty and silent.

'Do you think she's okay?' I asked under my breath and Vicky shrugged, ambivalent. Could it be we were wrong in our assumption she was holding up well? I made a mental note to get her on her own at some point, to gently suss it out.

Will chivvied everyone to go out to the hut, so he could start barbequing the meat. I brought up the rear and ended up slipping onto the end of the bench seat beside Ford. I wasn't sure if it was luck or by design he sat there, but I had no alternative. My only option would have been to make a fuss and get the others to move around. He smiled lazily at me as I sat beside him, deliberately leaving some distance between us. However, he meaningfully grazed my hand with his more than once and strayed closer, his thigh pressing discreetly against mine. It seemed his usual reticence in our spouses presence evaporated with each beer, and I was on edge all evening for fear he would say or do something incriminating. The air sizzled with such tension, it was surprising no one commented on it.

His wife chatted animatedly to our friends as I kept the glasses topped up. Kate had noticeably not received the memo to keep it subdued, as her volume increased with each glass of wine. Not for the first time, I thought she should learn how to hold her drink. However it helped us to forget the space where James should have been, which didn't remain empty for long as we spread ourselves out, unobtrusively filling the gap.

Will's face flushed redder and redder as he cooked the meat, and I was ashamed for comparing him unfavourably with the other men there. He seemed years older than he was. While the other three were tall, slim and fit, my husband looked fatigued and unfit. I suddenly felt an all-encompassing contrition at my meanness, and in need of air, I excused myself to collect plates from the kitchen.

We'd strung coloured lights around the hut and lit lanterns along the path. They created a dreamy ambiance to the garden and unusually I didn't feel unnerved by nightfall. Once I reached the kitchen, I had my back to the external French doors folding paper napkins and quickly regained my composure. I heard a footstep behind me and without turning, sensed Ford near though not quite touching. His breath was warm on the nape of my neck, and I could smell his musky aftershave, one I was intimately acquainted with.

'Do you need a hand?' His voice was the faintest whisper in my ear.

I swung round to find he was so close we could scarcely be

separated by a sheet of paper. My temper rose, disinclined to play games or risk getting caught. I felt his hand on the small of my back, pulling me towards him and my heart beat wildly in my chest. I should have moved away, but was stuck to the spot.

Before we could do anything irresponsible, Will burst through the door, demanding a dish for the meat and Ford stepped back, the spell broken. Wordlessly I gathered up the plates and fled back to the hut, leaving the men to sort out the dishes.

I was relieved to find the atmosphere was more relaxed now we had consumed a few drinks. Conversation, which had been stilted earlier in the evening, flowed. People began to laugh openly and even Laura seemed in buoyant form. When everyone had finished eating, I carried the plates back to the kitchen, then withdrew into my bedroom to refresh my make-up and have a rest from playing hostess. I stared at myself in the mirror of the en suite, and thought how tired I looked tonight. And every day of my fifty years. Vacant eyes stared back at me, fine lines by my eyes and lips were accentuated by the harsh light. Feasibly it was shame rather than tiredness that lined my face and dulled my eyes.

Resigned to my fate, I left the solace of the house and returned to the hut. There I ensured no one wanted a top up and relaxed. Matt unthinkingly raised the subject of the dinner dance towards the end of the evening, receiving a sharp dig in the ribs from Annie. Silence descended as we nervously awaited Laura's reaction. Annie shushed furiously at Matt who blushed with embarrassment.

'I would hate for you all to miss out on the night, and especially Annie, as it's your charity. So I was thinking.' Laura hesitated briefly before ploughing on. 'Would it be all right if I brought a friend to it with me? To even up the numbers.' She studied her Pinot intently.

'Of course it would,' said Kate, reaching out to lightly touch her arm.

Sharply I intervened. There would be no hand pyramids tonight to bring the mood down, when it had all been going so well.

'Absolutely fine with me. Us.' I recovered swiftly from my error, then glanced at Will. 'The more the merrier.' Which I understood too late was the wrong thing to say. I'd been thinking of her as the merry widow, and it inadvertently slipped out.

Everyone assured her it would be fine, though no one queried who her friend was. It only occurred to me later she hadn't told us and no one had asked. I never did find an excuse to pull her aside and quiz her about how she was doing. I failed that night and would forget all about it in the coming days, distracted by my own worries.

The remainder of the evening passed in a haze of alcohol and laughter and I admitted that, despite my instinct not to get too close to them, these girls truly were the best friends I'd had in years. Decades. I recollected everything we as a group had survived over the years; ill-health, bereavement, issues with our children. Fun filled nights, long summer days in foreign cities, cocktails on rooftop bars.

All too soon the first taxi arrived and our guests prepared to leave. I found myself alone again with Ford before they left. We'd hung everyone's jackets in the utility room on arrival, and I was rummaging through them trying to find Laura's, when someone moved close behind me. The lightest caress of my waist and a whispered 'Sorry' as he reached past me for his wife's coat. He pushed the door slightly closed with his foot and bent to briefly kiss my neck.

Hurriedly I stepped apart from him, the imprint of his mouth scorching me. Outraged, I shook my head and returned to the kitchen. By the time I reached our guests, I had a phoney smile in place and again thanked everyone for coming. I dodged Ford and his wife, disquiet settling somewhere beneath my ribs.

A few minutes later Will and I stood together at the front door, watching the taxis' taillights disappear from view down the driveway. He reached for me and flung an arm around my shoulders, before pulling me close.

'I think the evening went well, don't you, darling?' He exhaled stale beer fumes over me as we returned indoors, shutting out the cold air and the starless night.

'Yes, you did a great job of the barbequing,' I replied, locking the door with a firm turn of the key.

Will went into the bedroom and I walked around the house blowing out the candles and checking all the curtains were securely closed. Before I retired for the night, I swallowed the last of my gin, and leaned against the breakfast bar, unseeing, considering the evening.

As we lay in bed a short time later, Will's solid body moving on top of mine, I squeezed my eyes tight shut, the voice in my head screaming. *I don't deserve him. I am poisonous.* It required all my willpower not to push him off me, sink to my knees and beg his forgiveness.

Then unwelcome memories.

Raucous laughter. Hands restraining my arms. Snip. Snip. Snip.

My resolve hardened and I dug my nails into my husband's back. Snapshots flashed. Perpetual clamour.

Jeering and catcalling. Handsome face contorted in hysterics. The Coven.

As he neared his end, the last image exploded in a mighty bang.

Kissing with tongues. Abject humiliation. Abandonment.

Sweaty and breathless, I gazed at the ceiling as Will rolled off me and disappeared into the bathroom. Despite my best efforts to keep the reunion and its associations from invading my thoughts, it was seeping into them more often.

My hatred was as extreme as it had been when I was sixteen, rejected and abandoned.

It may have been a lifetime ago, but to me it was as fresh as if it had happened yesterday.

CHAPTER FOURTEEN

I woke the morning after the barbeque and stretched a hand over to Will's side of the bed. It was empty and cold, and I hazily recalled he had organised a round of golf. Sleepily I reached over and retrieved my phone from the top of my book, which had lain unopened for several months on the bedside table. The screen lit up with numerous messages against my wallpaper photo of Will and the girls. I propped myself up against the oak headboard to scroll through them, and relaxed back on the pillows.

Eva and Poppy had both messaged to ask if I would pay for tickets to see some awful band in Dublin. A double-pronged attack which made me smile, for I found it hard to deny them things we could afford.

There were several messages from the Book Club, thanking us for the barbeque. Laura also sent a private text, anxiously enquiring if she'd put a dampener on the evening. Poor Laura, she lacked such confidence, and I wondered where it stemmed from. I messaged back to reassure her of course she hadn't, and we were glad she'd come.

And lastly:

You were looking good last night.

My instant response was, *Yes I was.* I didn't type it of course. Instead I debated what I should do. Such a comment would have thrilled the teenaged me; now it barely fazed me. With a small fortune and a lot of grooming, anyone can be the best version possible of themselves.

Intentionally I didn't reply. Buying time, I set my phone back on top of my book, reached for my dressing gown and got out of bed. Pulling open the curtains, I found the weather had changed, and in typical Northern Irish fashion the beautiful sunshine of yesterday had been superseded by thick clouds and drizzle. Fat raindrops dripped continuously from the roof of the barbeque hut onto the grass and the lanterns were half full of water. Today the weather didn't match my mood, which was oddly positive. My phone remained beside the bed, Ford's message unanswered. I ate a bowl of granola at the breakfast bar and charted a vague timeline.

First the dinner dance, followed by our night at the cottage. The school reunion in early December, provided I uncovered exactly who would be attending.

And then what would no doubt be my last Christmas night out with the Book Club. I was under no delusions that I would be included in another one. Admitting it to myself for the first time, my stomach involuntarily lurched. Sorrow. Contrition. Sadness. I had to think of something else, for I couldn't contemplate the isolation which awaited me.

The final piece of this tangled web I had weaved would unfold at a hotel, either immediately before or after Christmas. Initially, I had planned for it to be after, to allow me the grace period of Christmas with my family. Now I was less certain, for the sooner the better in many respects. I would have to confirm the date with Ford and soon.

Once I finished breakfast, I went back to the bedroom. The phone's screen stared blankly at me, only Will and the girls' smiling faces when I tapped it. I replied to Ford, stripped off my nightwear and dressed in my Lycra gym kit. I'd never exercise without make-up, though I'm at great pains to appear like I'm wearing none, therefore I dutifully applied my warpaint.

Make-up sorted, I was filling my water bottle with chilled water from the fridge when I heard a car engine rev outside. Curious to see who it was, I opened the door to find Vicky depositing Tom and David on the drive, so they could collect their cars. The rain had stopped, and the sun's weak rays had broken through the dense clouds. I was relieved I'd taken care with my appearance as the only person who ever sees me looking less than my best is my husband, and he doesn't mind. Tom and David called their thanks for the barbeque before getting into their respective cars and driving off.

Vicky apparently had something on her mind, as she lowered her passenger window and waved over to me. She was dressed casually in a hoodie and jeans yet was still beautiful, and I felt dowdy in my T-shirt and leggings. Straight away she remarked on Laura's decision to bring a friend to the dinner dance.

'Who do you think it will be?' Nosiness was gnawing at her.

'Someone from work probably,' I replied offhandedly, as I had no idea. Vicky was brimming with excitement, eyes glinting and smile wide. I found myself grinning back and acknowledged it was intriguing.

'Apart from asking Laura directly, we'll have to wait and see. Maybe we can ask in a roundabout way at yogalates next week.'

Vicky shrugged before saying, 'I suppose so. I can't wait to find out about her secret friend.'

We talked on for a short time about last night, then I made my excuses, explaining I was about to go to the gym. I had made enough small talk; my social battery was depleted after the barbeque. Vicky waved goodbye and I forgot about Laura and her friend. The next couple of hours were spent working out and releasing endorphins to lift my mood.

On Tuesday night, Laura joined us for yogalates and as we drank our cappuccinos after the class, Vicky soon asked the question she'd been champing at the bit to since Saturday night. Her lovely face shone with both the exertion of the class and delight at getting to snoop.

She leant forward and said, 'If you don't mind me asking, who are you bringing to the dinner dance, Laura?'

Laura's pale face coloured as she replied, 'An old friend I bumped into recently.' She faltered before rushing on. 'His name is Sam.'

'Is he a work colleague?' For someone as smart as Vicky, she could be exceedingly slow on the uptake at times. Laura had said she'd bumped into him recently, meaning he definitely wasn't a work colleague.

Now her cheeks were distinctly pink. An unattractive stain right across her face which spread down her neck.

'No, he's someone I went to school with.' Laura tried to shrug it off, as though it was inconsequential, but I knew with conviction there was more to this story than she was admitting. A good liar can spot someone else's lies a mile off.

Vicky became distracted as her phone vibrated, and she dropped her eyes to study it closely. I raised my eyebrows at Laura, with a tiny tilt of my head towards Vicky. We had discussed more than once how absorbed in her phone she had become recently and how she could barely hold a conversation without it interrupting. The silence became uncomfortable and Laura cleared her throat in a non-too subtle manner.

'Sorry,' Vicky replied, setting her phone face down on the table with a thump. 'Tom's somewhere with work again and says he's been delayed. It will be Friday afternoon now before he's back. It means I'm on my own a bit longer.' I found it hard to read her expression, was she angry or relieved? Her exasperation with his workload was a common grievance.

'What a shame,' I said. 'When had you been expecting him?'

'Thursday morning. Something to do with staff sickness. He says he's got to cover.' As a pilot he was often absent for days at a time.

Conversation ebbed and flowed as I listened to them discuss the dinner dance. Laura informed us she would be wearing a silver maxi dress with a split up the side. She nervously giggled when she told us, as it was far from her traditional demure style. I was more interested in what Vicky was wearing. An amethyst purple halter neck. Inwardly I relaxed. No competition this year, unlike last, when I had felt second best all night as she was so much more attractive in her red dress than I was in mine. I envied the ease with which they could gossip about anything and everything. Before long it was time to leave and we said our goodbyes in the car park. Laura had driven them both in her Mini. I suspected she had sold James's Range Rover, however I didn't like to pry.

As I slipped behind the wheel, my phone buzzed with a message. Ford wanted to meet me this week. My lip curled when I read it.

So much for cooling things between us. He was as predictable as ever and, I was learning, manipulative too.

Since I had made the decision to never again use my home for our illicit trysts, it fell to me to find somewhere else. Clearly we couldn't always book a night away, so I figured there were limited choices; either the uninhabited houses I was showing or I had to find a viable alternative. He had made it abundantly plain it was my problem to solve.

I mulled it over as I sat in the office the next day, faking work. An idea struck unexpectedly, I'd recently shown a house about a mile from my home, right at the fringes of the forest. The forest was huge and not especially popular in bad weather, therefore there must be a remote, disused car park we could make use of.

I messaged Ford, who eagerly replied it sounded perfect. We made a date for late Friday afternoon, as the daylight started to fade, and we would be safe from prurient eyes. And the distasteful chance of getting caught in flagrante delicto by some unsuspecting hill walker.

We were like teenagers evading vigilant parents with no place to go. It was a bit sleazy and although someone else might have found all the sneaking about invigorating and thrilling, I didn't.

To take my mind off it, I booked Crofters Cottage for two nights in the middle of November for me and Will. The days would be short, we could light the log-burner, and indulge ourselves with some R&R before the frenetic Christmas period. It was something to anticipate during the bleakest months of the year, which I generally disliked. Some people adore the chance to light candles and pull the curtains, shutting themselves inside with a roaring fire. I much preferred long summer evenings and balmy, sunny days.

I'd spent some time thinking about moods recently and the swinging pendulum between depression and high-octane highs I'd been experiencing over the past year or so. For months the Book Club had been dissecting menopause and HRT in minute detail. Kate had been trying to manage her symptoms by skinny dipping and chewing raw garlic. Actually, it wasn't skinny dipping, it was wild dipping. Or something equally as uninviting. As uninviting as her garlic breath must be for her husband David.

Laura had been having a rough time with menopause and she sometimes got rather too enthusiastic about sharing every intimate detail. I had begun to suspect I may benefit from a wee patch of hormones. Possibly it would help prevent the pits of despair I was frequently prone to, or the flushes which caused me to strip naked at the window during the night. The fact my life could be dictated to by my hormones frustrated me greatly. Depression and anxiety, up and down, like a rollercoaster without the adrenaline rush. I reconciled myself to booking an appointment with the GP.

Before I did though, I had to meet Ford.

CHAPTER FIFTEEN

Friday was an overcast, gloomy day and I would have much preferred to remain in the warmth of my house over meeting Ford in an exposed car park. Nonetheless, I had committed to it and somewhat irrationally, despite my misgivings, I refused to cancel at short notice. Will would be home around seven and the girls had texted earlier in the week to say they would both stay with us for the weekend. They would be my excuse not to linger.

I had spent the morning at the gym in an effort to relieve the tension I was feeling. A headache had settled behind my eyes and painkillers barely eased it. Since Hilary's message last weekend I'd been preoccupied about the reunion; if I should go, who would be attending, what would ensue if I did. Over and over, round and round, incessant thoughts scrambled my mind. It was exhausting inside my head and exercise provided the tiniest respite from it.

I forced myself to eat a bowl of soup at the breakfast bar. My nerves were ragged and I eyed the gin bottle longingly as I gulped sparkling water. I would never drink and drive, but could virtually taste the fresh piney flavour and yearned for the quick relief which follows the first mouthful. My resolve waning, I deliberately turned my back and hastily went into my dressing room to get ready for my liaison with Ford.

The bottom drawer of the unit was tightly closed. Nevertheless I could envisage the envelope and its corrosive contents. Through sheer willpower I resisted yanking it open, extracting the envelope and obsessively staring at the photos.

I dressed with care, each item calculatingly preselected. I was by now intimate with what Ford preferred and my aim was to please. Silk lingerie. A sheer blouse. Stilettos. The opposite of how his wife dressed. More what I imagined a high-class escort would choose.

Scrutinising myself in the mirror before I left, I confirmed not even one hair was out of place. Deep red lipstick and a spritz of perfume. The grubbiness of it all adhered to my every pore and an inherent fatigue swept through me as I drove along the twisty road towards the woods. I persuaded myself my distorted logic was in fact, reasonable. The strain of my double life was beginning to show, both outwardly and inwardly.

It took about ten minutes to reach the part of the forest where we had arranged to meet. A rutted track led up to the car park, which was as expected, small and isolated. If I had been interested in the impressive view, it would have been the ideal spot to observe the river snaking through the valley below. In the distance the Irish Sea lay sleek, smooth and mesmerising. I parked the car and turned the engine off. It was then I appreciated the bleak isolation of the car park, hidden in the hills, miles from anywhere. Behind me the trees huddled together, a gravel footpath disappearing between them into the murky dimness. Far below, along the roads and in the village, slivers of light shimmered in the twilight.

Too late, I realised the car park was a mistake, as I was innately afraid of the dark. It scared me in a way which was irrational. I peered out at the dense forest while nerves unfurled within me. The dark elicited a primal response in me that I had unsuccessfully tried to master. It made me jittery and I tore ceaselessly at the raw skin at the edge of my thumbnail until dots of blood appeared, and I patted them absentmindedly with a tissue.

Fortunately, I wasn't on my own for long, for Ford arrived with a squeal of tyres and grinned as he pulled up alongside me. Lasciviously he beckoned me with his finger so I stamped down my qualms and obediently got out of the car. An icy wind rose from nowhere, and I was shaking by the time I got into the passenger seat.

However it didn't take long for me to warm up.

Afterwards, he lay back on the driver's seat and we discussed our planned night away. There were so many topics of conversation which were out of bounds between us. Our families. Plans for the future. Where this was going. Conversation never flowed, instead it spluttered in fits and starts, barely a pretence at anything meaningful. Some nights I lay awake creating a mental list of topics we could cover. I rarely made it past 'How are you doing?' 'How's work?' or sporadically, 'Any holiday plans this year?' Small talk was not my forte and especially not with him.

Suddenly I had an almost irresistible urge to demand why he was doing this. I guessed it was for the forbidden high, his mundane reality a burden, our secret assignations a break from routine. For all his talk, his marriage was not platonic. His wife may be blind to his betrayal, but she often spoke lovingly about him, something I doubted she could invent. I couldn't fathom why he would risk it all. And with me of all people.

On the face of it, one of his wife's best friends.

Was he doing it to pay her back for some reason known only

to himself? Or was he utterly unscrupulous and thrived on the deception?

Realistically, he would never reveal his reasons.

I swallowed my questions, and instead rehashed the same conversations about Crofters, the barbeque, the dinner dance. His eyes gleamed as he suggested what I should I wear under my formal dress, a salacious smile tugging at his lips. Not remotely contrite nor penitent. I played along with it, while appraising this man I had become embroiled with. Despite an end of day shadow on his jaw and a tiredness around the eyes, he remained exceptionally handsome. A fact he was fully conscious of. He was king of the humble brag, seemingly self-effacing, but the longer this relationship had lasted, I discovered the real Ford. He was a man who knew his own mind and pursued whatever he desired, irrespective of the cost. I now believed he was immune to culpability or shame.

The air between us cooled quickly, my clothes thin and insubstantial. I never complained nor would I ask him to warm me up. Instead I used the excuse I couldn't be late back as the girls would be arriving home this afternoon. Which was a fib as they weren't due until much later. As expected, he didn't question it, or ask about them. I left him reclined back on his seat, eyes closed, unperturbed and disinterested in my life beyond the tenuous boundaries of this affair.

The house was empty when I arrived back and I helped myself to a large G&T before stripping off and bathing. I had no time to wash my clothes, so bundled them into the linen basket, covering them with benign jeans and a sweater. By the time Will arrived in from work I had soaked myself clean, was tipsy and had buried the afternoons activities in the Do Not Enter area in my psyche. Once we'd eaten we waited for the girls, as my mind flitted about and I was unable to concentrate.

For I had an altogether more troublesome worry.

After an excruciating delay, Hilary had answered my question about who would be attending the reunion. Before I could reconsider, and somewhat fuzz-headed after the gin, I had replied to say I would be glad to confirm my attendance. Glad to attend and share with them all how successful my life had become, in spite of their best efforts to thwart it. Inevitably once I'd sent the message, my mind hurtled into overdrive about all the abysmal things which could hypothetically befall me on the night.

Will and I sat together on the sofa, waiting for the girls, who were late as usual. He stroked my hair and dropped kisses on the top of my head as we listened to Amy Winehouse's haunting voice informing us she was no good. The irony was not lost on me and I masked my uneasiness.

Will had raised his eyebrows when I confided I would attend the reunion. The unspoken question *Are you mad, putting yourself through that?* clear as day in the downward curve of his mouth and set jaw.

I had smiled in what I hoped was a brave manner, and dismissed his disquiet with a brief kiss. My decision was made, nothing he could say or do would dissuade me now. It was necessary for him to be on my side about this, despite the holes in my story.

Luckily Poppy and Eva soon arrived, quarrelling good-naturedly and not so subtly asking their generous dad for money. Their happy chatter hushed the worry in my mind and my fears about the reunion were quashed by clatter and light and love.

Will, always attuned to my moods, was careful to keep me included in the girls' nonsense. They wanted to watch *Dirty Dancing*, one of our favourite movies, and Will had made his excuses before disappearing to watch sport in the conservatory. I knew by his worried glance as he left, he was uneasy about the reunion and the cost it could have on my state of mind. While I watched Baby and Johnny getting down and dirty, memories fluttered, then Eva and Poppy got up to dance and as usual their very presence pulled me back from the brink. The memories became cloudy, then dissipated altogether. I giggled at them both and not for the first time, mentally gave thanks for them and my husband.

Overnight, like clockwork, I woke in a cold sweat with Will beside me, murmuring platitudes and rubbing my back. The nightmare was worse than ever, wisps of it lingering as he held me gently. For once my father's invective was not aimed at my mother, rather at me and Liz, huddled together on the carpet beside the bed we shared. Looming over us, faceless, shouting and punching the wall above our heads. I couldn't be sure if it was a real memory, or the product of a strained mind.

More importantly, I couldn't comprehend why I continuously dreamt of my father when other scenes from my youth were much worse.

Long after Will had dozed off, I stared at the ceiling, the dim light from a lamp in the hall giving relief to the blackness. In all likelihood, despite my growing resolve, the reunion was a bad idea as it wouldn't matter how amazing I looked or how successful my life was, I would never shake off the past.

As sleep once again evaded me, I rolled over onto my side and stared at the shadows, one sharp thought carved through my musings.

My world had started to unravel. It was as though I had picked at a thread and pulled it, gently at first but now with greater ferocity.

My life was in freefall and I was powerless to stop it.

CHAPTER SIXTEEN

The couple of weeks leading up to the charity dinner dance were filled with beautician appointments, work, one meeting with Ford and exercise. Although the next few weeks were bound to be difficult, I hoped for a fresh start by the time New Year was ushered in. It was so close now I could almost reach out and touch it.

Past atoned for, future brilliant with promise.

On the night of the dance, I readied myself for the function of the year with a large G&T and plenty of crushed ice, which I sipped as I dressed. I longed for another, but I forced myself to stick with one.

I slithered into my new dress, then scrutinised myself in the full-length mirror before carefully applying my lipstick. I had spent a small fortune in order to feel like a million dollars. I admired my midnight blue sheath dress, trimmed with hundreds of tiny raindrop crystals, with its plunging neckline, spaghetti straps and a split to mid-thigh, twirling to ensure I was perfect from every angle. I acknowledged all the exercise, dieting and self-denial was worth it. If I discounted my trembling hand, I could pretend it was an ordinary evening with friends, rather than another taxing evening in the company of the Fords.

The chasm between my façade and my reality was glaring.

When I could delay no longer, I sashayed into the hall, where Will was waiting in his slightly straining tux, grinning widely with pride at his wife. He gave a low whistle of admiration as I shimmied towards him and I was overcome with affection for him, so pleased with himself, with his cat who got the cream smile.

'You look stunning, darling,' he declared, reaching to embrace me, before cheekily caressing my butt. He gave me a peck on the lips as I heard the rumble of the taxi on the drive.

He helped me into the minibus and clasped my hand, as we squeezed onto a double seat. My stomach was a mass of butterflies as we drove down into the village to collect the others. The hedges and gates whizzed past and before long we reached the lights of the village.

Laura and her friend Sam would meet us at the hotel; the minibus would collect the other couples from their street. No pre-dinner drinks this year for some reason. No one had suggested or organised it. Misgiving mingled with nerves as we waited in the taxi outside David and Kate's house, and I was acutely aware it was the first time we would all be together since the barbeque. Rain began to fall, drops splattering the windscreen and the taxi driver flicked on the wipers. Squeak, squeak, squeak, like nails down a chalkboard. I ground my teeth, desperate to get the night over and done with. Will incessantly rubbed my thumb and I itched to remove it from his sticky grasp, tension making me irritable as the seconds ticked over.

Kate and David climbed in first, Kate breathlessly laughing about a lost clutch bag, David surreptitiously rolling his eyes behind his wife's back. Next were Vicky and Tom, whose body language shrieked of angry words and a half-hearted attempt at a cover-up. Annie and Matt brought up the rear, brimming with excitement the big night had finally arrived, commiserating about the rain starting at the wrong moment.

'I can't believe it's a year since the last one!' Annie's lovely face was split by a huge grin. Unusually for her, she wore her hair up, tendrils of chestnut curls escaping from their pearl pins. This was her cancer charity formal, raising valuable funds for a worthy cause. Five years cancer free and it was evident she appreciated them all.

'I've been so looking forward to tonight!' exclaimed Kate, suspiciously bright-eyed. David rested his hands on his thighs, face impassive. I gave him a sympathetic smile and was rewarded when the corners of his lips twitched in response. Wryly he looked away, as Kate roared about something hilarious.

Vicky sat across from us, studiously snubbing Tom, who was at pains to make small talk with anyone other than his wife. I was fascinated, as they normally presented a united front. Annoyingly, the amethyst purple dress I had dismissed as unthreatening, was in fact stunning on her, fanning flames of envy. A slinky halter neck, it emphasised every curve of her statuesque frame. It seemed unrealistic having won the genetic lottery, she could not fail to be like Narcissus and in love with herself. If she was though, she never so much as hinted at it.

The Melville Hotel was situated in Belfast city centre, beside the River Lagan, near to where the *Titanic* had begun her disastrous maiden voyage. The taxi pulled up outside the opulent hotel as close to the door as possible. Lights burned brightly within the ornate foyer and I stared upwards to the iconic glass domed roof. Will gripped my hand as we hurried through the fine mizzle, and the eight of us crammed together in the lift to go up to the drinks reception on the first floor. We were offered glasses of cheap bubbly on arrival and I downed Will's as well as my own.

The room was beautifully decorated in the charity's colour of pink, with balloons in various shades from palest pink to cerise. Annie must have matched her dress to the balloons, as she complimented the décor. There was no sign of Laura or her mysterious date as yet. We chatted and my senses tingled as I unobtrusively monitored our group. The men gravitated towards each other and the bar, like moths to a flame.

A sudden movement caught my eye as Laura stepped out of the lift, her date out of sight behind her, only a black enclothed arm visible. She was radiant in her glistening silver column, like a butterfly emerging from its chrysalis. Glancing over her shoulder, she smiled at him before he too was in my line of vision.

The attractive silver fox she had been immersed in conversation with at James's funeral.

Before she noticed us, all our eyes were drawn to them. We watched in a hushed semi-circle clutching our lukewarm drinks, while Laura and her 'friend' walked over to us. For this was no simple friend, the very atmosphere crackled between them, as he hardly lifted his eyes from her and she basked under his attention.

James had never once made her glow like she did tonight.

Shyly she introduced Sam, and as he said hello, barely seemed to register our names, his eyes flying back to her. They didn't touch but they had no need to. When she led him over to meet our husbands, the air was thick with the whispers of my friends, buzzing about the surprise addition to our evening.

'She kept him quiet!'

'Who knew Laura had such a handsome friend!'

'He looks like he wants to coat her in chocolate and lick it off slowly!'

Like schoolgirls, we tried to smother our giggles and I humoured the charade they were only friends, for it was harming no one. Also, I was in no position to judge.

Laura didn't abandon him to the men, but instead remained beside him at the bar, ensuring he was included in their conversation. If it was a test to see if Sam would be accepted into our circle of friends, I could have told her the answer. Men couldn't care less who you're sleeping with, as long as it's not their own wife. Yes, it was quick after James, but what did it matter. If Sam made her happy, there was nothing wrong with it in my opinion.

We were called to take our seats and walked as a group into the spacious function room. Our round table was near the back of the room, far from the dance floor, beside giant windows offering a spectacular view over the city centre. The solid bulk of Cave Hill towered above the intricate web of roads, streetlights casting a flattering glow over quietening streets.

Laura and Sam sat to my right, giving me the chance to find out more about him. Tonight he wore no glasses and there was the nagging certainty I recognised him from before, but it still escaped me. He chatted politely, and although there was no physical contact at all between them, it was obvious they knew each other intimately, occasionally finishing each other's sentences, laughing together at a story about someone called Nigel. I was sincerely delighted for her, for she shone with an inner happiness which transformed her pale face.

I perused the table and Ford refused to catch my eye; instead he spoke animatedly with everyone else. It allowed me to covertly study him; so handsome, self-assured and gregarious. Perhaps he too felt prickles of discomfort about our immoral secret, although I doubted it.

Husband. Lover. Cheat. Liar.

Wordlessly I ate my vegetable soup and hid my gaze from

the table, convinced my emotions were transparent on my face. I didn't know if we would speak to one another tonight, but it was inconsequential. Eventually I flicked my hair back, and surveyed the table. My friends and their husbands conversed enthusiastically together and the volume escalated. Good-natured joshing, glasses always full. I had no appetite and barely finished my soup as the tumult in my head jarred ever louder. The pervasive undercurrent of being never good enough when we were all together.

I sought the solitude of the foyer and was about to make my escape, when Will asked me a question about our trip to Crofters Cottage in November. Swivelling to face him, I answered tensely in a low voice. I couldn't risk Ford overhearing I'd booked the same cottage on the North Coast for Will and me, so soon after our own night there.

My eyes darted across to him, but he was immersed in conversation on the other side of the table, and my shoulders sagged with relief, definite he hadn't heard.

For I couldn't face hostility tonight of all nights.

Too late now to retreat to the foyer, I smiled and nodded along as my husband extolled the virtues of a weekend in a secluded cottage, and shame curdled within my stomach.

Wife. Lover. Cheat. Liar.

CHAPTER SEVENTEEN

The Melville Hotel is renowned for its fabulous food, but I nibbled my way through course after course, hardly tasting it. Instead I pushed it around my plate while drinking copious glasses of wine. Not once did Ford hold my eye and I occupied myself by talking to Laura and Sam. They gave the impression they had been a couple for years. I made a mental note to ask her more about him when I got her alone, and then I realised where I had seen him before. He leaned forward, I caught sight of his side profile and it slotted neatly into place.

A few months ago I had been at a local outlet village which had a cineplex and various restaurants. While sitting in the car before my shopping spree, I had spotted Laura exiting the cinema. I was mid-text to Ford and sank low in the seat, as though my deceit was splashed across the bonnet. She would not have noticed me anyway, as she was intent on the smiling man near her. I had dismissed him at the time as some random person who'd been to see the same movie as her, leaving at the same time. My vision was clearer now with the benefit of hindsight. It had been a smokescreen.

I was unsure of the timescale, but it was certainly before

James died. I regarded Laura now through new eyes, thinking she had mysteries of her own. I bit my lip, amused to see them studiously avoid even the slightest of touches and marvelled at the secrets we hide from even those closest to us.

With the dishes cleared away, I excused myself as the silent auction began, and I retreated to the sanctuary of the ladies' loo. Locking the cubicle door behind me, I lowered the toilet lid and sat down, yearning for space from so much babble and din. Traces of the last year swirled incessantly, faintly reproving, whispering their disapproval.

'Claire, are you in here?' A voice I knew well cut through my contemplations.

'Yes, I'm here,' I answered, stood and flushed the toilet, pretending I had used it. I exhaled slowly and opened the door. Vicky waited outside, an uneasy expression on her face. I noticed a dark stain on her dress, as if she had split something and tried unsuccessfully to clean it off. One minute flaw in the otherwise faultless exterior.

'Is everything all right? You've been a bit subdued since dinner,' she asked kindly.

I moved past her to wash my hands and replied as cheerfully as possible, 'Yes, I'm grand thanks. Just a bit of a headache.' I dried my hands on a soft white towel and continued. 'Thanks for checking on me, it was thoughtful of you.'

'No problem,' she replied, turning towards the mirror. She rummaged in her bag, then carefully applied her lipstick before casually enquiring, 'Can everyone tell Tom is furious with me?' She blotted her lips with a tissue, while concentrating on her reflection.

'No, I don't think so,' I fibbed, as I leant against a nearby hand basin and folded my arms. 'What happened?'

'Nothing important. We were supposed to be going out to

dinner with my parents next weekend, but he's working. Again. He asked me to rearrange, and I refused.' Her cheeks were a deep crimson as she spun to face me. 'He's always bloody working. I'm sick of it and I told him so. He's going to have to miss another family meal.' A smile which settled on her lips, did not reach her eyes.

'Join the club,' I replied immediately, turning to reapply my own lipstick in the mirror. 'Will's work takes precedence too. I have to plan everything well in advance to fit in with his schedule.' Which was a white lie, but I said what she needed to hear. 'Why is it men's jobs supersede everything else?'

Then Annie and Kate came crashing through the door together, giggling at something.

'We didn't know where you'd gone!' Kate called loudly. 'We presumed you'd run off with some big ride!' One of the straps of her dress had fallen down and her neat chignon had come loose. She hoisted the strap up, and it promptly fell down again.

Thankfully there was no one else in the toilets with us, or it would have been mortifying. Annie laughingly tried to shush her, apprehensive someone else should come in and overhear her. They joined us at one end of the bathroom and Vicky confided in them about her row with Tom.

Annie interjected straight away, saying, 'Matt doesn't work shifts but he eats, sleeps and breathes rowing. Weekends. Evenings. Early mornings. Whenever!' She acted as though he was never home.

Kate seized the opportunity to criticise David as well, complaining about his predilection for the gym and increased travel with work, which occasionally included 'necessary client schmoozing' in the evenings. She even did that irritating thing of air quotes with her fingers, like a six-year-old.

I let them complain and moan about their husbands, one of them unwittingly grumbling about time her husband was spending with me. Self-reproach like a red-hot poker charred my chest. Cheating is one thing; it's quite another to be accosted with the effects.

Before I said or did something I later regretted, Laura burst through the door, face flaming, hands on hips and demanded, 'Are you all bitching about me bringing Sam?'

Slickly I answered, 'No, we're all grousing about our husbands, and thought it would be too painful for you to be reminded of... well, James,' I finished lamely.

'So you're not discussing me and Sam?' She looked sceptical, primed for a fight.

'No, of course not,' cried Kate, hiccupping discreetly behind her hand. 'He's very nice. We want you to be happy. Please don't think we're discussing you, I couldn't bear it.'

Guilt melded into exasperation as one by one, everyone assured Laura they were grateful she had such a good friend to lean on. Obviously it ended in a group hug which made me want to scream, for the superabundance of oestrogen was suffocating. Well, mostly lab-made oestrogen. I flippantly exclaimed we'd better get back to our other halves before they sent out a search party.

'You girls are the absolute best,' said a dewy-eyed Laura, as we left together.

We'd missed the silent auction by the time we arrived back at the table, and the band was starting to play. Although I was not much inclined to dance to Abba's 'Waterloo', I pasted a smile on my face and joined in with the girls, as if I didn't have a care in the world. The five of us danced together to a mix of songs from our youth and classic disco hits. To anyone watching, we must have seemed the perfect friendship group, tightknit and unbreakable.

Out of breath after a dozen dances, I signalled I wanted

some air and returned to the table to tell Will. He offered to accompany me, but I insisted he finish his pint.

Alone, I headed out to the foyer and found the same deep, leather sofa I had sat on last year. It was far from the furore of the boisterous guests, with faux greenery in giant terracotta pots, perfect to conceal me from snooping eyes. The pillar obscured me from the rest of the room, and gave me the respite I needed.

I heard footsteps on the marble tiles, and Ford rounded the pillar jacketless, tie missing. The top button of his white shirt was open, allowing a glimpse of the tanned notch between his collarbones.

'I thought I'd lost you,' he said in an undertone, eyes boring into me.

I lounged back and crossed my legs, allowing my dress to fall open. 'Really? I didn't think you were bothered where I was.' I hadn't expected him to come and find me, as I imagined he was too unnerved by the chance of his wife discovering us together.

He stepped towards me and said in the same low tone, 'Come here.'

Compliantly, I did as I was instructed. He was so close now I could smell his scent emanating from him. In a gentle movement, he twirled me, so my back was pressed hard against the pillar, and then he was right before me. He ran a finger down my bare arm, leaving a trail of fire in its wake.

'Don't ever think I'm not bothered,' he breathed into my ear as his hand dropped to my waist, and he pulled me tight against him.

As swiftly as he had arrived, he disappeared. With every nerve ending blazing, I watched his retreating figure. Annoyed at the ease with which I surrendered to his probing hands and mouth, I needed time to compose myself before returning to the function room. Will was immersed in a sports game on his phone, unconcerned how long I had been missing. He tore himself away from it long enough only to enquire if I wanted another drink. I shook my head and sank onto the vacant chair beside him, watching everyone dance along to 'YMCA'.

Laura was letting her hair down with Sam, getting the dance moves totally wrong but who cared? Her pretty face was suffused with joy, for all her dancing left a lot to be desired. Vicky, Annie and Kate danced about beside them, doing a better job of keeping time.

Then the band played a slow set and Will drunkenly insisted on dancing with me to Sam Smith's 'I'm Not the Only One'. Throughout the song I was conscious of eyes on me, drilling into my back. Ford sat on his own at the table, eyes fastened on me and my insides flipped. Not with longing or desire, but with the knowledge despite my best intentions, this was not some insignificant fling.

This was real life, and actions had consequences.

The night drew to a close, and I needed one last visit to the bathroom before the drive home. The others were enthralled by the Clarins goodie basket Matt had won for Annie in the silent auction. I had silently watched as she had thrown her arms around him to thank him, and I held his gaze momentarily before turning away sharply.

The cool anteroom was a welcome reprieve from the almost frenetic atmosphere of the function room. I walked towards the bathrooms and realised I had been followed out, when I heard the squeak of a shoe behind me.

I turned and Ford almost walked into me.

'Sorry!' He laughed, holding both hands up in front of him. We were barely outside the room, in full view, therefore we maintained a discreet distance from each other. Leaning over towards me, he spoke so quietly I hardly heard him, 'I'm looking forward to the cottage.'

'Me too.' I smiled tightly, as Annie made her way through the glass doors.

The three of us amiably continued on together and I hid my discontent.

Not long now.

CHAPTER EIGHTEEN

The secret to a good lie is to keep it as close to the truth as possible. When Will enquired what my plans for the weekend were while he was in England, I could honestly reply I would be walking by the coast, cooking something tasty and having an early night. I lied by omission. No mention of Crofters Cottage or who I would be spending time with.

I waved him off on the Friday morning, closed the door behind him, and rested against it despondently. I was going to be spending time with someone who was gorgeous, witty and good-natured, yet I was sickened by my duplicity. The transitory feelings of remorse towards my friend at the dinner dance had long since evaporated.

I slowly went through into the bedroom and retrieved my suitcase from the bottom of my wardrobe. Last night I had been tormented by another bad dream, which left me awake for hours listening to the house creak and groan.

Since I had confirmed my attendance at the school reunion, my sleep was increasingly disturbed. I was consistently getting less than five hours a night, prowling around the house on noiseless feet while Will slept on regardless. By day, I felt strong and invincible. When at last I fell asleep, self-doubt struck, and the dreams were in vivid technicolour. No longer the exclusive domain of my father, other scenes featured callously now.

Mandy. Shirley. The glint of scissors. Mocking laughter. Torn pages. Napoleon's Nose.

I purposely emptied my mind as I finished packing my case, instead contemplating my plans for the weekend ahead. Unbeknown to Ford, I would remain alone in the cottage when he left on Saturday. Before I dressed, I retrieved my second phone from its hiding place in my dressing room. Thanks to watching spy movies with Will, I had learned about pay-as-you-go phones. Burner phones. No contract. No bills which could be unearthed by a spouse. And I had discovered the clever way to tape it to the back of a drawer, along with the charger, meaning it would take a special ops team to discover it. The battery was nearly flat, so I charged it while I packed my toiletries.

However I couldn't resist flicking through it as I perched on the edge of the bed. It had never been used to send texts, or emails or WhatsApps. It had only been used to store photos. Incriminating photos. And one video. One day soon though, it would be used to send messages to the single recipient in the contacts.

Packing finished, I had a quick lunch of roasted aubergine soup with a flatbread, and transferred the food I had bought from the fridge to the cool box. I stored it in the boot of the car alongside my small case, locked the door behind me and got in without a backwards glance.

Despite the cold air and darkening clouds on the horizon, I put the top down on the Audi. I sped along the curving coast road, between steep hills on one side and an angry, writhing sea on the other. The sky was thundery by the time I arrived in Ballydunn and passed the Stile and Donkey pub. There were a couple of parked cars on the main street and one lone walker strode purposefully towards the shoreline.

I was so intent on catching my first sight of the cottage, I again missed the driveway's entrance. Once more I had to find the turning spot a few hundred yards along the road where I could safely do a three-point turn. Driving back from that direction I spotted it easily and as I slowly drove down the tree lined lane, I couldn't help but smile. No matter what happened over the next couple of days, this was a perfect location for a short break.

I put the top up on the car, got out and stretched, while inspecting the cottage. Although an old building, it was well-loved, with pots of fading flowers and a freshly painted exterior. The lock system for the door was operated by an app on my phone, and cautiously I stepped inside, hopeful it was as inviting as the website had proclaimed. I needn't have worried: it was impeccable. Decorated in the Swedish style, all bare wood and white walls, rattan and rugs, a vase of cut flowers sat on the coffee table in the living room, the delicate fragrance fresh and welcoming. I loved it on sight, gratified with the ambiance.

It didn't take long to explore; the living room and kitchenette, bathroom and one bedroom with a king-sized bed. I glanced out of the sash window in the bedroom to find the ocean a stone's throw from the cottage, at the bottom of its small garden. The quintessential white picket fence and gate was the cherry on top. Retracing my steps to the living room, I checked my watch. It was half past three, so Ford was due soon. I retrieved my small case from the boot of the car, unloaded the wine, crusty bread and other bits and pieces I'd brought for dinner. Tonight we would have a Marks and Spencer's dinner. Thinking ahead, I decided when I came here with Will, we would eat dinner in the pub, snuggling by the open fire, huddled together at a table for two.

I unpacked my case and secreted my burner phone on the floorboards at the side of the bed, to charge it further. I reprimanded myself I should have been better prepared, as it wasn't as if I were a novice at hypocrisy. Satisfied it wouldn't be noticeable, I returned to the living room and waited impatiently on the sofa. Rather nervous, I rose several times, to pull the curtains, check the parking space, use the bathroom. Occasionally I would hear a car engine, listening until it passed by, before it faded into the distance.

Will rang me around four o'clock to say he had arrived safely at his hotel and was going out for a drink. Hoping I was okay without him. Aware I'd been on edge since my decision to attend the reunion.

I reassured him I was fine and not to worry, then hung up, unable to bear his loving words of concern. A few minutes later I heard a car which did not pass by, but crunched over the stones on the driveway, headlights sweeping past the kitchenette window. The engine cut and I turned on the sound system. Lewis Capaldi crooned about someone to love while I lingered by the floor lamp, casting a single, long shadow on the wall behind the sofa.

The door opened and Ford filled its frame, bringing with him a blast of cold air. Wordlessly he smiled and stepped forward, I met his lips with mine and we barely made it to the rug on the floor in front of the stove. Later as we lay together, I laid my hand on his chest, feeling his heart rate gradually slow. We lay in silence for a few minutes, then he turned his head, made a casual remark about his log stacking abilities and shrugged me off, asking where the bathroom was. I pointed to it and he disappeared, closing the door with a firm thunk. Rolling onto my back, I shivered, reeling at the extent of my self-hatred. How easily I had forgotten my phone call with Will.

Hurriedly I pulled my clothes on and was fully dressed by the time Ford returned. Once he too was dressed, he said, 'I need to bring my things in from the car, then shall we have a glass of wine and something to eat? Or would you prefer a walk on the beach first?'

I couldn't have cared less, but smiled back. 'I'd like a walk on the beach first.' A crescent moon had risen from behind the headland, and we walked along the sand, commenting on what a beautiful spot this was. Moonlight guided us, glittering on the surface of the water, no sounds other than the waves splashing on the shore. The moon was bright enough to keep my dread of the dark at bay, faint enough to conceal us from inquisitive eyes.

When we returned to the warmth of the cottage, he lit the log-burner, laughing as it needed several goes before it caught light. Meanwhile I heated M&S's crispy aromatic duck, which we ate at the small round table, my appetite huge for once. We shared a bottle of white wine, stretched out on the sofa, watching orange flames dance within the stove, chatting about insignificant things, music filling the gaps in conversation.

Then his phone rang constantly and he had to answer it.

'Hello,' he replied smoothly, unpeeling himself from the sofa. No hint in his tone of anything out of the ordinary. He strode into the bedroom, leaving me staggered at how normal he sounded, as he told his wife everything was fine and he would see her tomorrow. The call was short and it highlighted what an accomplished liar he was. Even better than me I'd say. I squirmed at that thought and the reminder of it tainted the rest of the evening for me.

He fell asleep within minutes in the giant bed, the sleep of the innocent. Such a deep, uninterrupted sleep he didn't even stir as I retrieved my second phone from its hiding place, and took a few photos. It was particularly good of him to forgo clothes: I couldn't have asked for better. I barely slept, terrified I would have a nightmare and wake him with my whimpering and shuddering. I could only imagine his revulsion if he saw the true me reflected in the sweaty sheen on my face or the terror in my eyes.

Next morning we had a leisurely start to the day as we brewed fresh coffee in the cafetiere and heated the croissants I'd brought with me. Almost like an authentic couple. He informed me he had to be home for one o'clock, so before he left, we wandered along the deserted stretch of shore again. The strong wind buffeted us, and the threat of rain from the leaden clouds overhead ensured no one else ventured out. As we picked our way over scattered seaweed, I snapped photos of our entwined shadows. He unquestionably expected me to delete them before I went home. And I definitely would. Once I'd saved them to my other phone.

On our return to the cottage, I indifferently said, 'How would you feel if I booked a night at the Averie before Christmas. An early Christmas present if you like.'

Tensely I waited, as everything hinged on his answer. If he refused, my grand plan would need to be reworked. If he agreed, we were on the final countdown. My back to him, I washed the few dishes we had used and he dithered before answering.

'I could manage one night in the middle of December. There's a thing I've been invited to I could miss.'

Lightly I replied that would be good. If he could let me know the date, I'd make my excuses at home and get it booked. He didn't care what I would do to make it work or what lies I would have to tell.

He drove off a short time later and I watched him exit the lane to return to his wife. I was glad I had chosen to remain at the cottage, with Will in England and the girls occupied with a twenty-first birthday party in Belfast. It was absurd going home to spend another night alone, when I could remain here. I would walk into the village to buy more food and another bottle of wine, impatient to explore further. I pulled on my long coat and bobble hat, before walking along the coastal path to the harbour and then the shop.

I meandered along, inhaling the sea air, the freshness contrasting with the warmth of the cottage. This was a beautiful part of the world, waves smashing loudly on the black rocks, towering cliffs rising majestically. It dawned on me why people loved the sea here. It was untamed and wild, with the threat of a sudden storm blowing in from nowhere. Its fierceness appealed to me.

Back at the cottage, I restocked the log basket from the outside store, showered, then towelled my hair dry with one of the luxurious towels. The rest of my time stretched ahead of me as I lit the stove, changed the music to something more cheerful and rested on the sofa with a cup of coffee. Subconsciously I listened for noises outside the cottage, as the sun set. I'd pulled all the curtains and ensured the doors were locked, nervous of being so isolated on my own.

I had wanted this night alone to untangle my past. To revisit what had brought me to this point. It had been flickering on the margins for so long, I needed to remind myself why I was doing this. I could put it off no longer.

Even if it tore me in two.

CHAPTER NINETEEN

1988

It was the summer term, only a few weeks until our GCSEs. I'd been studying hard, though faked it with Mandy and Shirley, maintaining I was uninterested about passing them and getting back into Lower Sixth for A-Levels. I believed the three of us were as tight as ever and fretted about how I would survive without them in sixth form, as they were adamant they couldn't wait to leave school and start working. I was not really friendly with anyone else in my year, friendships groups having been formed and cordoned off long ago. A good day was one in which no insults were directed at me. A bad day was one in which the name calling and barbs began in the morning and ended only with the last bell.

I found the folded piece of paper pushed into my locker one Thursday after lunch. They were standing beside me, waiting while I retrieved my maths book from amongst the detritus in the metal box. They looked baffled when it fell at my feet as I opened the locker door.

'What's that?' asked Mandy, brown eyes shining.

'No idea,' I replied, stooping down to lift it up. Unfolding it, I read it with mounting disbelief.

*Fancy going for a walk in Belfast Gardens tonight?
Wear the earrings I told you I liked in chemistry.
I'll meet you at the climbing frame at 7.*

He signed his name at the bottom.

'What on earth?' asked Shirley, mouth open in shock. Girls like us didn't get notes like that in our lockers. The three of us stared in awe at the note.

'I told you!' I crowed. 'The Hunk. He told me he liked those dangly green earrings I bought in C&A!'

'No way,' squealed my friends in amazement. Mandy jumped up and down, giddy at this startling turn of affairs.

'Are you going?' asked Shirley inanely, pushing her thick black fringe out of her eyes.

'What do you think?' I asked, almost light-headed with elation.

The moment I had been waiting for my entire school life. He had noticed me after all, irrespective of my lowly position in the hierarchy. Giggling together we made our way to maths class, my cheeks burning with pleasure at him sitting on the other side of the classroom. My heart beat so loudly I was surprised no one could hear it as I walked over to my desk. He leaned forward to speak as I passed him.

'Did you get my note?' he mumbled, so quietly no one else could hear. Nodding, I held my breath as he smiled and asked, 'See you there at seven?'

Nodding like one of those dogs which sit on car dashes, I took my seat. I had no idea what the maths teacher said, or any other teacher in my remaining classes either. All I could think was, *He likes me, he really likes me.* Over and over again, I wanted to shout it out loud, but knew I had to contain my excitement.

What should I wear? What would I say to him? Would he try and kiss me? Maybe Liz would let me borrow her frosted pink lipstick. Mandy and Shirley were as excited as me, insisting on walking me home and helping me to choose my outfit. We selected a white T-shirt with lacy sleeves and a pink rah-rah skirt I had bought in Primark. It made me feel like Molly Ringwald in *Pretty in Pink*. It was the first time either of them had come into my house, and I was relieved to find my dad had not yet returned home. From work, or the pub, I wasn't sure.

They ran home to get changed and arrived back at six, staying with me as I got dressed, applying my green eyeshadow for me, and stealing Liz's lipstick.

I was a bundle of nerves, so afraid of saying or doing something stupid when we were alone. What if he tried to kiss me and his lips got stuck in my braces or my glasses hit him in the eye? I couldn't eat I was so nervous, and the three of us left the house together, nattering and laughing. I was going on my first date ever. With the Hunk. The most gorgeous boy in the world, who had chosen me above all others.

We reached the edge of the park and Mandy and Shirley stopped at the gate like we had planned earlier. They would leave me to go it alone from there. Suddenly Mandy reached out for my hand, glancing uneasily at Shirley. 'You don't have to go in there, Clare,' she exclaimed, stumbling over the words. I thought I had misheard her.

'Of course I'm going in there.' I was incredulous.

Two bright red spots warmed her cheeks. 'Please don't go, I think–'

She never finished her sentence because Shirley elbowed her sharply in the ribs. 'Shut up, Mandy,' she said harshly and Mandy obeyed, though she seemed upset. Reluctantly she released my hand.

She's jealous, I told myself. *She wishes it was her he had chosen and not me.*

I turned my back on them with a last nervous giggle and continued on alone. The climbing frame was in the middle of the park, a lush oasis in the centre of the city. Leafy trees, grassy lawns and vibrant flowerbeds defied the barbed wire and armed police on the streets. I waited for him at the climbing frame, anxiously checking my watch. Seven o'clock exactly.

I was still alone at ten past, the first twinges of insecurity he was going to stand me up nipping me. I stared around, panicky now, heart hammering, armpits damp. Then I saw him strolling down the gravel path, wearing stone-washed Levi's with matching denim jacket, white T-shirt and aviator sunglasses. Sauntering over, he looked even better than Tom Cruise had in *Top Gun*.

When he reached me, I shyly said hello and he simply stared at me like I had two heads. 'Did you really think I would go on a date with you?' he asked spitefully, a sneer on his handsome face as he removed his sunglasses.

Flustered, I looked into his eyes, then became aware of sounds, laughter and sniggering. There were so many people, hidden behind trees and bushes, all revealing themselves, while I stood stupidly staring, confounded. I recognised face after face of the other kids in my year, pointing and jeering at me.

I heard 'Hefty Lump' from behind and swung round, spotting the Coven, clutching their sides from laughing so hard. At me. They were all laughing at me. He too began to laugh as Tori stepped away from the gang and walked over to him. For my benefit, he kissed her. With tongues. Pulling apart, he slung his arm casually around her shoulders.

'As if he would look at you twice.' She flicked her shiny hair away from her clear, spot free brow. 'He's my boyfriend, you pathetic sod.'

We were surrounded by so many people, they seemed to fill the park. I was mortified and wanted the ground to swallow me up, to run and hide under my bedclothes.

Shortly, I became aware of the deepest betrayal of all. Mandy and Shirley standing with the rest of them, laughing, pointing at me. They had colluded in this set-up.

The tears started then, though I tried to stop them as I pushed my way through the crowd and began to run, my cheap sandals slapping against the ground. I could scarcely see where I was going, I was blinded, as the scornful voices got fainter and fainter behind me.

When I could run no more, I ducked behind a rickety wooden shed, before I collapsed on the ground. Nauseous, I vomited my agony until my stomach was empty. When I was done, I sat with my back against the shed and cried until I could cry no more.

They hated me so much they weren't satisfied with calling me names. They had to belittle me and remind me I was so ugly no one could ever fancy me. I was unlovable. And friendless.

Was I such an awful person? Was I grotesque? Any shred of dignity or self-belief I once had, was now lost.

I hated myself with a passion which was frightening.

Deep down, I was astonished anyone could loathe me this much.

How was I ever going to face any of them again?

CHAPTER TWENTY

Alone in Crofters Cottage, I grieved for my younger self. So gullible, so naïve. Betrayed by the only people I had believed truly liked me. They had sold me out at the expense of our friendship, to curry favour with some of the nastiest people I had ever crossed paths with. A challenging homelife and rejected by everyone else. A victim of the brutality of youth.

Was it now time to forgive that miserable girl and move on? For too many years I had despised her. Now I commiserated with her and felt protective of her memory. I had been given the opportunity for justice, and would not fail her again.

I shrank from unveiling more, emotionally shattered. I swopped my coffee for wine and threw a log into the stove. As the flames leapt and flickered, I recalled Mandy and Shirley. I had trusted them absolutely. Their treachery resulted in such innate distrust of female friends, I had purposely protected myself throughout my adult life.

The one person who had trampled over my defences was Laura. For I recognised my old self, my lost self in her. The intrinsic kindness, her almost painful quest for acceptance and friendship. A people pleaser. The person I had been was forever gone. Sacrificed at the altar of self-preservation.

I had intentionally obliterated the episode in the Belfast Gardens and its repercussions almost entirely over the years. Never facing it, at least in daylight. Now I was tearing down my defences, inch by inch, ripping them apart with such force it took my breath away.

About five years after I left school, I bumped into Mandy waiting at a bus stop in the city centre. My transformation had started, glasses replaced by contact lenses, braces gone, hair well cut and highlighted, my face healthy and tanned. I had developed a modicum of self-confidence from working in an estate agents, and had gradually moved past those difficult school days. She and Shirley had come to my house the day after everything had happened. On my instruction, Mum had sent them away and they never tried again. She didn't reveal what had been said, but they avoided me both in school and out of it afterwards.

That gloomy, dull day I saw her smoking at the bus stop, face pale and wan. I walked down the busy city street, wavered for a moment, then locked eyes and strode over. I grabbed the chance to challenge her before my courage trickled away. 'I hope it was worth it,' I said thickly, holding her shifting gaze.

'I'm sorrier than you will ever know, Clare,' she replied, blushing a deep red, dropping her eyes and rubbing the toe of her dirty trainer on the footpath.

It was too little too late.

I didn't respond, I simply turned away. Fresh tears stung my eyes, and I was glad she couldn't see them. I had no idea what became of her and Shirley, nor if they would be attending the reunion. It was irrelevant if they were there or not; there was no chance we would reconcile, despite it having been over thirty years ago. They were collateral damage in the whole grubby thing.

Soft music played in the cottage, lamps throwing shade and light around the snug room as I stared at the ceiling. I rose stiffly and laid out a plate of bread and cheese, although I was not hungry. The food I had bought in the village store earlier remained in the fridge, uncooked and uneaten. I returned to the sofa with a fresh glass of wine and slowly chewed the food.

By recalling the episode in the Belfast Gardens, I had opened Pandora's box and now permitted myself to consider my father. Properly recollect him, not simply as the tyrant from my nightmares. I found though my memory was sketchy after consciously repressing thoughts of him for so many years. I could see him in my mind's eye, but I couldn't be sure what was real or figments of my imagination.

My early years had been happy, playing with Liz in our small back garden, where Dad had built us a sandpit. We had two bikes and there was a play park behind our house where we spent long hours with the other kids from the street; on the swings, the slide, the roundabout. There was a strong sense of community in our area, lives woven together, caring for one another. Everyone knew everyone else's business, or at least, knew enough to keep their lips sealed and a concerned eye out for each other. We were in and out of the other houses, playing imaginary games and, it seemed, always laughing, fingernails black with grime from outside.

In our front garden grew the most beautiful cherry blossom, incongruous against the chipped paint and dirty wooden fence. Every year the delicate flowers would bloom, despite the bombs and terror in the city, thriving against all odds, raining down on our garden and the street to herald the beginning of summer.

I couldn't remember exactly when Dad's behaviour escalated and he hit the bottle with such rank determination. It seemed to me he had always been explosive and fist-happy. Yet there had been a definite change in him when I was about thirteen, a few months after he had started a new job with a different building company. Initially we'd reaped the benefits of his better pay, and there were less bad-tempered, drunken outbursts.

Gradually though, the outbursts grew more frequent; raging, roaring, fists through the kitchen door. Living in fear of provoking his hair-trigger temper. There had been a continuous, pervasive threat of physical violence within our home, though I couldn't be certain if he'd ever hit me or Liz.

As I considered the past, a deeply buried, extraordinary scene sprang to mind. After the incident in Belfast Gardens, and what happened next, I had resorted to spending long hours in my bedroom at home, pretending I was studying for my imminent exams. I sneaked downstairs one evening when Liz was at her boyfriend's, and heard crying from the kitchen. Automatically I supposed it was Mum after another row as I soundlessly approached the half-closed door.

Surprisingly it wasn't Mum who was crying, it was my father. His head in his hands, bent over the table with Mum leaning over him, rubbing his back and whispering to him. Shocked, I watched this immensely private moment between my parents, embarrassed at witnessing such an intimate act. Quietly I crept back upstairs, shut my bedroom door and got back into bed, pulling the covers over my head.

I never mentioned it and the next day Mum behaved as though it had never happened. I ached to question her, to ask what had caused the tears, but never found the words.

My phone began to ring and I mentally lugged myself back to the cottage. Will was in a noisy bar and had to shout to make himself heard. His team had won and they were celebrating. He kept it brief, words slurred and endearments many. He was an affectionate drunk who would lavish anyone and everyone with love after a few. I told him how much I was looking forward to him coming home, and that I loved him. Paying lip-service to our marriage.

Though my body was dull with fatigue, it was only eight o'clock, and too early to retire to bed. I retrieved a blanket from the wardrobe in the bedroom and reached down beside the bed to grab my second phone before returning to the living room. I topped up my glass for the last time and demolished the remains of the bread.

I then settled under the cheerful multi-coloured woollen blanket and sent a message to my daughters. They replied with a selfie, on their way out to the birthday party. Poppy in a clinging, short black dress, Eva in red. I was overjoyed they were such great friends, that they had an unshakeable bond. They relied on each other and knew they had each other's backs.

Which led me to reflect on my own sister Liz and the offences we had committed against each other. Tit for tat. I was as much to blame as her and deeply regretted my actions. Her offence had been committed when she was a teenager, whereas mine occurred when I was an adult, and should have known better.

She had failed me when I needed her most, my big sister who had thrived in the school of my nightmares. Good-looking, self-assured, with many friends and even a boyfriend, she too had shunned me when I hit rock bottom.

And years later I had screamed abuse in her face, justifying my verbal bashing of her by reminding myself she had married an alcoholic who treated her like Dad had treated Mum. Unable to comprehend how she could have tolerated the cycle of drink, fight, sleep it off, repeat. It was all my fault though, according to Liz. I lacked the capacity to appreciate addiction. Which was amusingly ironic, as I was addicted to obtaining payback, no matter who accidentally got destroyed in the process.

Basically we let each other down and I knew she had frequently tried to make amends to me over the years. In my wretchedness, I had been unable to forgive her.

Impulsively, I sent her a text:

Do you want to meet for coffee?

If she told me to get lost, I wouldn't blame her. If she wanted to meet, I would apologise. Biting the skin beside my thumbnail, I stared at the screen, willing her to reply. Unexpectedly, it was essential we met up.

She sent a response within a few minutes:

Only if its yr treat. 🙂

It was going to be all right. One debt paid to the past. Grinning as relief flooded through me, I asked where she wanted to meet. I didn't want to get off on the wrong foot by unintentionally insulting her. She selected the time and place and I agreed readily.

Completely spent from trawling through my past, there was one last thing I wanted to do before I sought the reprieve of the bed.

I scrolled through the photos I had taken this weekend, and sent the most contentious one to my burner. I then browsed through the photos and video already stored. Only ten photos in total. Each told their own story of a sordid relationship, plainly taken over several months. No words were needed, no explanations required. Objectively I watched the short clip, its meaning unequivocal.

My main phone pinged with a Book Club WhatsApp

message. Ford's wife had sent a cute photo of the two of them together, raising a toast to something. My lips lifted in a smile at them, blissfully ignorant as to what the future held. Soon it would be time to end this charade.

I sent a cheery response back to her photo, quashing the desire to reply with a photo of the log-burner and the rug, as a reminder to her husband of what he had been doing a few hours ago.

Fun, happy, faithful friend Claire replied *'Fantastic! Hope you two enjoy!'*

Cheating, two-faced, dishonest Claire sat on the sofa and raised a toast to herself and her future.

I flopped into bed a short time later, leaving a small lamp in the corner of the room burning dimly. Afraid of the dark and the dreams which were sure to haunt me, after this rummage through my history. At first I lay awake with my eyes open, mind capering, but it didn't take long for sleep to come.

Curiously I slept through the night, undisturbed by nightmares. In their place, I dreamt Liz and I chased each other through a leafy garden with water pistols. Light-hearted and lively, only the two of us. I woke to find my cheeks wet, yet didn't feel sad.

Strangely I felt the unfamiliar sensations of happiness and hopefulness.

For too long, this had all been one massive mess, but a thin sliver of hope now penetrated it. Tantalising hints of a happier future lay ahead of me.

Lying in the comfortable bed, glimmers of positivity filled me.

CHAPTER TWENTY-ONE

Before I left Crofters Cottage, I had another solo walk along the sand and through the village. It occurred to me I could become addicted to walking by the inclement Irish Sea, wind whipping my hair, savouring the tangy taste. Content, I gazed out towards the horizon and recalled Laura doing the same thing a few weeks ago. Then I had been unable to comprehend her thirst for fresh air, salty breezes and a choppy ocean. Now it made perfect sense. Nature has a way of soothing the soul. Even bruised and battered souls like mine.

On my return home late morning, I vowed to be the best wife I could be to Will over the next few weeks. Therefore when he arrived home, I met him at the door to the kitchen wearing a wide smile and little else. I held him close, startling him with my ardour.

'I'm going to have to go away more often if I get this welcome when I get back,' he laughed gleefully, his face grey with fatigue. Worn-out by the late nights and overindulgence in alcohol.

'You better not!' I replied instantly, turning to pour him a beer and offering him supper. The best wife I could be.

Uncharitable criticism of him had to be shut away with all the other things I felt ashamed about.

On Tuesday, Kate sent a message suggesting a Book Club meeting at hers, supposedly to discuss our upcoming Christmas night away. After much discussion, we had ultimately settled on a Saturday night at the start of December at the fabulous Mourne View Hotel in County Down. It included use of their spa facilities and a five-course meal followed by music featuring a 'famous' DJ Big Bert. Which didn't exactly inspire me with confidence. When I googled him, I discovered he had once played a gig as The Waterboys' support act in 1992. Famous indeed.

We duly met at Kate's house the following Friday night, when it was pouring with rain and the wind raged as I drove down into the village. I would leave my car overnight in her street, and Will would pick me up after work. I'd been ambivalent what to wear with my dark blue skinny jeans and after much internal debate, chose a plunging ivory silk blouse with a layered gold necklace nestling in my cleavage. Over the top for a casual Book Club evening, but I was not going to feel second best tonight. Forever comparing myself. Rarely satisfied with the results.

I stepped out of the car and observed the silent houses, dim light spilling out of some, others in darkness. One by one I studied them.

Annie's. Vicky's. Kate's. Laura's.

What lay behind those walls?

Unfaithful spouses. Unhappy wives. Unfulfilled dreams. Secrets and lies.

I shivered before I turned briskly and walked up Kate's drive. I pressed the bell, hoping she would hurry as my wet hair dripped down the back of my neck. However it was David who opened the door with a smile. It was almost as if he had been waiting for me behind it.

I grinned back at him, brushed my hair back and leaned in to kiss his cheek as I said a cheery hello. We always greeted the men with a peck on their cheeks when we socialised, a habit I enjoyed as I appreciated rough cheeks and soft lips.

'They're all in the sitting room,' he said, before asking, 'Can I get you a drink first?'

'Yes please, G&T if you have it. Wine of any description if you don't.' It was our habitual greeting.

I followed him through into their kitchen, the voices of my friends barely audible from behind the closed door. I glanced around their kitchen with a critical eye, noting it would benefit from some TLC. I became aware of David watching me and he shrugged, before reaching into the freezer for ice.

'We have three untidy kids who leave everything lying about.' He coloured slightly as he handed me my drink, subconsciously defending the mess.

'You don't need to explain anything to me,' I said as I accepted the glass, ensuring my fingers grazed his, holding his gaze. He really did have the most mesmerising eyes, reflecting almost black under the spotlights above the kitchen island. Just then their youngest daughter Sophie burst into the kitchen, demanding food as she was '*starving*', and the moment passed. Her dark eyes glared as she went straight to the fridge, without acknowledging me. Their tricky child.

With a rueful smile, I walked alone to the sitting room, where everyone was chittering animatedly. Kate and Vicky sat together on a sagging green sofa while the others had taken the mismatching armchairs. I perched on the sofa, squashed between Vicky and Kate, uncomfortable at our enforced closeness. Kate's perfume was cloying and it caught the back of my throat, making me cough.

I realised too late I wasn't in the mood for them tonight; giggle, chit-chat, smile. I didn't much care what we should wear to the Christmas party night, or how Vicky's receptionist had upset her yesterday. I gritted my teeth when Annie griped yet again about the long hours Matt spent rowing and Kate's vocal concern about Laura. The evening stretched interminably ahead with only the gin to dilute my tetchiness.

Laura was the only one who didn't agitate me that night. Who slyly winked at me when Vicky became distracted by her phone, and Kate got over-the-top excitable on a single glass of wine.

We decided, as if there had been any other option, we would dress to the max for the party night at the hotel. We'd go as early as possible so we could make use of the spa and we'd travel together in Vicky's car. And we'd all bring some bubbly with us to drink in our rooms. I'd volunteered to have a single room, declaring 'hot flushes' kept me awake and I wouldn't wish to disturb the others. Primarily I was unnerved in case I woke in the night snivelling, and dripping in sweat from a night terror. Unfortunately though there was a shortage of available rooms and we had booked a twin Laura and I would share, and a triple for the others.

If I'd known as a child I would one day become jaded by the ease at which I could spend three hundred pounds on a single night's dinner and entertainment, I would have scoffed with derision. Three hundred pounds was a fortune then; it may as well have been one million pounds. The unpalatable fact was, I had become accustomed to it, for I had been spoilt by a husband who could see only the good in me. Who was blinkered to my faults.

And the worst thing was I stupidly took it all for granted, assuming the adulation would never end and the money tree would forever keep giving.

No matter what I did.

The evening dragged and I repeatedly checked my watch. How could the minute hand move at snail's pace tonight, when it usually sped so fast, it made me dizzy.

As the clock crept close to midnight and the possibility of my escape, Laura anxiously asked the question I'd been half expecting. 'So, what did you all think of Sam?' She lowered her eyes and became fascinated by her nails, the dark red polish a departure from her standard nude tones. I noticed for the first time she no longer wore her wedding band, and now wore a silver Claddagh ring on the middle finger of her left hand. A ring which signified love, loyalty and friendship. I briefly wondered if she had bought it herself, or if it had been a gift.

'He's absolutely lovely!'

'Gorgeous!'

'So kind. Imagine, a hospice doctor devoting his life to caring for others.' That was Kate, who was trying her best to cry at the astounding emotion of someone doing their job.

'And is he just a friend?' I threw it out there, as the others were hesitant to ask. The words left my mouth with little consideration, as I softened them with a smile.

Laura tentatively looked at me and I raised my eyebrows in a question.

'He's an old boyfriend who's been a rock these past few weeks. Friends now. Who knows in time...' her voice tailed off and her smile wobbled, as if anticipating a barrage of shock and outrage.

Which, I was relieved, didn't come. No scandalised comments, no gasping with horror. To reinforce I was on her side, I said quickly, 'We all want what's best for you, Laura. No one would ever judge you for finding love again. Would we?' Here I meaningfully glowered at the others, daring any of them to disagree with me.

No one did. I didn't care what their real opinions were, but no one derided Laura, or made her feel embarrassed about Sam and I smiled at them all. They would bite their tongues and accept him. To Laura's face at least.

Will messaged to let me know he was outside in the car and I gratefully said my goodbyes. The others stayed on to finish their drinks, but I didn't want to keep him waiting. I left without seeing David again, though I could hear a raised voice in the kitchen as I slipped out of the front door.

Will looked at me wearily, having come off another long shift, and was visibly hankering after some rest.

'Did you have a good evening?' he asked, as I clicked my seat belt into place.

'Great thanks,' I answered him with a smile, filling him in on the evening, glossing over my touchiness.

The exterior lights were on at home, shining bright over the driveway and garden. I scurried inside and headed straight into the kitchen to pour a large glass of water. Will was not behind me as I'd expected, so I opened the text which had been sent to me while I was with the Book Club.

When can we meet?

True to form, Ford had messaged when I was with his wife. I exhaled slowly and didn't immediately reply. I called out to Will, but silence reverberated back at me. Wondering where he was, I searched for him down the hall, and found him asleep on top of the bed. He was fully dressed, shattered by his long shift and not yet recovered from his weekend away. His face was blameless and a sudden, sharp pain made me catch my breath. Contrite once again, I pulled a blanket over him, turned off the light and went through to Poppy's double bed.

I retrieved my phone and stared at the message, questioning

once more why he insistently contacted me when I was with his wife. However, it changed nothing.

His reasons were unimportant. The outcome would be the same.

Destruction of the thing they held so dear.

CHAPTER TWENTY-TWO

I woke late the morning after Book Club with a thumping headache, as I'd hardly slept again. Despite the comfortable bed, I'd lain awake for hours, my mind active. I'd fallen asleep at some point during the night's darkest hours, after Ford had messaged repeatedly, sending an explicit photo among the texts. Ultimately we had arranged to meet late Friday afternoon, when I hoped Will would be at work and lies and excuses weren't required.

There was a gentle knock on Poppy's door, as Will arrived in his dressing gown with a breakfast tray. He kissed me on the forehead and apologised for falling asleep so quickly last night. Undeserved atonement about such a minor thing. As recompense, he'd made me a frothy coffee and hot buttered toast, dripping with my favourite orange whisky marmalade. I eased myself against the velvet headboard, thanked him and patted the other side of the bed, encouraging him to join me.

As I chewed on the toast, we discussed our imminent weekend away to Crofters Cottage, our plans for Christmas, how well his golf swing was coming on. Mundane married chatter.

While he talked, my thoughts drifted. I assured myself yet again when he learned what I'd done and my reasons behind it, he would undoubtedly feel some degree of hurt or even anger. He always forgave me and surely this time would be no different. His love was unequivocal and my selfishness knew no bounds.

Still guilty over falling asleep so quickly, he asked me what I wanted to do for the rest of the day. It lay enticingly before us with no plans. We had the luxury of whiling away the day exactly as we pleased.

'Whatever you would like,' I answered, remembering my vow to be the best wife ever, eager to please. I snuggled into him, swallowing my discomfort at the recollection of the photo Ford had sent me in the early hours. I'd hastily screenshotted it, forwarding it to my burner phone, before deleting it. My guilt was not so easily deleted.

Will proposed lunch at Jennings, a fantastic local fish restaurant on the coast. I instantly agreed, pleased to see his face break into smiles. He lifted my dirty dishes and retreated to the kitchen, while I had a hot shower, scrubbing until I felt reinvigorated.

Concentrating only on my lovely day out with Will, I dressed in an emerald jumper dress, complete with knee-high black leather boots. Even with a two-inch heel I'd only reach his chin, something I revelled in as it made me feel small and cherished. I viewed myself objectively in the mirror, pleased with the results.

After I applied my lipstick, I joined Will, who was flicking through the sports channels on the television in the living room. He'd dressed in a navy rugby shirt and cream chinos, thankfully no old man trousers today. I dropped a kiss on his forehead before we left, laughingly having to rub off the pink stain of my lipstick. His hands roamed over me and I hugged him close, my mind shuttered and still.

We drove together in companionable silence from our haven in the hills to the coast. The restaurant was one of my favourites, overlooking the Irish Sea and serving the best Brambles in the area. I relaxed onto one of the patterned tub chairs in the stylish bar area while we waited on a table to become free in the restaurant. I slowly sipped the delicious drink, making it last as long as possible. While I would have preferred several not one, I was determined not to surrender to the delights of alcohol, my automatic go-to when stressed. I would not succumb to the appeal of the demon drink like my father before.

Will and I chatted companionably, and then he asked if I thought Laura and Sam were an item.

'Definitely!' I was shocked he could think anything else, having witnessed their chemistry in action.

'Don't you think it's a bit soon after James?' He looked at me quizzically, eyes intense.

Incredulous at his naivety, I wanted to snap at him not to be so dramatic, but instead mildly replied no. James had been a prize prat and if Sam cared for her, no one should complain. I stamped down my dissatisfaction, and clarified it by saying she deserved happiness and we shouldn't judge.

Will nodded once, before asking in a mournful voice which riled me, 'If it was you, would you move on so fast?'

'No way,' I replied quietly, taking his large, warm hand in mine. 'We can't blame her if she's been offered a second chance at happiness. And please don't talk about you dying, I simply can't bear it.' Will was occasionally prone to whining defeatism, a trait which exasperated and annoyed me equally.

He seized my tiny, cold hand in both of his and looked at me. Sadly I think, as if he could read my mind and see the brittleness which resided there. 'I love you, Claire,' he pronounced as he studied me, like an insect under a microscope.

'I love you too, Will, please don't ever question that for a second.' And of course, it was entirely genuine.

Something must have caught his eye, for as he leaned forward to kiss me, he moved back and raised his hand in welcome. The beginnings of a smile hovered at the corners of his mouth.

I swung my head round to find Mr and Mrs Ford coming into the bar area. My heart sank with dismay, an image of the photo he had sent me last night flashed bright like an electric shock. Mechanically I fixed a rictus smile in place, and rose to receive my chaste kiss on the cheek from both of them. Floral perfume from her, musky maleness from him.

There was no denying how good he looked in a white shirt and jeans, she in body-hugging leggings and a caramel coloured blouse. Ford positioned himself on the chair beside mine and casually enquired if we were planning on lunch or just a drink. Typically good-natured, Will proposed they join us for lunch and we get a table for four. Great.

Ever the actress, I replied it was a lovely idea, and only if they didn't mind company. I could tell by the glint in Ford's eye he didn't mind the idea at all. Much more fun than simply having lunch with his wife, why not include his lover and her husband too. He not so subtly complimented me, the slightest overstepping of the mark. Shrewd enough not to raise suspicions. Innocent flattery of his wife's friend to deflect from his leg touching mine. I refused to engage with him. Acutely aware of the undercurrents between us, I resolutely conversed with my friend, moving my leg so far from his, the gap was unbridgeable.

I'd unwisely forgotten he enjoyed nothing more than the chase, and rather than discouraging him, I belatedly realised it was turning him on. By the time we were walking through to our table, I sensed him daringly close behind me, the lightest inappropriate touch on the small of my back. Will chatted obliviously to us all, including everyone in talk about the dinner dance, the Book Club night away at the Mourne View Hotel and then he walked with both feet straight into the shambles of my making.

'Claire and I are going to a wee place called Crofters Cottage on the North Coast in a couple of weeks' time,' he bumbled on, heedless Ford had grown motionless beside me. 'It looks fantastic and is right on the beach near a traditional Irish pub which plays live trad music on a Saturday night. We're planning on shutting out the rest of the world and spending some time together before the madness of the Christmas rush.'

'Sounds idyllic.' Ford gave a humourless laugh and a sidelong glance at me. 'We should think about going somewhere like that.' He faced his wife and ostentatiously reached for her hand.

'We absolutely should. You two are so romantic.' She beamed at me. So much for their platonic relationship. Nevertheless, I knew all was not as it seemed.

I could stomach it no longer, so made the excuse I needed the bathroom, as Will started a monologue about coastal walks. Blood pounding in my ears, I unsteadily made my way to the ladies' toilet, where I hastily locked the door behind me. I leant my head against it and it took every ounce of self-control I possessed not to bang it until I drew blood. For at that moment I hated him, myself and this situation I had contrived in the name of vengeance.

A few moments later I felt calm enough to flush the toilet, wash my hands and go into the corridor.

Where of course Ford was loitering with intent. Without

speaking, he snatched my hand and swiftly led me into the vacant baby change room.

'What an interesting choice of holiday home,' he said flatly, locking the door behind us. I leaned my back against the wall, silently regarding him. He lowered his mouth close to my ear and rested against me, hands placed either side of my shoulders.

'Perhaps you two could book it for yourselves,' I hissed, furious with us both.

'Perhaps we could,' he replied darkly, before bending to place feather light kisses on my collarbone.

'I need to get back,' I whispered, before he covered my mouth with his own.

Pulling apart curtly, he regarded me with narrowed eyes, and asked, as if bewildered, 'What are we doing, Claire? Really, where is this going?'

'I don't know,' I mumbled, anxious to leave.

I could have answered we had a one-way ticket to chaos and bedlam, but I didn't. I placed a conciliatory hand on his cheek and said delicately, 'Let's not worry about it now. Why worry about what the future holds.'

He nodded, before saying firmly, 'I'll see you at the woods as planned on Friday.'

He opened the door, ensured no one was around, and I returned alone to the dining room, mind swirling.

'All okay?' asked Will, and I fabricated a long wait for the ladies' toilet.

Ford reappeared a few minutes later and the four of us sat in the bay window of the restaurant, a watery sun casting its dull light over the sea nearby. It was flat calm today, no hint of the swirling eddies and currents beneath the surface.

We sat together, the four of us, looking like the ideal group.

Friends. Lovers. Enemies.

The calm before the storm.

CHAPTER TWENTY-THREE

The day after our lunch with the Fords, I had planned to meet my sister Liz and woke to Will's gentle snores beside me. It was only 4am, the middle of the night for anyone except insomniacs. Bone-tired, yet unable to get back to sleep, I gave up on the pretence and crept out of bed. It was pointless staying there while my mind bounced about like the proverbial cat on a hot tin roof.

One minute I was replaying the last ferocious fight with Liz; the next I was remembering the initial cause of our tattered relationship. Occasionally snippets of good memories sneaked through. I would recall the years when we were each other's best friends, the two of us against the world.

Rather than going into the living room, I went into our underused playroom. We had called it the playroom when the girls were small, a hangout for teenagers when they outgrew dolls, and since they were now adults, we'd furnished it as a small sitting room complete with a sofa bed and floor-to-ceiling bookcases. To me, it would always be the playroom. I generally shunned this room as it reminded me of a golden era when I knew where the girls were at all times, and their biggest dilemma was if they should wear pink or purple that day. Wistfulness for those carefree days was so powerful it could incapacitate me at times.

The bookcases were neatly stacked with books purchased primarily because of their aesthetics, not their contents. I'd never read any of them and neither had Will. However all the featured houses in the home magazines had extensive bookcases, so we duly cast original opinion aside, and filled ours with books which had pristine spines and impeccable dust jackets.

I lay down on the comfortable sofa, tucked a dark blue throw over me, the lone tripod floor lamp emitting a warm glow. I knew if I was to repair my relationship with Liz, we must both admit our faults. To forgive each other once and for all. Though I pined for reconciliation, I was unsure if it was possible, as the cuts may have been too harsh.

I was afraid of unleashing further recollections, but to move forward, I knew I must confront them. From the safety of my home in the hills, I thought about what had occurred the day after my humiliation at the hands of the Hunk and the Coven. Even now, it made me want to rail at the injustice of it all. The memory I had shied away from for so long was laid bare before me.

1988

I had tearfully slunk home after the scene at the Belfast Gardens, and had a sleepless night. Miserably I had listened to Liz's deep breathing in the double bed beside me, ignorant to my turmoil.

Next morning, I pleaded with Mum to let me stay at home,

claiming I had a headache, a stomach-ache, anything I could think of. She refused, asking me only what was wrong.

How do you find the words to tell a parent they have produced such a repellent human being that everyone despised them? Even their so-called friends. I couldn't tell her what had happened, and neither could I ask for her help.

I plodded to school with my head down, trying to make myself as inconspicuous as possible, leaving it until the last second before dashing alone into the assembly hall. Keeping my eyes on the ground, I slunk onto a free seat at the end of a row, and could hear the suppressed giggles and gossiping as the news of my great stupidity spread like wildfire throughout the school. Anyone who hadn't known before school now did.

No one spoke to me. No one defended me. Those at the bottom of the pecking order were now above me. Even they couldn't afford to be seen to be friendly to the idiot who believed the school heartthrob would deign to notice her. If they had, they would have suffered the same or a worse fate than me. Public shame. The social pariah.

At breaktime, my big sister Liz came to find me crouching alone in the corner of the locker room. Surely the one person who would have a kind word for me.

'Follow me,' she instructed, pulling me roughly into a nearby unoccupied biology classroom.

'You stupid bitch,' she spat in my face. 'You're such an embarrassment. I cannot believe you would think for a minute any man in his right mind would look at you twice. For feck sake, Clare, do you know how ashamed I am? You're my sister!' Her hand shot out and she shoved me so roughly I stumbled backwards, almost falling over a wooden stool.

She strode from the room, leaving me sobbing and in pain from where she had pushed me. I sank down onto the floor of the deserted classroom and stayed there for the rest of break, before sloping along the corridor to my French class. Normally I shared a desk with Shirley, but she had moved up the ranks from the bottom of the food pile to the next tier. As a thanks for her betrayal. Today she sat beside a pale faced girl with BO. Emboldened, I scowled at my former friend, who had the grace to drop her eyes, unable to hold my stare, face flushing.

I sat on my own opposite the teacher's desk, trying to ignore the sneers from behind me.

'Enjoy your date, Hefty?'

'Even Pervy Purvis wouldn't look at you twice and he's got a glass eye.'

Snigger, snigger. Whisper, whisper.

I sought refuge with some first years in the library at lunchtime. They didn't speak to me, but didn't scoff either. I was unable to face the canteen, or the lockers, or the school tennis courts where my year liked to hang out. Eventually, the school day ended, and I crept into the girls' toilets, planning on hiding there until it was emptied of pupils. I heard the door creak open and they followed me in, half a dozen of them at least, surrounding me. Someone produced a pair of scissors. Alarmed, I assumed they were only hassling me, pretending they would do me harm. Someone grabbed my arms, then another and soon I was pinned with my face flattened against the cold, unforgiving wall tiles. My glasses dug into my nose as I felt tugging on my ponytail, hands forcing my head to be still. I couldn't even shout for help, I was so panicked.

Hesitation for a moment, then snip, snip, snip.

It seemed to last both forever and merely seconds as the hands released me, and I swung round. Tori held my ponytail in her hands. Her shocked look changed into something akin to pride, as her friends laughed wickedly at her spoils. The only crime I had committed was to fancy her boyfriend. As if I had ever been any competition for a beauty with money and brains.

She could have been flattered by my teenage infatuation with him, but instead she had been single-minded in her efforts to teach me a lesson I would never forget.

Nothing but complete humiliation would do.

How anyone could be quite so cruel was beyond me. They ran out, laughing together, my mousey thin hair lying in a heap on the tiles, like roadkill. Racing to the nearest mirror, I stared at the damage they had wrought. Jagged ends, a hotchpotch of lengths. I couldn't help myself, I started to howl, and stuffed my hands in my mouth to try and temper the agony. On and on it went, I had no control, until Maggie the cleaner came in to see what was making such a primitive noise. Looking at the hair on the floor and my contorted face, she intuitively grasped what had happened. Without speaking she came over to me, and rubbed my back, shushing me like a baby, murmuring meaningless words until my anguish lessened.

'You poor wee thing, they are a bunch of bitches. Complete bitches.'

She stayed with me until the tears dried and my sobs had subsided. Then she snatched the hair from the floor and beckoned me to follow her into the corridor. Head turning side to side, alert for anyone lurking, she padded down the hallway towards her private room on muffled feet, me sniffling behind. Once there, she reached for an ancient kettle and flicked it on. The hair was swallowed by the bin in the corner. Two chipped cups were produced, and she offered me tea, before instructing me gently to sit on the only chair.

I nodded and collapsed down on it, as the shock was wearing off and my legs felt like jelly.

'I hate that bunch of wee snobs,' she declared, waiting for the kettle to boil. 'Elodie and her mates. What a prize git she is.' To my shock and secret amusement, she lit up a cigarette and offered me a drag. Silently, I shook my head. 'You're worth ten of them, you know. They have no manners or balls. Bullies always run in a pack.'

Sniffing noisily, I listened to the friendliest person in the school as I suddenly understood. They were bullies. Pure and simple. They might be pretty and well-dressed, with the latest clothes and accessories, but they were bullies.

However at sixteen, I was at a loss to know how you dealt with bullies. Nor did I know how I was going to stay there day in, day out. Even thinking about it made me cry. Everyone detested me and I couldn't face any of them again. I drank the strong tea, but I couldn't stomach the biscuit Maggie offered me.

'You come in here any time you want,' she said sympathetically, as I rose to leave. 'Doesn't matter if I'm here or not, you're welcome any time. And I'll back you up if you want to tell a teacher. I saw them all running out, Elodie and her hyenas.'

I thanked her again for her kindness and glumly returned to the lockers to get my schoolbag, where it lay scuffed and discarded on the floor. A folded sheet of paper was propped on top, with my name written in swirly letters on it.

Feeling sick as I opened it, I read –

We all hate Hefty Lump

And it was signed by dozens of names, some scrawled, some signed with a flourish, some cramped.

They all loathed me.

But not as much as I loathed myself.

CHAPTER TWENTY-FOUR

After recalling one of the worst days of my school life, I was dry-eyed. Numbed to the core. More than thirty years had passed, yet it seemed I was that unattractive sixteen-year-old again, friendless and desolate. At the end of my tether with a world which reviled me to such an extent, even my sister was mortified to be associated with me. She had stated in no uncertain terms I was an embarrassment who deserved nothing but absolute disdain.

That experience had shaped me as an adult and not for the better. No one knew the true me and I was too afraid to reveal her. It wasn't the end of it, but there were only so many skeletons I could exhume at once. At some point I must have fallen asleep, for when I woke, weak daylight edged around the curtains and my neck ached from lying awkwardly on the sofa in the playroom.

I checked my watch, and found it was already nine o'clock. I was surprised Will hadn't come to wake me so, grimacing at the crick in my neck, I swung my legs over the side of the sofa and stretched. After tidying the room, I went in search of my husband and found him toasting pancakes and chopping fresh berries in the kitchen.

'Bad night again?' he asked, hunting for the maple syrup in the cupboard.

'Yes, I woke at four and didn't want to disturb you,' I answered, rubbing my neck.

'Were you worried about meeting Liz?'

Tersely I nodded, then reached past him to retrieve the maple syrup from the back of the cupboard. While he finished buttering the pancakes, I made coffee, his a strong black and mine with plenty of milk.

'You can cancel, darling, you know,' he said seriously, setting the food between us on the island. He wore a worried expression, with deep grooves between his eyes, a grimace replacing his usual smile.

I pretended a composure I did not feel, my voice firm. 'It's time Liz and I met up to discuss everything.'

He pretended to believe me, and we breakfasted together before he left for his beloved golf game with a last kiss on my cheek. After my coffee with Liz, I planned to meet my daughters for a catch-up and to lift my spirits.

Liz and I had arranged to meet at half past twelve, so I showered and dressed down in a pair of bootcut jeans, trainers and a navy sweatshirt I normally only wore around the house. Liz had always been vocal about her opinion on my marriage to a relatively affluent man, and I was at pains not to antagonise her by wearing expensive clothes. Whilst she'd never directly said it, I knew she believed I was a snob who looked down on her life.

Which was so far from the truth, it was laughable.

Liz had always fitted in, no matter where she went or who she was with. She had a natural magnetism which drew people to her. Throughout her life she had been almost universally accepted. And if she wasn't, she called them out and moved on without a backwards glance or a second thought. Truthfully, I had always envied her. In order to let bygones be bygones, we both had to concede to our failings and apologise for the years of misunderstandings and upset.

I was jumpy, but enthusiastic too, encouraged we could improve our recent non-relationship. We'd arranged to meet at a café near her house and I left plenty of time to drive there, not sure where I could park. It seemed many of the roads in her part of the city were one-way and it took me longer than anticipated. The café had three parking spaces of its own, so I parked in full view of the window tables. I stepped out of the car and pulled my padded jacket around me as a bitter wind caught me unawares. I shivered as I looked around, noting piles of rubbish tottering on the edge of the pavement, fast-food cartons scattered about and graffiti daubed on every available wall.

The air was penetratingly cold, so I hurried into the café and appreciated both its heat and smart décor, belying the exterior. Painted a midnight blue, with oak tables and copper accessories, it wouldn't have been out of place in the smartest of city streets. Nervously I sat at a table by the window and waited for Liz, scanning the menu before ordering a green tea to pass the time. My heart thumped irregularly and I took relaxing breaths, for fear I would hyperventilate otherwise.

Five minutes later a short, peroxide-blonde woman threw open the café door, and looked anxiously about. Her face brightened when she saw me and she raised a hand, before threading her way through the tables to me and I steeled myself for what was coming.

'Long time no see, sis,' she said, before leaning down for a quick hug, taking me completely by surprise. Half-heartedly I hugged her back, inhaling the smell of cigarettes and washing powder. She was wearing a pair of black jeans and a black sweatshirt, with LOVE embossed in red rhinestones across the front.

She took the chair opposite me, and we didn't get a chance to say more as the waitress arrived to take our order.

'They do a great sausage bap here,' Liz commented, and to please her, I ordered one, though my breakfast pancakes already sat like a stone in my stomach. She also ordered a pot of tea and once the waitress had left, leaned back in her chair, folded her arms across her chest and simply smiled.

'You're looking good, Clare,' she said, and though I searched for it, I could find no hidden barb in her statement.

'Thanks, so are you.'

She sniffed loudly, possibly aware she looked every day of her age and then some. There were vertical lines around her lips from a lifetime of smoking, dark rings under her eyes and a sorrow her cheery demeanour couldn't hide.

'I'm really glad you agreed to meet me.' It came out in a torrent. 'I wanted to say sorry.' Subconsciously I ripped at the already raw skin by my nail.

She raised her eyebrows before saying, 'Go on.'

'You're right, I was a judgemental cow about Pete. I couldn't grasp how you stayed with him after Dad.'

'What was I supposed to do? Leave him? Max was only a kid, and I didn't want to be on my own. And he's always been a good dad, Max adores him. He's an addict, but hasn't touched a drop in three years.' Her pride in her husband was obvious, adding to my regret. Undeniably, she was right. Who was I to say she should have disowned her husband at his lowest point when I knew nothing about it.

'How's Max?' I changed the subject because I knew I was in the wrong about my brother-in-law. Heat spread across my face when I remembered how unsupportive and nasty I'd been about him. Liz rolled her beautiful green eyes, and launched into a monologue about her only child, making light of the fact he was soon to be a dad himself, worried about the responsibilities it would entail, unsure if he would be equipped for them.

The sausage baps arrived, and I suddenly felt ravenously hungry. Now Liz and I were talking civilly and she was unlikely to launch herself across the table to grab me by the throat.

We talked about Will and the girls, about my life in the country and how I loved the solitude. Ultimately though, we had talked about every subject except the reunion, and it hung over me like a guillotine ready to drop.

I swallowed my last mouthful of bap as she asked, 'Are you really going to the reunion?' It was gentle, said with concern.

I nodded when I found myself unable to speak.

'I know I've said this before, but I'm really sorry for being such a bitch to you when, well, you know. I can't forgive myself for it.' I lifted my eyes and saw hers were glittering with unshed tears.

'You were only a kid, Liz, we both were. It's so long ago now.' It was barely audible.

'How do you think you'll feel when you see them all again? Have you seen any of them over the years?'

Naturally I lied, unable to admit I had.

'Once or twice. I'm ready to face them now.' Convincing us both with daring words, overlooking the hollow ring.

'Will you confront them about their behaviour?'

'I haven't decided.' Which was true. 'Maybe they'll prostrate themselves at my feet and beg forgiveness.' I grinned at the prospect of my teenage torturers on the floor before me.

'I wouldn't count on it,' Liz replied sagely. 'I think you'd better prepare yourself to be disappointed if you're hoping they'll admit to bullying. Remember, they were convinced they were better than everyone else and Daddy's bucks would get them out of anything.' Her face was set, eyes brilliant now with barely contained fury, as we both recalled the gang which had been the source of so much heartache.

'No doubt you're right,' I exhaled. What if I went to the reunion and they refused to acknowledge what they had done was wrong? Despite the outcome and the pain they'd caused. There was a chance it was the only way they could live with themselves. I knew I had to be ready for any outcome, for if I went to the reunion and was rejected again, I still had to move on once and for all.

We parted outside the café with a warm embrace and a promise we would meet again soon. Mum would be jubilant we were on speaking terms, and Liz suggested we both visit her in the near future.

She declined my offer of a lift, stating she was itching for a cigarette and wouldn't want to smoke in my shiny, expensive car. She said it with a cheeky grin, and I realised at long last, we were making tentative steps at a full rapprochement.

Truly, I needed all the people I could find on my side.

I got into the car and debated about whether I should take a detour down a street I hadn't visited in decades, or if I should drive straight to the city centre.

Feeling bolder than I had in years, I started the engine and revisited the past.

CHAPTER TWENTY-FIVE

When I was a young girl, I didn't know places existed where there were no soldiers on the streets, no bomb threats, no terror stalking the alleyways. Belfast is a beautiful city with a chequered past. From the rows of closely packed terraced houses to the leafy suburbs, so many families were touched by those years of unrest, and the past simmers still within some hearts and minds.

My family home was a short bus journey from the opulent City Hall, which presides over the centre of the shopping and business districts, although it could have been a different universe from where I had lived. Back then we had rarely crossed the lines between communities, the peace walls in place to protect families from rioting. Neighbourhoods had intentionally been separated to reduce the risk of trouble.

Without needing to check Google Maps or the satnav, I drove down the streets I grew up in. Safe now from the spectre of terrorism, children rode their bikes and scooters, calling out at some imagined game. Pristinely kept gardens, elaborate artificial floral displays in the windows, these were the homes of my neighbours until I married and moved away. Purposely, I steered clear of Shirley's street, determined not to resurrect those particular emotions today.

At last I rounded the corner into my own street, a long terrace of red-brick homes. I was surprised to find not much had changed, only the makes of cars and satellite dishes now fixed to houses. Wheelie bins had replaced the old metal dustbins, but the painted kerb stones remained, a testament to the parades of the summer.

I parked a short distance from my old home and admired the cherry blossom tree which grew broad and strong now, its leafless branches reaching towards the cloudless sky. Our chipped wooden front door had been replaced with a modern white one and a gaudy plastic wreath hung from a hook. I had no idea who lived here now, and wondered if they were ever woken in the night by the sighs of unhappy spirits from a time long gone.

The door of the house next to ours opened and an older version of Mrs Peoples, who had lived beside us, emerged. She had offered refuge from my warring parents with home-baked biscuits and a glass of lemonade. Her wrinkled face screwed up against the biting wind and she tucked a checked scarf securely round her neck, before turning her back to me and setting off at a slow pace, shopping bag in her hand. She had seemed ancient to me as a child, so who knew what great age she had reached now.

I watched until she disappeared around the corner, and was reminded of the red phone box at the end of the road, the games of hopscotch we had chalked out on the pavement and roller skating along the path after Santa surprised both Liz and me one Christmas. Not all memories were sad, I thought as my eyes drifted up to the first-floor windows, curtains neatly closed now. Our bedroom had been at the back, our parents' overlooking the street. My mind was filled with memories, both happy and unhappy, as I pictured my family in the house all those years ago.

Exhausted reminiscing, I put the car into gear and sedately drove off without a backward glance. I would not visit the house or the street again. My time there was done. For a brief moment, I considered driving on to my old grammar school. Even thinking about it caused an intense pressure in my chest, and I knew I was not brave enough to face it.

I drove down busy streets until I reached the centre of the city, where visitors filled the footpaths, admiring the architecture and enjoying the busy bars and restaurants. For Belfast is now a popular holiday destination. No one would ever have imagined there would be tours of the streets and historic murals which used to make the world news for a completely different reason.

After I had parked in a multi-storeyed car park, I put the past back in its box, looking forward to meeting my daughters. Today I'd booked a table at one of the smart bistros in the city centre, which overlooked a wide street thronged with traffic. I was early and characteristically they were late. Therefore I occupied my time scrolling through social media until Poppy burst through the door on her own. She was wrapped up in a long pink jacket and bobble hat with two pompoms.

She stripped them off and threw herself down onto the banquette seat opposite me, then started a long story about some 'prat' called Ethan who treated her like dirt, slept with her friend Mina and yet expected her to date him. I couldn't comprehend all the convolutions of modern dating. In my day you went out on a date, went steady and then dumped them, two-timed them or married them. Dating nowadays was a minefield; 'talking', 'exclusive', 'relationship'. No wonder the younger generation seemed so confused by everything. It was as if they spoke a foreign language I had no phrasebook for.

I let her ramble on, until at last she thanked me for listening. Drawing a deep breath, she looked directly at me and her face changed, lips thinning and brow knitted.

'You're very pale, Mum. Are you feeling all right?'

'And hello to you too.' I smiled to let her know I was fine and evaded her question. 'Where's your sister?'

'Probably not out of bed yet, she had a late one last night with...' Abruptly she stopped speaking. 'Her friends,' she finished impotently, with a dismissive shrug of her shoulders.

'I don't need to know the ins and outs of your lives,' I commented wryly. 'As long as you're both happy and not doing anything illegal.'

Poppy rolled her eyes, announced she was ravenous and asked if we could order before Eva arrived. Of course I allowed her. As she studied the menu, I furtively studied her. She looked tired and washed out. We should surprise them both with a short break somewhere hot in January, before their term resumed after the semester break. Once everything was over. I made a mental note to speak to Will about it.

Eva had not arrived by the time Poppy's smashed avocado on sourdough toast was served, so I sent her a quick message instructing her to hurry up. Poppy chattered on and I relished having her alone for once, as they typically came as a pair. Eva texted to say she'd be with us in a few minutes and before she arrived, Poppy commented on our weekend away to Crofters.

'I haven't been on holiday in ages,' she whined, conveniently forgetting we'd spent two weeks in an all-inclusive resort in Turkey in July. Specifically it had been a treat for Eva's birthday in July and hers in June.

'Do you know I'd never been abroad until I met your dad?' I said impetuously. I rarely mentioned my childhood to my children, in an effort to whitewash it completely. Poppy shook her head and said nothing, waiting for me to continue. 'He treated me to a few days in Barcelona to celebrate our six-month anniversary. Until then I'd never been any further afield than Portrush for a day trip.' Suddenly it was crucial my daughter knew how blessed she was, and life hadn't always been a bed of roses for me or her gran. 'He wanted to spoil me, to make me feel like I was the luckiest girl in world.'

'Who was the luckiest girl in the world?' Eva's voice cut through my reminiscing, as she plonked herself down on the seating beside her sister, before helping herself to the crusts of Poppy's toast.

'Me. I was when I met your dad.' I smiled at her, and she grinned back. Her face glowed, eyes bright. Either she'd been on tap water last night, or she'd met a boy she liked. I hoped she wouldn't get her heart broken again. Eva was quick to fall and slow to recover when her relationships ended. I wouldn't meddle, so changed the subject. After she had ordered food, we spent the next hour discussing what they wanted for Christmas, how much studying they had to do before their exams and I surprised them by revealing I'd met their Auntie Liz for coffee.

'Wow, I've forgotten what she even looks like!' exclaimed Poppy, brown eyes widening. 'Does she have grey hair and lots of wrinkles?'

'No! She's got blonde hair and lots of wrinkles,' corrected Eva. Irreverently I giggled, though I should have chastised them. Anyone over the age of thirty had lots of wrinkles in their book.

'Your cousin Max is going to be a dad.' Various reactions sped over their faces, ranging from disbelieving to pitying within a few seconds.

'How lovely,' Eva replied tentatively, awaiting my opinion.

'Yes, it's lovely though it will be a bit of a struggle for him as he's only on apprentice wages. They've been together since they were at school and Auntie Liz will help them out.'

'Is Uncle Pete still an alkie?'

'Don't call him that please, Eva,' I barked. 'He's a recovering alcoholic.'

'Sorry, Mum, I didn't mean to cause any offence.' Mutinously she stared at me from lowered lashes, mumbling under her breath, 'You always called him an alkie.'

'I did and I'm sorry.' Warily I observed my daughters. 'I was wrong and I was unkind. It's an addiction and I should have been more tolerant.'

'Okay, well good then. Will we be getting together with them soon?' Poppy the peacemaker tried her best to smooth things over.

'You never know.' I smiled at them before changing the subject. 'Do either of you want to go shopping?'

They needed no persuading, and we browsed the shops until it was dark and I offered them a lift back to their student digs. Remarkably they refused, saying they would take the bus together. I hugged them tight before they headed towards the bus stop, and had to bite my tongue, for I wanted to reassure them I loved them and to apologise in advance for what lay ahead.

Would they ever look at me the same way again? Would they be able to forgive me when they learned what I had been doing? I fervently hoped so as it was unthinkable to envisage a time when they might look at me with disgust.

Traffic was uncommonly heavy for a Sunday, and I seemed to catch every red light in the city. I marvelled how drivers dealt with it every day without losing their temper. I fumed as I sat stationary at another set of lights, eager to reach the less congested country roads where the worst thing to happen was getting stuck behind a sluggish tractor.

When I reached the motorway, I glanced up at the sheer face of Cave Hill, keeping its vigilant watch over the city. It had been many years since I'd climbed up there, and the cold hand of dread made me tremble slightly. So benign looking and yet potentially so treacherous.

I prayed I would never feel the urge to climb up there again.

CHAPTER TWENTY-SIX

It was early November, heralding the shortest days of the year. Too soon for Christmas decorations, too early for fairy lights to brighten our rooms. Winter scented candles raised my spirits, as did lush furnishings, after I swapped cotton covers and curtains for textured velvets and tweeds. Each evening I lit the fire and piled on the peat, the smell wafting through the house, mingling with the appetising aromas of rosemary and thyme from my cooking. Shortly it would be cinnamon and orange for the festive season.

Ruthlessly time marched on, and each day brought me a step closer to the end. I was by turns relieved, then afraid. Afraid of change, of what the future held. However I was equally terrified of the past, and longed for the morning I would wake and this too would be a vague memory.

I continued to join Laura and Vicky at the yogalates class in the leisure centre on Tuesday evenings, unwilling to break the routine even as I retreated further into myself. The stretching and gentle exercises helped to quell the onslaught in my mind, and I fleetingly experienced peace afterwards. One Tuesday in November, we gathered up our exercise mats and water bottles, and moved without discussion towards the café. The sole customers were two women and six boisterous children, who were eating chicken nuggets and chips. Immediately their noisy cries and incessant hubbub made my head throb. Harsh overhead lights illuminated the laminate tables, and the screech of metal chair legs being pulled along the tiles increased the nagging pain in my temples.

We occupied a table as far from them as possible, and Laura patently had something important she wanted to discuss. She was fidgety, eyes zipping around nervously as we waited for the coffees.

Once they arrived, she tripped over her words in her haste to voice them. 'I'm considering selling the house!'

Blue eyes observed us searchingly, while she unconsciously wrung her hands on the table in front of her.

'What? Where would you live? Why? Have you had an estate agent out? Claire, did you know about this?' Vicky demanded in a volley, eager to learn everything as quickly as possible.

'It's early days yet, but it's too big for me. And it holds so many memories,' Laura replied, eyes drawn to the exuberant kids who were now loudly demanding ice cream from their frazzled mums.

'I can appreciate that.' Rapidly I intervened before Vicky could hijack the conversation again. 'Have you somewhere else in mind?'

'Would you stay in the village, or would you move into Belfast? Will Robbie move in with you?' Vicky fired the questions without pausing for breath, eyes dancing with excitement.

Laura simply laughed good-naturedly at the relentless barrage. I envied her patience as I suppressed my umbrage at the constant interruptions. Laura should be allowed to tell us at her own pace. She tucked her hair behind her ear, sipped her steaming coffee and flinched as it burned her mouth.

'I don't know the answer to any of those questions yet. I'm only beginning to work it out. I love the village, however I dislike being on my own in the house. Robbie doesn't stay often and that's quite right, he's got his own life to live.'

All of a sudden, I became conscious James had not been mentioned. Not once had she uttered his name since the day on the beach with me and Kate, and it was weeks ago. I questioned how happy their marriage had been. Laura seemed particularly upbeat for a new widow, her life effortlessly moving on, his presence ostensibly unmissed.

'Only you can make the choice, Laura. Our opinions don't really come into it.' I smiled at her reassuringly. If she wanted to move from her five-bedroomed detached house into something smaller, it was her prerogative. I'd miss her living close by, but even if she moved into Belfast, it was barely a twenty-minute drive away. I watched her closely, about to ask if she would be moving nearer Sam, but the words died before they reached my tongue. She was in charge of her own destiny.

I leant over and gave her hand a gentle squeeze. 'If you need any help with valuations and so on, I know a good estate agent.'

'Thanks, I'll keep you in mind. Now I really need to get going. Do you mind if I head on?' She had barely touched her coffee, but we shook our heads, and I offered Vicky a lift home. With a small wave she tucked her yoga mat under her arm, smile in place. Vicky and I eyed each other across the table.

'Do you think this has anything to do with Sam?' Vicky enquired the moment Laura disappeared through the café doors. 'Is that why she's left early tonight as well? She didn't give a reason why she had to rush off.'

'No idea,' I replied, taking a mouthful of my cooling

cappuccino. I knew Vicky was only getting started on the subject.

'I know we all want Laura to be happy, but I would hate to think she's rushing into something she could regret.' She bored on for a while about the different stages of grief. The doctor who knew everything about every possible ailment. On and on she babbled, until I zoned her out. I wanted to ask her about medication and if it could help deep-seated misery. However, I already knew the answer. Not even a daily pill could help me now.

I nodded and grunted until she ran out of steam, my headache now like a vice, unrelieved even when the stressed-out mums departed with their unruly children.

'Have you any plans for the next couple of weeks?' I asked, keen to stop her discussing Laura further.

'Not really. Tom's working as usual, so I'm going to visit Flora at her uni halls next weekend. We also have a meal in Belfast planned with some other friends. Though to be honest, I could do without it,' she confided. 'It's one of Tom's pilot friends and his wife is a bit too interested in my husband for my liking.' Her nose wrinkled as she disclosed this.

'Too interested in what way?' I asked curiously, draining the dregs of my cup. Vicky rarely admitted to concerns about other women's attention in Tom, and my curiosity was piqued.

'Oh, she's always touching his arm, brushing his leg with hers in a not-so-subtle way, you know that bosom heaving way some women have.' She lifted her hair off her neck, before dropping it listlessly, and laughed humourlessly.

I rushed to reassure her she had nothing to worry about. 'For goodness' sake, Vicky, take a look in the mirror! No one compares to you. You must know that.'

She glanced briefly at me, clammed up and smiled vaguely. Deftly she changed the subject, asking me what my plans were over the next couple of weeks. I briefly filled her in, skipping the best parts. The café staff were unmistakably impatient to close, so we realised our time was up.

I dropped her off at her house a short time later and waited outside until she had entered her picture-perfect home. Welcoming outside lights, landscaped garden, Monoblock driveway with her Mercedes parked out front. Supposedly, she had it all. However, inside she seemed to be no different to the rest of us. Insecure, frustrated, even a bit down at times. I mulled it over as I drove past Annie and Kate's houses. I had never probed why they declined to join us for the Tuesday evening class, but now I wondered about their reasons.

Annie had no children and complained constantly about Matt's obsession with rowing. She worked full time for the charity and clearly resented any time Matt spent at the gym or training. Kate didn't have a job; she'd given up work as a dental nurse when she had the twins. I questioned how she filled her time. I'd never asked, and she never volunteered an explanation.

Latterly I had become so obsessed on my own agenda I had never bothered to find out.

When I reached the end of their street, I considered my circle of friends. As the lights of the village dimmed behind me, I sped along the country roads, brooding about the friends we had entertained and even holidayed with on several occasions. For their husbands were as integral to this sorry tale as they.

I debated if any of them would remain friends with me after. Unequivocally I would be excluded, spurned like I had been in school. The most insistent question. Did I even care?

Try as I might to fight it, the deepest part of me cared deeply. I had known when I first chose this path, what the potential outcome would be. Yet I had charged ahead, my sole aim to make amends for the past. The resulting ripples of hurt were secondary to my single-minded pursuit of revenge.

Moonlight guided me on my drive towards home. Stubbornly I reiterated the only people who mattered were my husband and children. I'd survived being friendless before, and I would do so again. It was, after all, the reason I had kept my emotional distance over the years. From those early Book Club nights when I agonised for fear of making a glaring error, to the nights the ten of us had drunk several bottles dry, and drunkenly assured ourselves we were the best friends ever. We were truly blessed. Throughout the years of confessions and confidences, when I had revealed little of any value, and no one seemed to realise.

I was fixated on the last point as I swung the car onto our driveway. The truth hit me with such force, it winded me. I killed the engine and my eyes misted over.

None of them really knew me. And none of them cared enough to peel back the layers to uncover the real me.

I had presented the painstakingly crafted version of Claire Collingswood and they had swallowed it hook, line and sinker. Without scratching the surface of me, or uncovering what made me tick. For actually, no one gave a damn. They had taken the bland, plastic façade of me, disinterested in what lay behind it. I grasped the steering wheel tightly, my thoughts careering out of control. Question after question drummed in my head.

How could I have been friends with them for fifteen years and not one of them knew Phil was not my biological father? Or why I had become estranged to my sister Liz. Or I had been so badly bullied in school I had dropped out after my GCSEs and never achieved my aspiration to be a teacher.

That I had known one of this group in a previous life. One who had not recognised the groomed, confident wife I now presented as the unattractive, shy teenager of yesteryear.

I relaxed my hold on the wheel and eased myself out of the car. I was seething with anger and resentment as I unlocked the door. If I had taken a moment to consider it logically, I would have understood they never queried my story because I had been hellbent on hiding my life before Will. Of course they had accepted the persona I had portrayed, for why would they not? My self-absorption was so great, I created an issue where there had not been one. I was filled with righteous anger as I stormed into the hall.

If Will had not been at home, I would have smashed every dish in the house or drunk myself into a stupor.

For despite my best intentions, I was drawn to the gin bottle on an ever more regular basis. It required great self-control not to surrender to the urge when my mood was as volatile as this. The small, rational part of me nagged me to speak to the GP about HRT or pills, rather than self-medicating with alcohol. The bigger, unbalanced part refused.

Carefully I took some calming breaths in the hallway, before calling for Will. No answer. I followed the low hum of the television and found him on the sofa in the living room, asleep. A half-eaten pizza was discarded on the coffee table with a half-drunk cup of coffee. Looking at his peaceful face, I felt my antipathy melt away. I shook him awake gently.

'Will, you're going to get a sore neck lying there,' I said, as he struggled to open his eyes. I leant forward to hug him and he sighed tiredly he knew he should get up, but he was so comfortable we should sleep there tonight.

So I joined him on the sofa, and we lay together for a while, as my mind raced, and I counted down the days which remained, living this duplicitous life.

CHAPTER TWENTY-SEVEN

On the Friday of that week I had to meet Ford. As usual the morning was spent at the gym, working out to cleanse my mind and fill my time. My temper towards my friends on Tuesday night had dissolved into nothing. I had become fired up over something petty and as a result of my own vulnerability. They didn't know to ask those questions because I had hidden the shameful parts of me so well, it was as if they never existed. The Book Club did not deserve my ire.

Late in the afternoon I waited in the deserted car park at the edge of the woods. Despite my previous reservations, I'd been unable to find an alternative place we could meet, and therefore found myself reluctantly there again. The shadows lengthened and the wind screeched through the barren trees. Rain poured tirelessly from the sky, saturating the ground, dripping from every surface and streaming in rivulets alongside the car park. I hated these woods in winter, bare branches harbouring who knew what. My mind fabricated all manner of menace hidden from me, imagining unblinking eyes staring. Shuddering, I switched on the engine to blow some warmth over me, barely suppressing the impulse to drive off and cancel our liaison.

Before I could hightail it out as though the hounds of hell were chasing me, Ford arrived in his shiny car. The headlights passed over me as he pulled up alongside me, and he grinned as I slipped into the passenger side of his. Wordlessly he leaned over to recline my seat, gently lying me back on it.

Afterwards he rested on his own seat, shut his eyes and spoke for the first time.

'How have you been?' Crisp.

'Great, never been better. You?' Calm.

'Good. Busy. You know, same old, same old.' Neutral.

The silence lengthened between us, at risk of becoming insurmountable. I tried to summon words, something, anything, but my mind was a complete blank. It was as if someone had reached in and removed my entire vocabulary. Brain fog, I'd heard it simplistically called, when it happened to a woman of a certain age.

Without opening his eyes he sighed, almost imperceptibly, before asking gruffly, 'Why did you chose Crofters Cottage for your weekend away with Will?'

I wavered for a second, then retorted sharply, 'Why are you asking me again?'

'Because I don't understand you, Claire. Why not book somewhere else, where we haven't stayed together?' His tone was hard and his glower now openly hostile. Tendrils of foreboding unfurled in my gut. If Will hadn't mentioned it, he would have been none the wiser.

I lowered my tone, reached over and gently stroked his cheek. 'It makes no difference to us. Please don't worry about it. You're right, I should have chosen somewhere else, it was wrong of me.' He must have found me convincing, as the tension drained from his face.

He was silent for a moment, then replied, 'I was serious the other day at Jennings. Where do you see this going?' Now he held my gaze, eyes stony.

'I never think about the future.' A blatant lie. 'This is enough for me. Why, where do you see this going?' Impulsively I threw his question back at him.

He moved away from me and studied the exceedingly exciting dash of his car. 'I don't know.' It was said quietly, just loud enough to ensure I heard. 'This is... exciting. Real life is monotonous. You are not monotonous.'

Glad to know it.

'No, I'm not! Have you ever done this before?' I blurted it out. Suddenly it was crucial I knew.

I watched him as he shook his head, before he regarded me with an unblinking stare.

'No never.' Said with complete authenticity. He reached out and touched my face, before he stretched out his arm and indicated for me to come over to him.

Unquestionably he was lying.

If I had been remotely invested in this, I would have been distraught. As it was, it merely stiffened my resolve the means justified the end.

I smiled my most friendly smile and lay uncomfortably in the crook of his arm, with the gearstick poking into my side. I reassured myself he deserved everything which was coming. The car seemed oppressive, and I suddenly yearned to gulp fresh air and feel the wind on my skin.

A short time later, we parted. It was pitch black now, hard rain pelting the windscreen, and I gripped the steering wheel ferociously as I drove home, a safe distance from his red taillights. The wipers made a sluicing noise as they beat back and forwards, barely clearing the screen and I processed what I had learned.

Ford was a cheat. He'd done it before and there was no

question he'd do it again, given half a chance. When I turned onto my driveway, his lights became fainter then disappeared altogether. He was returning home with no compunction, content with his deceit, sated and guilt-free.

I parked as close to the house as possible, then ran through the rain to unlock the door. I mindlessly stripped off my clothes in the bathroom and checked my phone to see if Will had messaged me. He was in work and would be home late, leaving me with a lonesome evening stretching ahead. Which was not what I needed or wanted. There was a short message, which I replied cheerily to. In an effort to keep my mind occupied, I played soft rock music loudly throughout the entire house.

'All Out of Love' by Air Supply blasted at top volume as I stripped off and wrapped myself in my fleecy dressing gown. I ran a bath and while it was filling, I went through into the kitchen to make myself a G&T. Dispensing with my usual berries and ice, I poured the gin into the glass without using a measure, adding a small dash of slimline tonic. I should really eat something, though I had no appetite and craved the oblivion of alcohol. I had the first one downed before Air Supply finished, so poured another while Don Henley sang the legend of 'The Boys of Summer'.

Wandering back to the bathroom, I tipped a hefty dollop of bubble bath into the piping hot water, before submerging myself. I sank back, sipping my gin, plotting my next move. The reunion was in roughly three weeks. Our night at the Averie after. It was as if a huge clock in my head was marking time to doomsday.

Slowly I relaxed into the suds, and an annoying earworm reminded me I could no longer overlook the rest of my story. Theoretically if I had only one more drink, I would work up the courage. My mind whizzed about, skirting the issue while I scrubbed my skin clean.

I had set my phone on the wash hand basin, and it buzzed incessantly with texts. Probably the Book Club with their silly chat and memes. Or my daughters demanding something. Or my husband ensuring I wasn't lying in the bath, drinking gin on an empty stomach and preparing to do something unwise.

When the water had cooled and goosebumps chilled my arms, I slowly rose. My head spun and I giggled as I stumbled, somehow invincible. Nothing and no one could hurt me while I was half cut on a miserable November evening.

Cautiously I stepped over the rim of the bath and reached for my towel. After drying off, I noticed my clothes from earlier remained in a heap on the floor. Lacy red lingerie, easy access dress. Repulsed, I gathered them up in a pile before going into the utility room, where I chucked everything into the washing machine. I switched it on before replenishing my drink.

The emotive soundtrack was still playing as I added ice to my glass. John Waite was singing 'Missing You', and I danced alone in the middle of my kitchen, clutching my drink and swaying slowly to his plaintive lyrics. Gradually I realised my cheeks were wet with tears, and as I raised the glass to my mouth, my father sprang uninvited to mind. He appeared in front of me, telling me he was so proud of me getting into grammar school.

'Go away, I hate you!' I screamed into the kitchen, my voice reverberating back to me in the vast space.

'Go away,' I begged, remembering him taking me by the hand to paddle in the sea one hot summer day.

'I hate you,' I repeated inconsolably, draining my glass. Why did I miss him tonight, when he'd been dead for so many years and haunted my dreams with only violence and unhappiness? I had to forget him, to keep hating him or my sorrow would overcome me.

The memory of him stuck obstinately to me in the kitchen,

and although I couldn't make out his face or hear his voice, his green eyes remained as vivid as in my dreams. Sad, grief-stricken eyes which hid who knew what secrets. The rest of him was like a puff of smoke, indistinct. Just those eyes burning into me with such intensity I wept harder than ever.

When I had cried until no more tears could flow, and after filling my glass one last time, I waveringly walked back to my dressing room and kneeled on the carpet. There I tugged hard on the bottom drawer and retrieved the envelope from under the T-shirts.

I opened it and allowed all the contents to fall onto the floor. One by one, they landed in a messy pile. I hesitantly reached for the folded scrap of jotter paper.

And the memories threatened to swamp me.

CHAPTER TWENTY-EIGHT

1988

It didn't take me long to decide what to do. Even my sister thought I was an embarrassment. I had no friends. I was unlikeable and unlovable. Years of insults and bullying had undermined me to such a degree it seemed there was no other way out. When I had been at my lowest ebb before, the idea had lodged and been stored away. Always before I had found a way through. But not today.

Rather than going home when I left Maggie's room, I turned towards Cave Hill, high above the city. It was a steep climb, but it would be worth it. Struggling for breath halfway up, I rested with my hands on my hips, numbly watching the busy streets far below me. Toy-like cars crawled along, and I could see a pair of army Land Rovers pull over to the side of a road, ant-like soldiers jumping out with guns at the ready. Everyday life in Belfast in the eighties.

My breath no longer ragged, I plodded upwards again, intent on reaching the top. Napoleon's Nose, the tall cliff which overlooked the city, so called because it apparently resembled the emperor, was my target. All of Belfast could be seen from its peak, and even Scotland and the Isle of Man on a clear day.

After a long while, I made it and walked as close to its edge as I dared. The sun was shining, and I watched as an aeroplane made its descent into the new Belfast City Airport on the other side of the lough. I waited until it touched down, then stepped closer to the edge. I reached into the pocket of my blazer and pulled out the torn sheet of paper I had found on top of my schoolbag. It swam in front of my eyes, all the people who despised me for simply being plain and timid.

I pushed the sheet back into my pocket and looked down. The ground was so far away. My hand shaking, I removed my glasses, everything blurred and made it seem less terrifying. Which was good.

I inched forward and drew a deep breath. Then I felt something nudge the back of my leg. It made me jump and I swung my head to find a golden retriever observing me with chocolate eyes. It had soundlessly padded up behind me and was now looking expectedly at me, tail wagging. I put my glasses back on to see more clearly.

'Go away,' I said. Instead it came closer again, and nuzzled its velvet nose into my hand. What was I going to do now?

'Poppy!' A gentle voice said from behind me. A woman with a frizzy perm had appeared from nowhere, lead in hand, jacket tied around her substantial waist.

'You need to get your dog away from the edge,' I called out. 'She might fall over and get hurt.'

'Poppy,' she unenthusiastically repeated herself. The dog sat down beside me, as if riveted by the bustling city below.

'Please, I'm worried she's going to fall!' I was feeling nervous now, for if she fell it would be my fault.

'I don't think she's going to come away unless you do.' The woman shrugged her shoulders, seemingly blasé.

I mulled it over for a minute, then nodded. If I moved back

now, then I could return when the dog was safe, and the woman had left.

With a last glance at the jagged ground below, I turned my back on the cliff edge and the dog followed at my heels.

Once we reached the woman, she patted the dog's head, nonchalantly stating, 'She likes you, otherwise she wouldn't have gone over to you.'

I snorted, retorting instantly, 'Well, she's the only one who likes me.' Uncomfortable at my unthinking admission, I glanced back to where I'd been standing a minute before. Right on the edge.

'Oh, she's an awfully good judge of character. If she didn't like you, she'd have bitten you,' the woman said with a grin. I imagined I could sense her relief, now there was a few metres between me and thin air. Had this been deliberate? The woman was about mum's age and didn't appear unduly bothered though, so it seemed I was mistaken. She was simply a passer-by with a disobedient dog.

However she didn't leave like I hoped and said, 'Why don't you give Poppy a pat.'

The beautiful dog lifted her head when she heard her name, tail wagging again. I could almost say she smiled at me. Tentatively I lifted my hand and patted her soft, silky head. The edge of the cliff didn't seem so appealing suddenly.

Without even realising it, I was walking alongside the woman and Poppy, until we came to a wooden bench overlooking the city, a safe distance back.

'Do you want a Mars bar?' she asked, as she sat down and did not insist I join her.

It was then I realised I had eaten nothing all day. I looked at the proffered bar and nodded. Smiling, she handed it to me. I didn't get many bars of chocolate, and as I ripped the paper open, the tantalising smell hit me in the face.

'My name's Eva,' she said, closing her eyes and lifting her face to the sun.

'What a lovely name,' I answered through a mouthful of chocolate. I was eating it so fast, it barely touched the sides of my mouth.

'I'm named after my gran. What's your name?'

'Clare.'

'Are you named after Clare Rayner?'

'Who?'

She smiled to herself. 'Oh no one. It's a pretty name.'

'Nothing about me is pretty,' I shot back, finishing the delicious chocolate.

'Actually, you have really beautiful eyes, Clare. You may not believe me now, but I guarantee one day you will. No one thinks they're pretty when they're young and living through the nightmare teenage years. I hated school,' she continued on, ruffling Poppy's head.

And so we sat there, in companionable silence for a bit and I thought about her words. Maybe this really was nothing more than a terrible, awful stage of my life and there could be something better waiting for me in the future.

Eva refused to leave me alone and unobtrusively stayed at my side. When she offered me a lift home, I found I couldn't refuse.

And I did what any sensible teenager living in Belfast knew not to do, I got into the car with a stranger. Who firmly insisted on coming to our door with me and speaking gently to Mum, as I waited pensively in the kitchen.

Mum came in a short time later, with tears running down her face as she hugged me, and the stranger drove off with her dog and I never saw her again.

But I never forgot them.

CHAPTER TWENTY-NINE

Will found me lying asleep on the carpet of my dressing room after he came home from work, and gently carried me through to our bed. I was only vaguely aware of his sighs in the half light, of muttering sorry as he pulled the duvet over me. He may have shared my bed, but was more likely to have spent the night in one of the girls' rooms. The only blessing from the whole sorry episode was I slept like a baby through the night, undisturbed by nightmares.

Next morning I woke alone with the mother of all hangovers, and gradually pieced together my self-pity party of one.

Sad music – tick

Maudlin wallowing – tick

Getting paralytic – tick

Something fuzzy needled me. It was just out of reach, yet its threat jabbed me. I tried to work out what exactly was filling me with foreboding. With mounting horror, I remembered putting my tacky lingerie and dress in the washing machine. Then I had forgotten to remove it before I overindulged in gin. I would have to rely on Will's allergy to laundry and wait until he was out of the house before retrieving it.

Hazy sunlight peeped around the curtains, therefore I guessed it was after nine o'clock. I lay rigid as with a sinking heart I recalled we had arranged to visit my in-laws for lunch, along with Will's brothers and their wives. I felt incapable of visiting anyone in my current debilitated state. My headache was intense and if I moved my head even slightly, nausea rolled within my stomach. Feeling distinctly sorry for myself, I called for my husband in a thin voice.

'Will, can you come here?'

No answer.

'Will, please!' I raised my voice slightly.

Still no answer.

I rotated my head with effort, spied the bedside clock and saw it was ten o'clock. Lunch was at precisely half past twelve. The notion of rising, getting washed and dressed, and looking in any way presentable was too great. I yearned to stay in a darkened room and sleep the clock round.

Will must have deduced I was awake, for he silently appeared at the door. 'How's the head?' he asked sulkily, as he leant against the doorframe with his arms folded. His eyes were guarded, his mouth downturned.

'Not great,' I said mournfully. Suddenly I was overwhelmed with agitation. What if I'd said or done something out of place last night? It wasn't in Will's nature to be so sullen. Could I have accidentally mentioned Ford? Or Will had seen my phone and read my messages? I experienced a creeping feeling of revulsion as I worried about the root of his coolness. Had I called him the wrong name? My pulse quickened, and I tried to raise my head from the pillow.

'What's wrong?' I felt obliged to ask, as he mutely glowered at me.

A pause before he spoke. 'You knew we had this lunch with my parents today. I don't ask much of you. Couldn't you have delayed getting stocious for another time?'

Ice-cold comprehension chilled me. Always keen to demonstrate his wife with the dubious background was as good, or better than his brother's classy wives, he was peeved I had a hangover when we were visiting his parents. It was nothing I couldn't remedy. I'd had years of practice.

I ignored my queasiness, sat upright and rested my thumping head against the headboard. We should really have opted for a padded, soft one, not an unforgiving wooden one.

'I'm a bit tired, so many memories...' I could tell immediately he wasn't buying it. A horrible idea struck me. Had I hidden the debris of my past back into the drawer before I fell asleep? Or had he arrived home to find a drunk wife and the evidence of her dismal history laid bare around her?

'Why were you sleeping on your dressing room floor? Couldn't you have gone to bed? And why weren't you properly dressed? I know the reunion is stressful, but this is...' A beat as he searched for the word, 'unacceptable.' He finished insipidly.

'I'm truly sorry, sweetheart.' The words were barely perceptible through my clenched teeth. For I wasn't sorry. I was only sorry I had got caught. It was his fault really, always working when he knew I was vulnerable. He should be home with me, not staying out late when I relied on his support. I dropped my eyes to conceal the quiet fury behind them, and said tonelessly, 'It's only a touch of a headache. Nothing a cup of tea won't sort out.' I raised my eyes to his, forced a smile, and he nodded before turning his back. Traces of his aftershave hung in the frosty air and I rolled my eyes. He could be such a paragon of virtue. I wanted to scream my frustration at his holier-than-thou act sometimes.

I threw back the bedclothes and queasily stood, then

shuffled through into my dressing room. I was desperate to ensure I'd left no incriminating evidence lying around. Nothing looked out of place. To be certain, I yanked open the bottom drawer to confirm the envelope was in its proper place under the clothes. Thank goodness I'd been savvy enough to do that. I rested back on my heels and the waves of nausea receded somewhat. Anxiety had been compounding the sickness. I reassessed my plan of action.

Obviously I had to stop drinking on my own. It was beginning to slide out of control and I couldn't afford a rerun of last night. Also, I had to rethink my eating. Although I seldom weighed myself, I could tell I'd lost weight through too much exercise and too few calories. I was skipping meals I could not afford to miss. I loved exercise, and it was crucial for my mental health to continue with it. Therefore healthy eating was no longer an option, it was a necessity.

Dejectedly I hauled myself up using the drawers, and returned to the bedroom, where Will had deposited a cup of tea and a slice of toast on the bedside table. No marmalade this morning. No sitting on the bed beside me putting the world to rights. I knew I would have to play the part of the dutiful, repentant wife today. I crawled back into bed and hunted in the bedside drawer for some painkillers, which I consumed with a mouthful of tepid tea. Afterwards I chewed the toast and eventually felt able to shower and dress.

In the bathroom I found the water still in the bath from last night. Slimy scum from the soap smeared the surface, like a waste product polluting a pond. Furious with my lack of self-control, I reached in and pulled the plug, watching the cold-water swirl down the plughole. Will must have seen it too, yet in his typical passive aggressive manner left it for me to find. I sighed with impatience, stepped into the shower and allowed the pounding water to pour over me. Although the headache had lodged behind my eyes and my stomach remained upset, I had to make an effort, no matter how ill I was feeling.

After ten minutes in the shower, I felt less like death warmed up. My sisters-in-law would be effortlessly elegant in their understated, expensive and demure way. The devil on my shoulder urged me to choose a clingy, red jersey dress which emphasised my surgically enhanced cleavage. Tempting as it was, I luckily remembered I was in penance mode and opted for a boring denim shirt dress and knee-high leather boots. Having my brothers-in-law salivating over my fake boobs at lunch wasn't the done thing.

I applied my make-up, at a loss as to why I was so angry with Will, as really he had done nothing wrong. My only plausible excuse was months of lying, cheating and duplicity had scrambled my sense of decency and logic. It seemed I had taken a sledgehammer to my moral compass and shattered it completely.

When I was ready, I found a surly Will watching football on the living room television. I swallowed my frustration, went over beside him and nestled in close. Kissing his cheek, I again whispered I was sorry and it wouldn't happen again. It was a stupid thing to have done, I was nervous, blah, blah, blah.

Lovely trusting Will, who only had my welfare at heart, solemnly informed me it was because he was worried about me. I wasn't much of a drinker and drinking alone was the road to nowhere. He didn't explicitly say *You don't want to become like your no-good father* but the implication was obvious. And I was completely, inexplicably furious with him once again, exasperated at having the spectre of my alcoholic father being used as a whipping boy.

I stamped down on my anger, murmured placatingly and agreed with him, while my insides churned. He hugged me and supposedly peace was resumed.

He drove me to his parents' house and I was silent, consumed with my musings. Sometimes it was wearisome being married to a saint. A man whose idea of breaking the rules was pinching a beer glass from a pub, who never parked on a double yellow line and whose sexual thrill was having sex with the lights on. I had to remind myself that was the exact reason I had chosen him, for his stability and steadiness. I had behaved badly last night, yet he believed all I'd done was get a bit merry on my own.

Which had warranted a mammoth sulk and a lecture on alcoholism.

Then the dawning awareness, so subtle I was barely conscious of it. If he discovered what I had really been doing, his moral outrage may be so great he would never forgive me.

With that axe hanging over me, he pulled into the driveway of my in-law's house. Suppressing my irritability, I placed my hand on his arm and smiled wanly. 'I'll drive home, sweetheart, if you'd like to have a glass or two of wine.'

'Thank you, that would be lovely, darling,' he replied, his broad face breaking into a smile.

I climbed gingerly out of the car, clutched Will's hand and forced a smile. My decent in-laws were completely oblivious to my underhand dealings, and I needed it to stay that way for as long as possible.

The entire afternoon, a small voice badgered me, saying that I had never been good enough and I never would be.

CHAPTER THIRTY

At last Will and I were going on our long-awaited weekend break to Crofters Cottage. In the intervening period, I worked out at the gym, cooked nutritious food and limited myself to two glasses of G&T each evening. They were doubles, but I restrained myself from having any more than two. Usually. My resolve to quit drinking completely fell by the wayside once the headache eased and my stomach had settled.

The morning before we left for the cottage, I drove to Marks and Spencer to stock up on essentials. We planned to eat pub grub in the Stile and Donkey on Saturday evening, though the rest of the time would be him and me, cosseted from the world.

Although only November, the shop was already decorated for Christmas; artificial trees decked with sparkling baubles, festive songs on repeat, the shelves brimming with gift ideas and scrumptious food to seduce. I salved my conscience by overindulging in gift buying for Will, the girls and my mum. I also purchased some of the demure white lingerie Will favoured, eyes skimming over the miniscule sets Ford preferred. Retail therapy at its finest.

Bags laden with the gifts, I decided to quench my thirst after my shopping spree. When I reached the café, I spotted Annie sitting on her own, nursing a latte as she flicked through a magazine. She glanced up before I could slip away unseen, so I mechanically smiled and waved back. I fervently hoped she wouldn't launch into a moaning session about Matt, for that was her favourite topic of conversation.

I carried my skinny latte over to the table, and sank onto the seat opposite her with a groan, depositing my many bags on the ground. She surprised me by immediately questioning me about Laura and her vague idea about selling the house. Her eyes shone with excitement as she quizzed me as to whether I knew the details. Mildly surprised by her avid interest, I was however relieved there was no hint of criticism in her tone.

Then she asked conspiratorially, 'Claire, did you like James?' Honest eyes seeking an honest answer.

'Not really,' I replied carefully, averse to saying the wrong thing, unsure what Annie was inferring.

'Me neither.' She dropped her voice, as though Laura was going to jump out from behind the potted plant in the corner.

I was taken aback, having presumed she would subscribe to the 'don't-speak-ill-of-the-dead' concept.

'Did you notice how he liked to tell her what to do, and was forever making snide digs about how she looked when we were together?'

I nodded as I supped my steaming coffee, waiting for her to go on. James's unpleasant comments about Laura used to infuriate me as her face coloured and she noticeably deflated.

'I wish...' Annie gazed pensively out of the window at the lough before continuing, '...I had been brave enough to say something when he was alive. Checked if she was all right.' Her frank gaze swung back to me, and she chewed her lip in consternation.

'Do you think she would have admitted if there was a

problem?' I asked faintly. Because I doubted she would have. The intricacies of a relationship could be hidden behind a smiling façade, the grim reality never revealed. Despair and discontent could remain a shameful secret, concealed from closest friends and family.

However once Annie voiced her concerns, I acknowledged to myself I had worried about Laura too, and now felt ashamed for not having pursued my gut feeling. I had sensed all had not been well in their marriage for some time, but I had buried my head in the sand, instead festering in my own mire.

Annie shook her head, curls bouncing, and smiled ruefully. 'Possibly not. She's like a different person now, and it can't all be down to the handsome Sam. It's like...' she hesitated as she searched for the words, before ending with a flourish '...she's thriving not just surviving!'

I grinned at her while remorse stabbed me. Deliberately ignoring it, I finished my coffee and made my excuses, explaining I still needed to pack for our weekend away. Wistfully she told me to have fun, before adding she had better leave too as she was due back in the office.

On the drive home a short time later, it crossed my mind a life with no children must be entirely different to the life of a parent, even when your offspring have grown up. The thought of never experiencing the unconditional love a parent both receives and gives, saddened me. I'd never enquired if it was through choice she and Matt were childless. It was simply too personal and might distress her.

By the time I pulled into the driveway, my brain had moved on from my chat with Annie, and was overcrowded with clamouring thoughts. Ford. His wife. The reunion. I packed the food into the cool box and tucked my new underwear into my case. I was relieved there was enough time to do an online workout before Will was due home. It might stave off my stress.

Sweating and panting after I had crunched, squatted and lunged, I stripped off and was about to step into the shower, when my phone beeped with a message. Cooling down fast, I wrapped myself in a towel, expecting it to be from Will.

Of course, it was from Ford.

Why am I annoyed about you going to Crofters this weekend with Will?

All of a sudden I felt trapped, the tightness in my chest causing my heart to race. My husband on one side, the progressively more suffocating Ford on the other. Since he had discovered I had booked Crofters for me and Will, he had exposed a different side of himself. It was as if it had insidiously unearthed his dark side; jealous, possessive even. His need to charm and cajole was now a thing of the past. My resentment towards this new trait escalated daily.

Furious with his mind games, I placed the phone on the edge of the sink, dropped the towel and stepped into the shower. Energetically lathering shampoo into my hair, I debated how to respond. Should I disregard it? Make light of it? Pretend I gave a damn? I tossed it back and forward as I exfoliated, shaved and soaped my body. I needed to keep him dangling for another while, therefore disregarding it was out of the question. Making light of it would provoke a flurry of indignant messages. I turned off the water, and feeling worse than ever about the entire situation, accepted I had to pretend I cared.

Words whirled, clouding my thoughts, leaving me unable to formulate a reply. Edgy, I debated what to do. Minutes passed before I devised my reaction. Pacifying with the hint of promise.

I typed:

We have our night at the Averie to look forward to. I'll make it up to you then.

He was online and I could see the three dots moving as he typed his reply.

I can't wait. What are you wearing right now?

I groaned with annoyance before snapping a photo of my damp arm. Hoping it would satisfy him, I prayed he would get offline and leave me alone. No such luck. He demanded more. Every word I typed was torture, every photo he demanded sacrilegious. I needed this to be over. I had minimal energy to think about a relationship I had devised, plotted and demanded. Defeated, I sank onto the hard floor tiles, fighting the urge to curl into the foetal position on the floor, put my hands over my ears, close my eyes and eliminate the world.

Part of me feared the pressure of my deception was leading me to lose control. I was fragile, close to breaking into a million insignificant pieces. Was it worse than the numbness I craved? Up, down, round and round, my mind spiralling, uncontrollable emotions and feelings and sounds and sights...

'Claire?' The voice of my rescuer loudly broke through the din in my head. Like a man offering a drowning woman a life ring. I replied I was getting dried off and would be out soon. I grabbed my phone and put it on aeroplane mode so I couldn't hear, see or think about anything other than my husband. I struggled to stand and caught sight of my image in the mirror.

Empty eyes, drawn face, ribs stark, mocking pert breasts.

Resisting my intrinsic negativity, I fought to regain my positive attitude.

A knock at the door made me jump as Will asked if he could come in. Unconsciously I wrapped the towel around me, smiled and opened the door. He had an optimistic look on his face and brandished a gift bag, dangling it from his fingers.

'What's this?' I asked, as I recognised the logo of an exclusive city jeweller.

'I saw it and thought of you.' He resembled an over-excited child on Christmas morning as he handed it to me.

I untied the black ribbon and withdrew a small velvet box. I gasped with astonishment as I revealed a delicate gold chain with a three diamond drop pendant. My eyes flew to his and I stuttered, 'This weekend is for your birthday not mine.'

He shushed me, instructing me to turn around so he could fasten it behind my neck. I lifted my wet hair and he stood behind me, hands resting on my shoulders as we stared at it in the mirror. It was the most beautiful and caring present I had ever received.

He whispered in my ear, 'The three diamonds are for me, Eva and Poppy. You've made me the happiest man in the world.'

The bile rose as we locked eyes in the mirror. In a moment of madness, I imagined confessing all. However sanity prevailed. Would he ever look at me this way again? After? I doubted it. Desolation and nostalgia for our happy life together, before Ford, stirred within me.

I allowed him to hold me as he kissed my neck, removed my towel and led me by the hand to our bed. The eyes are windows to the soul, and I shut mine, afraid Will would glimpse what lodged there.

When it was over, I watched him go through into the bathroom, my inner voice silent, yet reproachful. I heaved myself off the bed, and dressed in the jeans and fuchsia pink jumper I had selected earlier. Acting the part of the loving wife was not challenging. Performing the role of the honest, faultless partner was almost unachievable. But imposter that I was, act I must.

After drying my hair and tying it back loosely, I decided to be make-up free this weekend. The two of us. No gimmicks. No game playing. Momentarily I contemplated leaving my phone at home, until I dismissed that idea. However it would remain on aeroplane mode for as long as possible.

Will packed the car while I ensured the windows and doors were locked. With a final glance around my home, I banged the door behind me and slipped into the passenger seat. The weather was drab and miserable, with low hanging clouds promising a downpour. We had packed our raincoats and boots, and really it didn't matter what the weather was like. Crofters Cottage would be our oasis of calm in the midst of a churning wild journey.

Nothing would spoil it.

Not even the promise of a hurricane ahead.

CHAPTER THIRTY-ONE

We spent a blissful couple of days at Crofters Cottage. As forecast, a raging storm hit the coast late on Friday night. A ferocious wind howled outside as rain battered the windows, and we remained snug within the solid whitewashed walls, the wood burner flaming bright as we fed it all weekend. I recoiled from recollections of my previous stay there as best I could, drowning out unwelcome images with music and chatter. We rushed to the pub on Saturday evening for a hearty meal of scampi and chips. There the peat fire smouldered in the corner as musicians played live trad music. It was cheerful and warm, and we snuggled together like newlyweds in our booth by the bar, my mind free of recriminations for once.

We laughingly ran hand in hand back to the cottage later, stopping to kiss like teenagers in the shelter of a doorway. I tasted the sea spray on his lips and felt young and free, unencumbered by guilt or regret.

We shook off our wet coats and I unveiled Will's birthday present before unveiling my birthday suit. I'd bought him a Tag Heuer watch he had coveted for some time. The superstitious part of me agonised: gifting a watch signifies an imminent break in your connection, and I worried about tempting fate. Ultimately though I dismissed it as drivel, impatient to see his face suffuse with joy. We enjoyed our time there so much I rebooked for Valentine's Day before leaving on Sunday morning.

Following our return home, I calculated the Book Club night to the Mourne View Hotel was now less than a fortnight away. Which ominously meant it was barely three weeks until the reunion. I should be preparing for Christmas, but I was drained at the enormity of what lay ahead.

Before the Book Club party night, I wanted to meet with Eva and Poppy to finalise their Christmas lists. There was the long-awaited catch-up with Mum and Liz, which we somehow had not yet organised. Also I wanted to buy a new dress for the reunion. I had rummaged through my wardrobes, selecting then discounting dress after dress. Too dowdy. Too long. Too clingy. Too nondescript. At times my mind screeched with nerves.

Compounded by the proximity of the reunion, Ford had hounded me throughout our stay at the cottage. Message after message illuminated the screen when I switched my phone on. My blood had boiled at his dogged efforts to ruin my precious weekend with Will. His relentless bombardment with unwanted communication exasperated me. I had half expected him and his wife to roll up for a walk on the beach outside the cottage, and I'd been relieved when the gale blew, extinguishing any chance of it.

However he left me no choice. I had to meet him again before the Book Club night away. We contrived a meeting at a house I was showing over lunchtime on Tuesday, when he could slip away undetected for a while. It was easy to fabricate a strong work ethic when you had as many 'viewings' as I did at lunchtime. Of course, they never resulted in a sale, which in hindsight was a lapse in judgement.

Unwilling to use the forest car park again, I'd chosen a remote farmhouse in the hills. It had lain empty since the owner moved into a nursing home in the spring, and his son was keen to sell, as he had no inclination to farm. There had been scant interest, especially as the frigid winter days exacerbated its isolation. My colleague who was dealing with the sale was on sick leave, and I hadn't sussed it out before our rendezvous.

When I arrived in the badly maintained yard, it reminded me of a derelict site featured in a slasher movie. Outhouses splattered with mud and in need of repair, windows smashed, rusting farm machinery discarded about. Ford pulled up behind me, leaving me no chance to enter the crumbling house and work out which room we could use. He exited his car with ill-disguised irritation, slammed the door and strode towards the house. With barely a glance in my direction, he waited impatiently in the cold, while I fumbled in my bag for the keys.

The ancient lock protested and I had to push hard to open the door, which had swollen with damp. Ford stooped slightly or he would have bumped his head on the low ceilings. I brushed cobwebs out of the way as we moved into the front room. The dim half light wasn't improved by switching on the single fringed floor lamp. A musty smell assaulted my nostrils and dust motes lazily circled around in the feeble light. No one in their right mind would buy this place unless they had a bottomless wallet to renovate. No one in their right mind would undress due to the risk of contracting some dreaded disease.

He looked at me with annoyance, evidently of the same opinion. 'Was this the best you could come up with?' he demanded, fists balled at his sides.

Affecting nonchalance, I reluctantly placed my handbag on the grimy coffee table before responding. 'Yes, unfortunately it was.' I was wearing a pleated skirt, it shouldn't be unworkable.

He shook his head before replying, 'Let's look upstairs.'

Meekly I followed him up the steep staircase, each step protesting loudly. Loose floorboards were everywhere. The bedroom at the far end of the hall was the most presentable, with a reasonably clean quilt on a small double bed, scratched mahogany drawers and a mottled mirror on the wall. It had probably been the main bedroom in a previous life, however I would not risk touching the bed.

A few minutes later, Ford seemed to have forgotten his bad form when I heard the indistinct creak of a floorboard.

'Stop!' I said in his ear, but he carried on, oblivious. Another creak. 'Stop a minute!' I hissed louder, and this time, he obeyed.

There was no mistaking the tread of heavy footsteps on the stairs. Pulling apart, I promptly straightened my skirt as Ford whipped behind the door to sort himself out. To my utter dismay a rotund man appeared at the top of the stairs. By good fortune he glanced over his shoulder in the opposite direction first, leaving me enough time to lurch onto the landing.

'Hello,' I said loudly, obstructing his view of the bedroom. 'Can I help you?'

His head swung round and I could see a scowl on his florid face. 'What were you doing in my father's room?' he demanded, shoulders unyielding.

'I'm Claire Collingswood, the estate agent. I was giving Mr Ford a tour.' I smiled blandly at him, as Ford cleared his throat behind me.

'Didn't sound like it to me.' There was no disguising his distaste.

My stomach flipped and my mouth dried as Ford stepped around me, walking up to the stranger. Calmly he reached a squeaky floorboard and started to rock gently on it.

Creak. Creak. Creak.

It was a plausible imitation of a not so innocent cause.

'All these floorboards creak.' He gave his most devastating

smile. 'It could easily be mistaken for something else.' And he stuck out his hand, so the younger man had no option but to grudgingly do the same.

'Gavin Ford,' he lied effortlessly, shaking hands firmly. 'This place is so charming. I should get Mrs Ford to come and view it with me.'

His nerve was astounding, as was his completely sincere tone. Not for the first time, I was dumbfounded by his ability to convincingly lie under pressure.

The owner's son seemed inclined to believe him, so I allowed Eric – as he insisted we call him – to lead us through the dank rooms. The highlight of the tour was a dead magpie lying in the fireplace in the 'parlour.' What a hellhole. I couldn't shake the concept a dead bird indoors is an omen of death. A cold shiver snaked down my spine as I completed the tour, somehow stopping myself from running outside, starting the engine and driving as fast as I could to civilisation.

After an age we were able to leave, and Eric stood in the doorway with his arms crossed, watching us depart in separate cars. No sooner had I reached the end of the overgrown lane, than my phone rang, connecting automatically with the hands-free system.

'That was a first.' Ford laughed when I answered it. 'I think he fell for the old squeaky floorboard excuse though.'

'He better have, or I could lose my job.' I was inundated with resentment. He was so congenial now, the complete opposite of earlier.

'Calm down, Claire,' came his retort, which incensed me further. 'No one's going to lose their job. The fool fell for it.'

By now I was so irate, I disconnected the call.

My temper simmered as I sped back to the office, picking over everything Eric had said and done, worrying he had not believed our fabricated story. My mind moved on to Ford, who had shown his true colours at last. I was certain he abused his good looks to get exactly what he wanted from life. Over time, he had revealed that behind the front he presented to the world, he was much less appealing.

Charismatic. Suave. Attractive.

While he was all those things, he was also shallow, selfish and arrogant.

I was mortified at how easily I had been duped. Like everyone else, I had been deceived by his carefully curated front. His true self was only exposed when he felt comfortable in your company, and he erroneously presumed he no longer had to conceal it. How could I ever have dropped my guard with him? For I of all people should have known better. Momentarily, I felt almost sorry for his wife, then incandescent with myself.

However I had no time to worry about it, because when I arrived in work my boss Imelda immediately appeared from her office, bony fingers clasped in front of her.

Rigidly she studied me, before saying firmly, 'Claire, can you come in here please.' Her eyes blinked rapidly behind her glasses, her back ramrod straight.

Unsure why I'd been summonsed, Kevin at the desk next to mine shrugged to indicate he didn't know either. I rose slowly, smoothed down my skirt with clammy hands, and strolled into the tiny, windowless room.

'Close the door please,' she said sternly, and I felt a surge of anxiety.

Obediently I did as I was told, and she indicated I should sit on the uncomfortable metal chair opposite her desk. With no preamble, she started to speak.

And it became obvious I had a whole other problem to contend with.

CHAPTER THIRTY-TWO

Will was working that Tuesday night, leaving me painfully isolated when I arrived home. I was shell-shocked following the impromptu meeting with my boss. Imelda had been terse, pale eyes balefully staring as she listed Eric's accusations.

Evidently he wasn't quite the fool Ford had supposed, and my cheeks burned with humiliation when she asked me to leave, pending further enquiries.

I eased my shoes off in the hall and walked into the kitchen, stricken with embarrassment as I recalled the scorn in her eyes. I was at a complete loss what to do. I sank onto one of the stools at the breakfast bar, unconsciously tearing at the already raw skin beside my thumbnail.

Her steely tone and glacial manner had chilled me. Despite my best attempt to dismiss Eric's allegations as preposterous, shame had clung to me, tainting the airless room.

I glanced around the kitchen, and although my eyes stopped wistfully at the gin bottle, I instead boiled the kettle, selecting green tea. Getting drunk on an empty stomach was the craziest thing I could do while I sifted through my options.

I couldn't confide in Will, though I longed to. A burden shared is a burden halved, but I had no confidante. No one I could trust to be objective or non-judgemental.

I carried my mug into the conservatory and instructed Alexa to play soothing music. My mind careered around while I deliberated, and by the time I swallowed the last mouthful of tea, I had a plan of action. I returned to the kitchen, calm now, and popped the remains of last night's lasagne into the oven. I surrendered to my craving for gin, carefully measured it out and added plenty of slimline tonic. While the lasagne warmed, there something else I needed to do.

I walked down the hallway and into my dressing room, where I set my gin on top of the drawers. I kneeled down to repeat the ritual one final time.

Everything lay in a messy heap on the carpet. The newspaper cutting was what I sought and I gently lifted it. Delicate as a flower in May, it was brittle and yellowing. I handled the fragile paper carefully, enrapt in the wedding photo I'd cut from the *Belfast Post* years ago. Unseeing faces grinned at me and an intense hurt twisted in my heart as I stared at them. Two youngsters, who had pledged to love, honour and cherish one another till death did them part. Huge smiles on line-free, gorgeous faces, congratulating themselves on their fairy-tale wedding and honeymoon. I despised them both in that minute.

I gently slipped the cutting back into the envelope, then buried it in the drawer, knowing I had no reason to revisit it again. It had served its purpose. I returned to the kitchen, extracted the lasagne, and sat at the table, forcing myself to eat it. I listened to the music as my pulse slowed and I concentrated on my breathing.

When I had cleared my plate, I went into the conservatory and allowed myself to recall hot summer days with the threat of exams looming ever closer.

1988

The weekend after Eva rescued me, Mum, Dad and even Liz tiptoed fearfully around me. My parents insisted I talk to them at the kitchen table, refusing my pleas to be allowed to go to bed.

Ultimately I confided snippets of what had happened. The scissors. The note. I couldn't voice the insults I had suffered, nor the despair I was feeling.

Mum had brought me to her hairdresser on Saturday. She had trimmed what remained of my hair into an approximation of a pageboy style. All it did was accentuate my bad skin and giant glasses.

Eva had got it wrong, I stuck adamantly to my story. I was stressed, everything had got on top of me. Mum wasn't content until I had given her the names of the girls who had cut my hair, insisting she would be taking it to Mr Shaw the headmaster first thing. No matter how I begged her not to, she had made her mind up.

Monday morning was fine and sunny, and I listened to birds chirp merrily outside my bedroom window, praying Mum would have changed her mind. I suspected it wouldn't improve my situation and I was terrified it would only make things worse for me during those seemingly never-ending school hours.

Sullenly I dressed in my detested uniform and drank tea at the kitchen table, while trying to swallow a slice of toast which stuck to my teeth and the roof of my mouth. Mum's idea was to walk to school with me and meet the head first thing, but Liz managed to dissuade her. Half-heartedly she decided to wait until after assembly.

I dallied on my walk to school, my stomach knotted at having to face everyone, worried what the headmaster would do. Would he suspend them? Or would he side with them and believe their version? I didn't know and was petrified of finding out.

I crept into our form room after assembly and sat alone at a desk in the front row, listening to the stage whispers about my hair, my isolation. Not one person spoke to me, and I had to fight the impulse to flee screaming from the room.

Mrs Simpson, our form teacher entered shortly after and I noticed how she compressed her lips into a thin line at the sight of me. Did she know? If she did, she gave no hint as she painstakingly conducted roll call. Before we had a chance to scatter for our next class, there was a knock at the door and the school secretary bustled in, before calling out the names of the perpetrators.

'Elodie, Kathy, Tori, Michaela, Anya. Mr Shaw wants to see you in his office. Now!'

Possibly it was my imagination, but a hush descended over the classroom as their smug faces paled at the command. Hesitantly at first, they rose and mutely filed out after the secretary.

'What are you all staring at? Get to class.' Mrs Simpson took no notice of the hubbub which had started as soon as the Coven left.

Every moment of my English class was agony, as I awaited their return. About twenty minutes later, Elodie strutted through the door with Tori and Kathy trailing behind. They grinned and threw me looks of pure malevolence when passing my desk. Elodie brazenly knocked my pencil case on the floor, as the Hunk sniggered loudly from where he lounged in the back row.

Not chastened. Not repentant. Entitlement oozing from them.

As expected, my mum's meeting had achieved nothing. Mr Shaw evidently believed the Coven and their distorted explanation. It was five to one. Popular versus unpopular. There had been no chance I would be declared the winner. Mr Shaw didn't even bother to discuss it with me. I was persona non grata. They were omnipotent.

Punishment was swift and harsh as word spread I had tried and failed to get acknowledgement of their role in my distress. I was sent to Coventry by the entire year. Not only did they blank me, they also literally turned their backs on me daily, making it glaringly obvious I was universally despised. Anonymous notes littered my school bag and locker. Scissors were taken to my PE kit. Food was stolen from my Tupperware lunch box.

Each day I slunk into Maggie's room to spend my breaks with her. She would shut the door and feed me tea and biscuits, prattling about this and that while smoking like a train. Her good nature and sympathy enabled me to finish those last few weeks of classes, before we were granted study leave and I sat my GCSEs. Finally I could be free of education. Beaten by the system and the injustice of it all.

Now I had permitted myself to remember everything, I questioned my sanity in attending the reunion. Nevertheless, I belatedly appreciated how easy it was to rewrite the past. I conceded I had changed parts of the story to fit my own narrative.

Not everyone had been awful to me. A couple of girls, whose names I couldn't recollect, had shown me compassion. One had offered me her bag of crisps when my lunch had been thrown on the ground and stamped on. Another had wordlessly handed me a spare T-shirt for games, after my own had been butchered. They too were unpopular and were careful to have no witnesses to their kindness. I understood too late and only with hindsight, they risked being dumped into my silent hell for showing solidarity with the outcast. It was important to remember how they and Maggie made my life easier.

The headlights of Will's car swept past the windows, glinting through the wooden slats of the blinds. Instantly I commanded Alexa to play happy songs. By the time he came into the kitchen, I was washing my glass in the sink and Fleetwood Mac's 'Little Lies' was blaring from the speakers.

'What on earth are you listening to?' he asked, as he removed his wet coat and hung it in the utility room, an amused look on his face.

'Oh, I love a bit of Fleetwood Mac,' I replied airily, humming tunelessly along.

'I thought you'd be in bed,' he said, head stuck into the fridge, eyeing the contents for something to snack on.

'I'm not tired. I wanted to wait up for you.' I wound my arms around him from behind and closed my eyes while resting my cheek against his back. He lifted out a block of cheese and set it on the worktop, before turning to face me.

Gently he lifted my chin and looked directly into my eyes. I held his gaze. Apparently satisfied I was neither drunk nor miserable, he leaned down and gave me a quick kiss on the lips before turning back to the cheese and buttering some crackers.

'How was work?' he asked through a mouthful of food.

'Same old, same old,' I replied uncertainly, unable to look at him. 'Though if I'm being honest, I'm getting bored of Russell Estates. I might look for a different company in January.'

'Well you've been there years. They say a change is as good as a rest,' he replied unknowingly, and pushed me no further about it.

Good old Will who believed anything I said.

And on that wild and stormy November night, I was immensely grateful.

CHAPTER THIRTY-THREE

With precise planning, I cunningly hid my indefinite suspension from Will. If he was home on Tuesdays or Wednesdays, I would rise at my usual time, dress in workwear and leave him with a kiss and a sinking feeling in my stomach. I changed my clothes in the car and parked by the ocean, where I walked for miles on the coastal path. The rolling waves and stiff sea breeze eased my mind, giving me the freedom to mentally prepare for the arduous weeks ahead. Ironically as the end drew closer, I felt emotionally stronger and more capable of dealing with it all.

On my return home, I would work out, then shop compulsively online, purchasing a plethora of Christmas gifts for my family. I dismissed the experts' advice to combat insomnia and occasionally fell into an exhausted sleep on top of the bed or the sofa, as daylight dimmed to dusk. When I subsequently couldn't sleep at night, I no longer brooded. Instead I scrolled through social media, delving deeper and deeper into the lives of those I would see at the reunion. When I slept, my new recurrent dream involved Napoleon's Nose, though without Eva and Poppy to save me. There was only me, the sheer drop and the insidious yearning to jump.

I'd messaged Ford the day after my suspension, to inform him about my situation. I was not surprised his chief concern was for himself. Unremitting messages, grilling me as to whether Eric could uncover his true identity, alarmed his wife or employer could find out. Furiously demanding if there was any way of determining when we'd used the houses I was selling for our liaisons. No expressions of interest in me, or how I explained my enforced leave from work.

His self-absorption was astounding. Heatedly I confirmed it was not possible to uncover his real name, or for anyone to discover his dirty little secret. After several hours of increasingly feverish messages, he asked me what I was going to do. Not that he cared. All he cared about was saving his own skin.

The following week I met Eva and Poppy for coffee in Belfast. I'd carefully concealed my pale face with make-up, my weight loss camouflaged under a loose sweater and boyfriend jeans. I dutifully listened to their woes as I sipped iced mineral water and laughed at their blatant efforts to inveigle money from me. When they left me to go back to their student lives, I browsed the shops, searching for a suitable dress for the reunion. I found the perfect one in the boutique next to Boudoir Confidential, a clinging, cerise silk column, which I paired with high silver sandals.

They will never recognise Clare Hefton, I reassured myself, as I headed for home after my successful shopping trip.

Sleet was falling as I navigated the motorway, cars slowing to a crawl as nervy drivers fretted about overtaking. I got stuck behind a Fiat Punto dawdling at fifty miles an hour in the fast lane, and my temper bubbled with frustration. By the time I pulled into my driveway, I was completely spent. With each mile I had driven higher into the hills towards home, the wet sleet had turned to large flakes of snow, which floated gently onto the windscreen. I stepped out of the car and tilted my head skyward. Flurries of snow swirled in the cold air, cleansing it. I cherished the silence, and the beauty of the valley below, before I retreated into the warmth of the house.

There I unpacked my beautiful dress and stroked it admiringly before hanging it in the wardrobe. It was sumptuous, and I knew when I wore it, it would fill me with confidence.

Over the next few days, I shunned the Book Club, preferring my own company. I cancelled yogalates and a last-minute Book Club meeting at Laura's. I fabricated a crippling headache, no longer wanting to venture onto their street, nervous I would inadvertently bump into Ford. I was deliberately keeping him at arm's length, disinclined to see him until after the night at the Mourne View Hotel. His messages had tailed off as the days had passed with no bomb blast from Imelda's investigation.

As long as I replied to the Book Club messages, there would be no clue anything was amiss. Soon I became fixated that not one of my so-called friends cared enough to visit my house and check I was all right. Dourly I decided my misgivings about them had been correct all along. Female friends were unreliable, untrustworthy and most of all, unfaithful. As I watched the snow fall outside the windows, carpeting the earth, I considered them all.

Vicky and her perfect life.

Kate and her self-serving tears.

Annie and her griping about Matt having interests other than her.

Laura. I realised she had a perfectly good excuse for her preoccupation. Shamefully, I admitted I had been a poor friend to her since James died. I sent her a private text, asking how she was and although I did not offer to meet before our night away, I smiled with relief at her cheerful reply. She was going to be all right.

Ten days to the reunion. Fourteen days to our night away the Averie. Spikes of anxiety interspersed with eager anticipation. Generally I was cool, calm and collected, months of anguish now a distant memory.

Before either showdown, I arranged to meet Mum and Liz. Mum had been unable to control her pleasure when she learned we had managed to right some of our wrongs. She had become tearful, and it struck me how disturbing she had found our longstanding sibling war. Another thing to feel regretful and contrite about.

The day the three of us met up was a rare early winter day in Northern Ireland, with a diluted blue sky as far as the eye could see. No ferocious wind, no hint of rain in the air. The snow had melted, leaving wet slush staining the earth. From immaculate white to dirty grey in a few hours.

We arranged to meet at Mum and Phil's house, and as I pulled into their driveway, Mum stood apprehensively at the sitting room window. She was unable to wait for us in the kitchen at the back of the house.

The front door swung open immediately, and she pulled me into a tight hug. I heard the growl of a car engine behind me and Liz waved from a jaunty daffodil yellow Fiesta. Before I knew it, the three of us were embracing each other. My shoulders dropped as tension seeped from me, inherently sensing everything would be resolved between us now.

We sat together at the kitchen table drinking coffee and munching on chocolate biscuits, as though it was a regular occurrence. As I watched them chat, I realised how similar they now looked. High cheekbones, a strong chin and a neat, upturned nose. Their eyes were both wide-set, but that was where the similarity ended. Mum turned her blue gaze on each of us in turn, a look of wonder in her expression. She was struggling to accept we were cordially chatting following years of animosity. Time flew as six years were condensed into two hours.

As the sun dipped low in the sky, Liz broached the subject of the reunion. She was gentle initially, confirming I still planned to attend. Expressing genuine apprehension it may not turn out as I hoped.

'What do you expect to happen, Clare? They will acknowledge wrongdoing or apologise?' She lifted her head, green eyes bright and hard. 'I'm afraid it could make you feel worse about it all, and it won't provide the closure you hope.'

Mum was allowing Liz to take the lead. Her fair brows drew together, and she drummed her fingers on the table.

'I don't know,' I replied honestly. 'I suppose I would like some acknowledgement of wrongdoing.' I echoed her words.

Mum interjected. 'Of course we hope this will give you the closure you need. We want to make sure you are strong enough to deal with any, and all, potential outcomes.' A look passed between them, and comprehension cut through her deceptively harmless words. They had discussed me before today, written their speeches. I bristled with annoyance as I regarded Mum, then Liz, who had dropped her eyes and was now captivated by the floral tablecloth.

'You encouraged me to go,' I answered as mildly as I could, stating the obvious.

'Yes I did. Now it's closer, I have to be honest, I'm worried it's too much for you.' This was said in a rush, her cheeks reddened. 'You've lost weight, you seem jumpy and you've got puffy circles under your eyes.'

'Thanks, Mum,' I retorted instantly, then continued lightly. 'I'm fine. Never better.' Despite my words, I unconsciously scratched at the skin beside my nail.

Mum reached over to move my hand away, a squeamish look on her face. She had never been able to tolerate my compulsion to tear at my skin. She tried again. 'Clare, I'm worried about you. You know I will support you in any way I can. You need to be prepared in case it doesn't go the way you hoped.'

She glanced again at Liz, who listened intently. Mum handed the metaphorical baton to my sister who said, 'Mum's right. Think about it. I regret even contacting you about the reunion. I should have ignored the message, but it was an excuse to get in touch with you.' She cradled the mug between both hands, a frown darkening her features.

The three of us sat together in the warm, homely kitchen, and it fleetingly crossed my mind they were right. Possibly it was madness.

I released a slow breath. 'I'm glad you reached out to me, Liz, and I'm happier than you can imagine we're speaking again. I'm not the same person I was when I was at school. I have a good life. I'm married to a man I love who makes me very happy. Anyway, the person who caused the most problems for me isn't going to be there.' It tumbled out because I wasn't thinking. I should not have mentioned them. Mentally I kicked myself. Hard. Then I kicked myself again.

Liz pounced immediately. 'How do you know?' She didn't ask me who I meant as she assumed she knew, though I could bet money she would have got it wrong.

I inhaled deeply, choosing my words cautiously. 'Because I checked with Hilary before I committed to attending. When I heard they wouldn't be there, I felt able to face the others.'

Liz looked unconvinced, as well she might. One absence was not going to change things. However I stuck by my guns and even Liz had to admit defeat.

She then startled me by asking if I wanted her to come with

me. Deeply touched by the offer, I declined, insisting I was well able to attend on my own. I sensed Mum remained dubious, and I suppressed the impulse to tear at the skin at the side of my nail again. I tucked my thumb inside my fist, to reduce the urge.

Mum stared so attentively at me it seemed she was probing about inside my head and could see all was not as it seemed. I'd forgotten how perceptive she was and how she knew me so well.

At last Liz changed the subject, and she expressed her excitement at becoming a granny. Daylight was fading fast outside now and Mum switched on the lamps. When Phil came in from the garden to ask if we wanted another cup of coffee, I made my excuses, explaining I needed to get home to pack for my night away with the Book Club.

Before leaving I hugged my mum and barely refrained from asking if she would love me no matter what I did. For I knew she would.

Wouldn't she?

CHAPTER THIRTY-FOUR

Soon the long-awaited Book Club party night arrived. WhatsApp messages had flown back and forward throughout the days leading up to it, brimming with excitement and anticipation. I had answered a few of them, enough to arouse no suspicions. Methodically I packed my small overnight case with all the paraphernalia needed for a spa break at an exclusive hotel.

Ford had resumed his repeated messaging after a few days' respite. He had moved effortlessly on, an unsavoury reason like my suspension not curtailing his desires. Real life problems would not overshadow his fantasy.

He demanded we meet before our night away at the Averie, however for the first time in this chaotic saga, I refused. Soon it became apparent the more I withdrew, the more attentive he became. Fundamentally, I no longer wanted to spend time with him. Exasperated I wouldn't drop everything to see him, he was in turns petulant then placatory, demanding then imploring. It meant nothing to me.

As planned, Vicky drove us all to the Mourne View Hotel. I listened to the chatter and the laughter, allowing it to flow over me, my icy core melting at the camaraderie. It would have taken a harder heart than mine not to feel sentimental about the friendship I had squandered.

The twin room that Laura and I shared had a sea view, modern prints on the walls, two armchairs and a magazine-strewn coffee table. After I unpacked my case, I went into the bathroom and pulled on my black swimsuit with chain detail at the back. Inevitably I critically surveyed my reflection in the mirror. I was now a size eight and my collarbones protruded in a disconcerting way. Make-up free, my face was wan and drawn.

By the time I exited the bathroom, Laura was in her swimsuit, a flattering navy and white polka dot costume, with ruching detail across the stomach. She grumbled about weight gain and meno-belly, but I truthfully told her she looked amazing. Self-criticism was permissible only in the privacy of our own minds. We pulled on the opulent robes and complimentary slippers, grabbed our bottles of Prosecco and made our way down the corridor to the other bedroom.

A grinning Kate opened the door as soon as I rapped it. She brandished a glass of bubbly, while the others reclined companionably on the beds in their bathrobes. The triple room was barely bigger than ours and one of them would sleep on a sofa bed. I was relieved I hadn't volunteered for this room, as I could feel the intimacy of so many bodies bearing down on me. Forcing the brightest smile I could manage, I popped the cork of my bottle, and topped up the glasses, before settling on one of the chairs.

'To friendship,' I toasted, ignoring the bitter taste in my mouth.

'To the best friends anyone could ever have.' That was Kate, her chin trembling with emotion.

'Thank you for being there for me when I needed you the most.' Laura raised her glass to us.

'Sharing my life with my best friends is the most precious thing ever.' Indisputably Annie had been memorising the MAAF app. Or drinking early.

'Cheers.' I appreciated Vicky's brevity, nerves frayed by the interminable toasting.

I waited for the effects of the alcohol to kick in, as the volume increased. They were in high spirits, the break a release from the humdrum of daily life, the grind of work and family.

After we'd emptied three of the five bottles we'd smuggled in, we unsteadily made our way down to the spa. Thick carpets and plum walls led us to the spa complex; indoor and outdoor pools, a steam room and sauna, heated beds and deluxe furnishings. The alluring scent and soft music was the ultimate in tranquillity, and I was powerless to resist. While the others swam in the pool or sweated in the sauna, I braved the cold and headed for the outdoor jacuzzi.

I reclined alone in the steaming hot water, and stared out at the mountains the hotel was named for. A brilliant full moon hung over them, the sky clear with thousands of twinkling stars. Mist shrouded the peaks of the Mournes, blurring their edges, casting an ethereal glow. No wonder this was the land of myths and legends.

My contemplation was disrupted by Laura clattering through the door. Pink cheeked with the heat of spa, she discarded her robe and climbed down into the jacuzzi, before sighing contentedly.

'This was a great idea, Claire, so much better than a meal out.'

'It was you who suggested a night away,' I replied, smiling at her. There was something particularly refreshing about being in the frosty winter air while still feeling pleasantly warm. 'How are you doing?' I was conscious it had been some time since I had asked her.

'Good thanks.' Resting her head back as the underwater jets came to life, she closed her eyes, and remained silent for a moment before commenting, 'I'm getting used to everything now. I'm virtually certain I'm going to sell the house once all the legalities have been completed.'

'Are you looking for somewhere else?' I asked. Instinctively I knew her answer before she spoke.

She opened her eyes and with a quick check to ensure we were alone, lowered her voice. 'I'm going to move into Belfast.'

'With Sam?' My voice was barely above a whisper.

She nodded, daring me to challenge her with a jerk of her chin, eyes blazing.

I grinned at her and enquired if she was going to tell the others.

She firmly shook her head. 'Not yet. It's not going to happen for some time and I don't want to hear how it's too soon from Vicky and Annie, or get that disapproving look from Kate.' Here she contorted her face into a good imitation of the look Kate wore when James was mentioned. I giggled as Laura said, 'Sometimes she makes me feel like I should be sitting in a dark room crying incessantly about my widowhood.'

Miaow. Laura had the ability to surprise me.

'Why did you tell me?' I asked, curious.

'You're my closest friend but shush, don't tell the others.' Her smile was warm and I was inordinately delighted by her admission.

Even if she changed her mind in the coming days, I'd remember her comment. 'You're my closest friend too,' I replied impetuously, as I felt the telltale prick of tears.

Before we could discuss it further, the door opened and the others came tumbling out, tittering together. As Laura and I made room for them, she caught my eye before grinning at me in solidarity at our secret admissions.

Soon it was time to leave the spa and get ready for our evening. In the bedroom a short time later, I pulled on my cerise silk dress. I'd discounted all my other dresses, wanting to portray graceful, attractive Claire tonight. It was my armour. The clock was ticking on the Book Club. Our last night together should be memorable.

While Laura used the bathroom, I checked my phone. Multiple messages had buzzed through while I was using the spa, demanding answers.

From Will, anxious I had arrived safely and was enjoying myself. So caring. So smothering.

From Eva, who in her own inimitable way had something important to discuss with me, but had completely forgotten I was away. She stroppily messaged it would have to wait until she next saw me. She'd undoubtedly spent all her loan and needed money from me to buy my Christmas present.

From Ford. What was I doing? What was I wearing? Monotonous now.

I didn't respond to him and switched my phone to aeroplane mode after replying to Will and Eva. Laura emerged from the bathroom and once she had buckled the straps on her sandals, we were ready.

She tucked her arm through mine as we took the lift downstairs to the smart bar area. The others were already seated at a gilt table with yet another bottle of Prosecco. Yet again we toasted our friendship, the bubbles fizzing on my tongue. I covertly glanced at each of my friends, who grew ever more raucous as the alcohol loosened their inhibitions.

Vicky was marginally less glossy than usual, her eyes tired and skin blotchy.

Kate had a new puffiness in the face I'd not noticed before.

Annie had an aggrieved demeanour she couldn't quite hide.

Although they wore their finest party dresses, it appeared

something disagreeable lurked under the lustrous surfaces. I wondered what was going on with each of them. There was a simmering undercurrent of disgruntlement I had been too self-involved to appreciate earlier. I debated whether I should ask what was causing Annie's agitation and Kate's bloating. Or enquire if everything was all right in Vicky's perfect world.

We dispensed with peaks and pits, our annual rundown of the year's high and lows, as it was obvious the biggest pit was James's sudden death, and we were at great pains not to rehash it. To deflect from the tragedy, we drank too much and laughed too hard at nonsensical things, especially Big Bert the DJ, who was quite the worst DJ I'd ever heard.

The night passed quickly and I never did take the time to ask Annie, Kate or Vicky what each of them was masking. When I found myself alone with Ford's wife, I almost asked if she was all right, but the words got stuck and the moment passed. The opportunity didn't arise again.

Broad smiles. Forced laughter. Enthusiastic dancing.

My last Christmas party night with the Book Club played out like so many before.

In the small hours of the night and from my single bed, I listened to the white noise machine Laura insisted she needed for her tinnitus. My mind was active with a kaleidoscope of snapshots from years gone by. From the earliest nights with our young children running manically through the house while we attempted to eat dinner, to the later years when the ten of us would socialise in Belfast. When I had been included in a supportive group of friends for the first time in my life.

Sleep eluded me, and instead I reflected about how I had become intent on revenge. Why now, when I had made a success of my life, was happily married and had been able to overlook it for so long? How could the long-buried bullying from my teenage years have become such an obsession?

Was it this simple; the opportunity arose, and I seized it? Or was it more complex? The workings of a flawed mind that couldn't make logical decisions?

Before I surrendered to sleep, I deduced something profound.

I had allowed my past to jeopardise my future.

And it was too late to stop it.

CHAPTER THIRTY-FIVE

The following week Eva cancelled her visit home, blithely informing me her news was insignificant and would keep for another time. Ford stopped messaging as frequently, assuming I would pine for him if he eased off. Will remained oblivious to my work situation, as I feigned normality.

I busied myself with decorating the house for Christmas, cooking meals to store in the freezer and of course, exercising regularly. I now walked daily by the sea, exploring beaches and coastal paths I had scorned previously. The freezing air and stormy ocean calmed my nerves. I would pull on my padded jacket, fleece-lined hat and gloves and stride out, whatever the weather. I probably should have invited Laura, but my world constricted ever further as the reunion approached.

In the run-up to it, I sporadically returned to Ballydunn, and had an epiphany there one morning while sheltering from a squally shower. The rain stung my exposed skin like needles and the wind thundered in my ears, as the clouds emptied their load. Mesmerised, I watched breakers smash on the shore and a surprising thought became clear.

Nothing which happens on the night itself could be worse than my own fears.

As with so much in life, the waiting was the most gruelling part. It allowed imaginations to run riot, to conjure all manner of dreadful outcomes. I reassured myself life didn't always result in worst-case scenarios.

I huddled in the same doorway where Will and I had kissed on our return from the pub, and remembered the tremendous sense of love and security I had experienced that night. He was unaware of the game I had been playing, the game which soon would be at an end and I could then focus solely on my marriage.

Due to this newfound serenity, I slept solidly through the night before the reunion. I woke refreshed, positive I would get through the evening with my psyche intact and ghosts put to rest.

I spent the day at the hairdresser and the beautician before dressing with care. First my most flattering lingerie, then a spritz of my favourite fragrance, before I let the silky cerise dress fall over my body. Cautiously I added the diamond necklace Will had given me, the pendant sparkling in the deep V-neck of the dress.

Only the brittle look in my eyes belied my true feelings. I knew I would be able to disguise it though.

I kissed Will on the lips before I left, dismissed his anxious offer to accompany me and reiterated I was good. Great in fact. That I savoured meeting them and tackling my past once and for all.

On the drive into the city suburbs, I paid no heed to the Christmas lights nor the falling rain. My mind only on my driving, my stomach churned time and time again. No longer composed, now uneasy.

I will be fine. I will be fine. I recited it until I pulled into the car park. Regrettably, the hotel was now faded and scruffy, affording a glimpse of a once lustrous past. Its white exterior was chipped, there were potholes in the tarmac and the City Chic Hotel sign was damaged, as it was now the 'IT CH HOTEL.' A tattered Christmas tree lolled in a bucket by the entrance, and middle-aged smokers clustered in an insubstantial wooden shelter set a short distance from the front door.

I watched them from the seclusion of my darkened car and with a start recognised faces from my recent social media scrolling. These smokers were here for the reunion. Billy Black, who had once streaked after a rugby match and been suspended from school for a fortnight, held court. Next to him was a thin faced woman with cropped hair. My ex-friend Mandy. She appeared emaciated, though it may have been a trick of the light or the eerie glow from her cigarette. Next to her stood a tall, handsome man who gesticulated excitedly, the tip of his cigarette swinging dangerously close to Billy's bald head.

I had a visceral response to seeing the living faces from my past. Nausea swept through me and my sweaty palms slid off the steering wheel onto my lap.

Everyone else's features were contorted by the gloom and the smoke, and it wasn't long until they returned en masse inside. The waves of queasiness slowly eased and I could delay no longer. Resolutely I grabbed my clutch bag and exited the car. The wind whipped my carefully coiffed hair as a huge gust caught me and the stench of cooking fat increased my nausea. Breathing through my mouth, I wrapped my woollen coat tightly around me, and strode towards the door. No matter how I was feeling inside, I would present the illusion of self-confidence tonight.

Once I reached the porch, I checked my reflection in an oval mirror hanging on the wall. My hair was windswept, so I patted it down with trembling hands. I gulped deeply, and headed down the old-fashioned, patterned carpet towards a table in the foyer. Two middle-aged women chatted behind it, and I could hear the hum of conversation from the bar area to their right.

I recognised Hilary, who had sent me the original message, so I smiled and forced one leg after the other until I was standing directly before them. She looked happy and healthy, and wore a wedding band on her ring finger.

She glanced at me and paused mid-conversation with someone called Lynette McMeekin. I didn't recollect Lynette at all, but they were both wearing name badges, so it was easy to pretend I did. A cluster of badges lay unclaimed on the table and I spotted my own amongst them.

'Clare Hefton'

I would give no one an inroads to my new identity. For one night only, I would be Clare Hefton again. Except the new, improved version of her.

'Oh hello. Are you here for the reunion?' Hilary looked at me perplexedly, apparently unaware who I was.

'Yes, I'm Clare Hefton,' I answered politely, annoyed at the tremor in my voice when I desperately wanted to exude poise.

Her mouth dropped open a little before she recovered herself, and rushed to cover her tracks.

'Oh hi, Clare, you look amazing! I didn't recognise you at all.' She grinned at me, and I felt a rush of pleasure at her words. They were exactly what I needed to hear before I braved the rest of them.

'I didn't recognise you either.' The woman beside her smiled too, and once she revealed the small gap between her front teeth, I recalled her. As her round face crinkled, her features lightened and she said, 'I was Lynette Cowden at school.'

The name transported me back to the eighties, reminding me of an introverted girl who was called Cow every day for years. School had been tough for others too, not only me.

'How are you both?' I asked, lingering with these friendly faces as long as possible. I still had no plan, unsure what I should do. I could walk straight up to the Coven, or dally on the edges hoping they recognised me.

'I'm great, thanks' Lynette replied. 'Sore knees and menopausal, but otherwise grand!'

The three of us reminisced together for a few minutes, exchanging titbits of information about our lives post Belfast Grammar School. I asked them questions about themselves and let their voices drift gently over me. They pointed out the cloakroom where I could leave my coat, and I said I would catch up with them later, though I doubted it.

We were joined by another couple who had arrived for the reunion, and I made my excuses. I wanted to compose myself before venturing into the bar, where everyone was congregating. After handing my coat to the waistcoated attendant, I followed the signs for the loos. I pushed open the door and was greeted by a chorus of voices from inside. A woman called for Elodie and I came to an abrupt halt, as though my feet had grown roots. For a moment I felt too panicked to move, then recovered enough to race into the vacant baby change next door.

I locked the door behind me and struggled for control, closing my eyes. My back to the door, I inhaled and exhaled, counting my breaths, trying to take no notice of the prattling voices outside my safe haven.

It was them, they had hunted in a pack back then, and they continued to even now.

Their voices became fainter as they passed the baby change and peace descended. As my antipathy for them threatened to overpower me, I was relieved to feel tentacles of steeliness uncurl within me. I had decided what to do.

Go in, locate them, speak to them and leave.

I wanted to see the recognition on their faces as they

realised I not only survived them, but I had led a fulfilling life. Despite their best efforts.

I peeled myself away from the door, washed my hands and reapplied my blood-red lipstick in the mirror. The brittle look had gone from my eyes, replaced by a flintiness which would carry me through this night.

It was the beginning of the end.

CHAPTER THIRTY-SIX

I walked back down the corridor to the hotel foyer, my earlier nerves replaced by calm. Hilary and Lynette were deep in conversation and I slipped undetected through the doorway of the bar. Straightening my shoulders, I pulled the V of my dress lower, my pendent sparkling in the light. Then I stepped into the reunion. Heat and sound and the crush of bodies assailed me, the beat of a vaguely recognisable eighties hit thumped loudly from the speakers.

Small groups of people stood dotted about; laughing, talking, drinking. Some glanced at me, then looked away. Not a flicker of recognition. I braced myself, strode forward to the bar and waited to get the barman's attention. Beside me stood a short man with a full head of white hair, sweat patches staining the armpits of his shirt, half-drunk pint of beer in his hand.

'Why hello, now who could you be?' he leered, using the name badge pinned to my dress as an excuse to ogle my cleavage.

I skimmed his name badge and smiled back before purring in his ear, 'Hello there, Frank, don't you remember me?'

He squinted properly at my name badge before screwing up his face, seemingly struggling to place me.

'Clare Hefton? There's no way you're Hefty Lump.' He exclaimed, an astonished expression on his plump face. My nerves dissolved. If they were all as dim as Frank, I'd survive this evening.

'I am indeed. I'm sure you're no longer called by your nickname either. And it's been a while since I was Hefty Lump.' He had the grace to look sheepish, though I did feel a smidgen of sympathy for anyone who'd gone through life called F. Artt.

The barman saved me from further conversation with Frank, and I ordered a slimline tonic with ice. No gin for now. It would be my reward or my oblivion later.

While I was being served, Frank moved away from the bar and I stood alone, searching the crowd for the faces which had tortured me. I spotted the clique, sitting at two tables they had pushed together. The popular ones had gravitated towards each other, and as the years fell away, I watched them closely while leaning against the bar in splendid solitude. Elodie surrounded by her coterie, head thrown back, laughing riotously. My stomach didn't clench and my heart didn't pound as I surveyed them.

It was apparent while it might be thirty-odd years since school, it was as if it were yesterday. The Coven and their hangers-on reunited.

I had no time to scrutinise them further, as I was joined at the bar by two anxious looking women. Noting their names, I engaged in polite conversation, less awkward than when on my own. If they remembered my story, they were good-mannered enough not to remind me of it, and we exchanged titbits about our lives since our schooldays. I gave them the précised version of my life.

Successful. Content. Fulfilled.

Soon the room was crowded with countless middle-aged bodies, the noise increasing as more people piled in. Hilary took to the small stage at the end of the bar, and signalled for the music be turned down. Confident and assured, she delivered a witty speech before inviting everyone to mingle. The buffet would be served shortly.

This was my opportunity, for even the popular ones would appear churlish if they didn't mix with the rest of us. I was ready for them. Before I reached them, Mandy stepped directly in front of me, impeding my way.

'Clare, I didn't recognise you! Frank Artt had to tell me who you were. How are you?' She gazed at me apprehensively. She looked frail and ashen, the telltale demeanour of someone who was ill, and I felt an unexpected rush of pity towards her.

'I'm good, how are you?' My voice was loud in order to be heard over the cacophony, though my tone gentle.

'I've been better,' she replied grimly. 'Should have given up the ciggies years ago. Too late now though. Have you seen Shirley yet?'

Sorrow for my old friend tore through me and I struggled to maintain my composure. In all the possible scenarios I had considered, illness had never crossed my mind. She looked kindly at me, before touching my forearm lightly.

'It's all right, Clare, it's rubbish. In those infamous *Love Island* words, it is what it is.'

Before I could reply, we were joined by another woman. Shirley. She had hardly changed in the intervening years, simply older and a lot less diffident. The two of them had kept in touch, as they didn't reintroduce themselves, and I felt a stab of envy at what could have been.

'Hi, Clare, nice to see you. It's been too long.' Her words were heartfelt, and I smiled at her. It was time to let go of my hurt and anger. We spoke for a few moments, catching up in the most banal of ways, before I excused myself. It was essential to get this over and done with now, while I was in charge.

It could wait no longer.

I made my way through the crowd, stopping only when I reached Elodie. Her Facebook photos hadn't lied. The beauty with the cloud of blonde hair and huge blue eyes was now a dowdy and unremarkable fifty-year-old. Her cheap red blouse stretched cross her sagging chest, her black velour flares unfashionable. I was barely conscious of the others standing protectively beside her.

'Hello, Elodie.' My voice rang clear, so she couldn't fail to hear me.

Her eyes dropped to my name badge, then she indifferently returned my glare, expression shuttered.

'Clare Hefton.' She said it knowingly and shrewdly. 'I don't remember you. Were you in our year?' It was calculated and cold, and yet it filled me with fire, not ice.

'Oh yes.' I smiled straight into those frosty blue eyes. 'I was indeed. Have you forgotten the fun you had at my expense? The name calling and the bullying? For that is exactly what you were, Elodie. A bully. And your friends–' I casually waved my hand to include the group beside her, '–were bullies as well.'

Conversation dwindled around us, as she stared defiantly at me. No shame. No apology. Entitled younger Elodie resurfaced. The briefest discomfiture shadowed her face, before she rallied.

'I have no idea who you are, or what you are talking about. Do you?' She asked her friends, seeking support. Elodie had not matured enough to own her past behaviour, though it seemed the others had. No one answered her. Silently they watched us. She beseeched them again, and again not one of her gang replied. The question hung unanswered between us.

Her face reddened while I waited.

'I don't remember you and I was no bully.' Her words lacked the bluster of before, without the encouragement of her friends.

'Well, I've never forgotten and you were a bully, Elodie. You bullied me and anyone else you thought beneath you. Here we are, fifty years old and yet you haven't the decency to admit it. Do you know something? You're a nothing and a nobody. And you lot–' here I raised my voice and my eyes to include all her group, '–are no better. No doubt you preach about being kind, but none of you were. Have you honestly forgotten?' The words escaped their prison, fired with gusto, firm and strong.

However Elodie stood her ground, refusing to back down and it became obvious she couldn't lose face. She had built her life on being superior to everyone and anyone, while conversely achieving little. The only place she had achieved greatness, was to lead a group of bullies in school. There she had been a big fish in a small pond. She was firmly clinging to the brilliance of a long dead era.

When no one answered me, I found it didn't matter. Their silence told a thousand stories, as did the downcast lashes and rosy cheeks.

Then a lone voice. 'I remember Hefty Lump. You were a complete state, if I recall correctly. Anything which happened was because of your own stupidity. Don't blame the rest of us.'

I dispassionately observed the speaker, and did not bother to reply. For I was conscious of a rumbling anger in the room. Those who had once been too afraid to defy this clique were now free of them. Another voice spoke up from behind me.

'I think you should shut up and have some manners. Clare's right, you were bullies. Didn't your parents teach you if you can't say anything nice, don't say anything at all?' It was Mandy, eyes fierce, breath short. She'd always been quick-tempered and apparently still was. At her side was Shirley, who backed us, condemning their denial.

The three of us stood together as a small ripple of *Well said* and *Spot on* grew. Elodie turned and marched towards the table she'd been sitting at, as one by one her friends dawdled behind. Before long the crowd swallowed them and they were out of sight. I was conscious of many eyes on me as I faced Mandy and Shirley. My heart raced and my legs were weak, but there were the seeds of a foreign emotion.

Pride in myself.

I had defied them and while there was no apology, nor a hint of contrition, I was proud I had ultimately challenged their behaviour. They may never acknowledge what they had done. Hopefully though I would sleep easier at night.

Yet somehow it was a thundering anti-climax.

Years squandered agonising about them, hours wasted obsessing about them. Ruminating repeatedly about my experiences at their hands, and in a few inadequate moments, it was over. The massive denouement I had agonised about culminated in a pop not a bang. Scraps of conversation flittered about me, as I digested the enormity of it all.

After saying goodbye to Mandy and Shirley, I left the reunion, as there was nothing more for me to do. None of us suggested we keep in touch or meet again, by silent agreement that part of our lives was relegated to the past. There was no point trying to resurrect the fragments of a friendship which was long destroyed – yet a small part of me healed.

I sat in the car a short time later and despite the heater blowing full blast, a cold chill had penetrated me. I discerned something dreadful.

This grand plan for vengeance I had been hellbent on, and was wilfully seeing through to the bitter end. What if it had all been a terrible mistake. I should have confronted my past head on years ago. Never allowed it to get to this stage.

It was too late now.

The juggernaut was racing to the finish line and there was no way of halting it.

CHAPTER THIRTY-SEVEN

When I arrived home after the reunion, I shouted to let Will know I was back and stripped off my sodden coat. I hung it in the cloakroom as he appeared from the kitchen in his bare feet, jaw tense. Without speaking, he enveloped me in his arms and I gratefully buried my head into his broad chest, the soft wool of his jumper tickling my nose. From the security of his embrace, I took a shaky breath and answered his unspoken question.

'They were there and I called them out.' I lifted my head and stared into his warm brown eyes, concern and love shining from them. 'Some of them were ashamed and remained silent, and Elodie denied it all, pretended she didn't remember me. Even when Mandy and Shirley spoke up. It's over, Will. I did it, I have closure.' The barefaced lie was obscured by the truth.

This wasn't over and I did not have closure. It would come later when I faced my last demon.

'I'm so pleased, and incredibly proud of you, darling. Now you can move forward and forget them. You have your night away with your mum now to recharge your batteries.' He believed I was going to the spa hotel in Donegal again, some nameless place he wouldn't be able to check up on me.

I smiled automatically, unable to hold his gaze. Recharging my batteries was not an option.

Later that night, I lay beside him in bed, rerunning the entire evening repeatedly. It was as though a burst of fireworks exploded in my head, a flurry of light and sound which merged and tangled, but at the end provided release. The greatest barrier had been overcome and after the turmoil, came silence. My mind peaceful, sighing in relief.

No nightmares haunted me. No dreams at all.

The next morning and on subsequent days, I prepared myself for the finale. My mind divided, fighting pessimism on one side, subduing regrets on the other. I placated myself I was strong, in a good place mentally, and well equipped for it.

The temperature had dropped outside, the rain had finally relented, replaced by an icy wind from the east, bringing frost and a bite to the air. Still I walked by the sea, my breath a cloud in front of me, my nose red and thoughts settled.

Finally, the day of reckoning arrived. I woke to an empty house, as Will had left early to cover for sickness. He would arrive home later, when I was at the Averie and the last act was unfolding. I was instantly alert, as expectation pumped through me, sizzling with urgency. Prepared to spill my secret, impatient for the revelation. I leapt out of bed and hurried to Eva's bedroom, where my packed case was secreted from sight. I lifted it onto the bed and tugged the zip open, eyeing the contents, ensuring once again I had everything I would need. I returned to our bedroom and strode through to the dressing room. There I prised my second phone from its hiding place and charged it while I showered. I had no interest in what was stored on it.

With some difficulty I ate a slice of toast and washed it down with green tea. I was as ready as I would ever be. With a last check of the locks, I glanced around my home. A flutter of anxiety as I imagined my return, uncertain how I would confess my sins to Will. Although I had visualised this day a thousand times, the fallout was unknown, a void yet to be filled.

Ford and I had arranged to meet at the hotel, which suited me as I wanted to take a leisurely drive up the coast road. I had no plans to walk by the sea today and hoped the drive would calm my nerves.

Spontaneously I pulled into a lay-by and cut the engine. The winter sun hung low in the cloudless sky, pale orange stripes reflecting on the shimmering surface. The sea continued its relentless offensive on the beach, never tiring, never resting. Gulls swooped overhead, their cries drowned by the crashing of the waves. Soothing and repetitive, it alleviated some of my angst.

All too soon, it was time to leave, and I drove the last few miles with the radio on, music drowning out the static in my head. I listened to the lyrics, emptying my mind of anything else.

Soon I turned onto a narrow road, with high hedges and overhanging branches. It was beautiful in the summer, when the greenery teemed with birds, and flowers bloomed in the hedgerows. In midwinter, the starkness of the branches had an eerie splendour, enhanced by red berries and a smattering of frost. Before long I reached the tall pillars at the entrance to the hotel grounds. At the end of the sweeping drive, the white columned hotel hugged the banks of the river, its spa concealed by a high wall.

I drove on until I reached the car park and found Ford had arrived before me, discreetly parking in a secluded corner. I pulled alongside him and smiled over, suddenly anticipating what was ahead. His egotistical face broke into a wide grin, and I imagined it in a few hours, when the smug look had been wiped from it for good. I hadn't seen him since the disaster at the farmhouse, and he had been irked by my ensuing disinterest in meeting him. The look on his face suggested his aggravation had thawed at the prospect of a night together.

I climbed out of the Audi and watched as he uncurled his tall figure from the car. Jeans and a tight white T-shirt with a black leather jacket. All that was missing were aviator shades. We didn't embrace, but maintained the illusion of casual acquaintances as we strolled to the front door, past a row of brightly lit festive sculptures.

A log fire was burning in the welcoming entrance hall, the imposing mantelpiece bedecked with holly, ivy and giant candles. An ornately decorated Christmas tree stood at the foot of a winding marble staircase, and a few well-dressed guests were scattered about. I scanned quickly to ensure I recognised no one. It would be devastating, and maddening, to fall at the last hurdle.

After checking in as Mr and Mrs Ford, we made our way to our deluxe room on the first floor. A luxurious king-sized bed filled the space, and the room had a small balcony overlooking the river. On a summer's evening, it would be a sun-kissed haven to relax and enjoy a pre-dinner drink. However darkness was already falling that cool December day, and I drew the curtains before flicking on the lights.

Ford insisted we make use of the spa facilities, which I readily agreed to, having no wish to be alone with him if at all possible. I unpacked my case and pulled on my black swimsuit. The same one with the chain back I had worn to a different spa with his wife a few short days ago. Selecting it had been thoughtless, as the reminder of the Book Club trip at the Mourne View Hotel triggered my anxiety. I made vague excuses, then retreated to the bathroom. There I struggled to reduce my accelerating breathing rate, focusing on exhaling the stale air, until I was at last in control. I returned to the bedroom, to find him sprawled on a chair, flicking through a magazine. He raised one eyebrow and smiled lazily.

'Ready? You look beautiful by the way.' He rose and stepped over to me, lifting my chin and planting a kiss on my lips. My smile was forced and insincere, and I was surprised he couldn't sense it.

We were alone in the steam room a little later, and an internal battle raged. Possibly I should have sent the photos before we came down to the spa. Timing was everything and I was second guessing myself constantly. I decided to return on my own to the room, maintaining I needed to shower and dry my hair, encouraging him to remain in the spa for a while yet. He lounged back against the wall and didn't open his eyes, simply nodded in agreement. Hastily I rushed to our room, switched on my second phone and opened the contacts. Then I put his phone on aeroplane mode so his wife couldn't reach him, as I didn't want anything to spoil the surprise.

Wavering for a moment, I sent her the first photo, an exterior shot of the hotel, with the message 'Wish you were here.' Which would ensure she knew his location. The die was cast, I had no choice. One by one, I forwarded all the photos and lastly, the video. Their significance needed no explanation. Her cheating, lying, unfaithful husband was with another woman.

I grasped the phone firmly, my heart flying, my chest tight. Two blue ticks lit up each message. Three rolling dots and the response came through.

> What the hell? Why do you have those photos
> of my husband? Who are you????

I chewed my lip as I sat on the edge of the bed, not intending to reply to her. A few breathless moments before her next message pinged through. I could visualise her pretty face twisted in concern. Or wrath. Or upset. I didn't care. All she had to do was confirm she was coming to the hotel.

And she played right into my hands with her message:

I'm coming to find out who you are

I was tempted to reply with the shrugging emoji but dismissed it as puerile. With shaking hands, I switched the phone off and hid it in the pocket of my suitcase. It was of no further use to me and I wouldn't require it again.

I stripped off my wet swimsuit and stepped into the shower. Hot water cascaded over me, as I scrubbed myself clean. My mind was now at ease, no longer troubled. I had waited years to exact my retaliation and it was only a few minutes away now.

The time had come to face my fate.

CHAPTER THIRTY-EIGHT

It was a quick shower as I was apprehensive Ford would decide to join me. Fortunately he didn't appear and I sighed with relief. However he wasn't in the bedroom either when I went through to get dressed, and my stomach knotted. We were on borrowed time and I chastised myself for not having insisted he return with me to the room earlier. Now my friend was on her way, it was essential we were downstairs for her arrival.

Fortunately he sauntered into the room a short time later, while I dried my hair at the dressing table. I was already wearing my fuchsia jersey dress and high sandals. The choice of dress was deliberate, for I'd worn it the first night he came alone to my house. The night we had crossed the moral boundary into a cesspit of deception. It was a commemorative token in a way. Wordlessly he sidled up behind me and ran his hands over me, like a butcher handling a hunk of meat. I batted him off, finding his proprietorial groping objectionable.

Instead I encouraged him to get changed and casually suggested a pre-dinner drink in the bar once we were ready. He responded with a grunt, before nonchalantly stripping off and disappearing into the bathroom. Playing for time, making me wait. His speciality.

While perched on one of the chairs by the coffee table, I sent a patently dishonest text to my husband, claiming I was having a lovely time. Hating every invented word I typed, my deceit ate into my self-control. To distract myself, I scrolled through multiple WhatsApp messages from the Book Club. There was no hint from Ford's wife about what she had recently learned, and I had to assume she was en route to her own private hell.

Soon Ford reappeared and he dressed in navy chinos and a white shirt. I objectively watched him as he splashed spicy aftershave on his neck. There was no disputing he was a good-looking man, humorous when he wanted to be, but prone to self-importance. Then I recalled the look he had given me in the Melville Hotel, when my confidence had been at rock bottom, and I felt an unaccustomed softening towards him. It really wasn't all his fault.

Sharp pricks of remorse stung me as I went over to him, held his face gently with both my hands and kissed him for the last time. We stood in the lift together as it descended to the ground floor and as his warm breath grazed the back of my neck, I swallowed my discomfort. Everything I had contrived and designed over this past year was about to come to fruition, perhaps even as the lift doors opened.

However I had a short reprieve, as the corridor was empty. We walked together towards the bar and I scrutinised the other guests, searching for that one, well-known face. It was just over an hour since I'd sent the photos; she could appear at any time. My throat was bone-dry and I craved a drink. A G&T was needed and as I sank onto a plush velvet chair at the entrance to the bar area, Ford willingly went to buy me my usual.

Absorbing the luxurious décor and furnishings, I rested

against the back of the chair, perusing each passing face, awaiting my friend's appearance. Ford was out of sight around the corner. Time slowed as I spotted her enter the bar area, head pivoting frantically as she searched for her husband.

At last her gaze fell on me, and her expression changed to puzzlement. She suddenly stopped, and eventually, after what seemed like forever, made her way towards me.

I rose as she reached me, subconsciously balling my hands into fists, though keen to appear blasé.

'Claire, what are you doing here? You said you were going to Donegal with your mum.' She bit her lip, brow furrowed with anxiety and confusion.

I hesitated as her eyes slid past me, her expression changing from one of bewilderment to incredulity. Her mouth fell open, eyes widened with shock as she stared behind me.

I turned as though in slow motion, to see what she was looking at.

Her husband Tom.

He had come to an abrupt halt, a pint of Guinness in one hand, a large ice-filled gin glass in the other. There could be no doubt we were together. He threw me a distressed glance, his cheeks reddening as his gaze flew back to his wife.

'What? Why? I don't understand,' Vicky's anguished eyes flitted between us, her face a question she couldn't process. Then brutal comprehension.

'You're here together.' A statement not a query.

'Yes. I'm so sorry,' Tom replied, walking over to us and setting the drinks on the table, before standing uselessly beside me.

'Hello, Vicky,' I said, my tone light and inconsequential.

'You?' She barked furiously. 'How long?' She addressed this to Tom, her face now hard, initial shock tapering off.

'Not here, Vicky.' He shook his head. 'Let's go somewhere

quiet, please.' His pleading tone ingratiating.

'Yes, why don't the three of us go somewhere nice and quiet. Of course, our bed's not made and there's only two chairs, so our room's not exactly suitable.' I pretended to mull it over before purposefully continuing. 'Where do you think we should go, Victoria? Or should I call you Tori?'

I stared directly into the eyes of the person who had tormented me and who had declared me worthless. The person who coincidence had led me to years later, when our children attended the same primary school and her friends had become my friends. She had haunted my dreams, guaranteeing I was incapable of leaving the past behind.

When offered it on a plate, my thirst for vengeance had been so great I had become obsessed with destroying her perfect life, in the way she had almost destroyed me.

Tom hovered beside her, puzzled. He had no idea what I meant and Vicky mutely gaped at me. He perceptibly moved closer to her, reflexively taking her side.

He tried to intervene, asking bemusedly, 'What do you mean? You've never been called Tori. You've always been Vicky.' He was incidental to all this really: they hadn't even met until their twenties.

'I haven't been called Tori for years. How did you know? Who are you?' I had to strain to catch what she said, an appalled look on her beautiful face.

'Clare Hefton,' I answered unemotionally. 'Do you remember me from school? Hefty Lump you called me.' My stomach curdled as I waited for her answer.

'Yes, I remember you,' she stuttered, lifting her hand to her mouth as her face changed. Colour drained from her cheeks and she dropped her eyes, which had filled with tears.

'You bullied me, Vicky, you and your friends. Do you ever think about it? Why didn't you go to the reunion? Were you too embarrassed?' The words tripped over each other as I seized the opportunity to verbalise what had been reverberating in my head for so long.

She answered me with a question of her own. 'You sent me those photos of Tom?'

'What photos?' asked Tom, head careering wildly between the two of us.

'The photos I took of you over this past year. The ones you assumed I would delete, I instead kept to show your wife. In order for her to discover what kind of man she married.' I said it mildly as each word dripped poison.

'This past year?' Now Vicky looked horrified, as did Tom. There it was, laid out in all its sordid, lurid honesty. 'A year, Tom? You've been cheating with my friend for a year?'

'I'm not your friend and never was. I kept expecting you to recognise me. I waited for the day it all clicked into place and you realised I was that poor little girl you bullied mercilessly at school.'

'We are friends, Claire. We've been friends for years.' She was shaking her head, as if to deny it all, as the enormity of the situation sank in. 'Do you hate me that much?' She whispered it, piteous now and I hardened my heart.

People at neighbouring tables were unabashedly enjoying the cosy, domestic scene in front of them, therefore I didn't answer her. I didn't want an audience, so firmly said, 'Let's get out of here. There are empty alcoves down the corridor.'

Tom tenderly reached for Vicky's arm, and led her from the bar to the alcoves, concealed from inquisitive eyes. I carried my gin glass, my mouth made arid by my words, seething with barely restrained anger. Vicky was playing the victim, weeping so prettily and inviting kind words.

I sagged down in the nearest alcove, gulped the gin and

wordlessly watched Vicky and Tom. Angrily she pulled herself free from his hold, turning to face me.

'If I was so nasty in school, why did you become my friend? Why didn't you tell me who you were the first time we met at Laura's?' She was starting to babble, wiping tears from her face as she flopped down opposite me. Tom stood mutely at the end of the table, and I wanted to tell him to get lost. This was between Vicky and me. Really it had nothing to do with him. I'd used him to pay Vicky back, nothing more.

It quickly became apparent his only interest was begging Vicky's forgiveness. He had not looked me square in the eye since she had arrived. It was plain he cared as little about me as I did about him.

As I was about to speak, she admitted dejectedly, 'You're the latest in a long line of women you know, Claire. Tell her, Tom, she's just one of many.'

Tom crouched down beside her, before pleading, 'I'm so sorry, Vicky, I'll never do it again. Please forgive me. This time I mean it.'

If I wasn't so enraged I would have laughed out loud. He was even more despicable than I imagined. The façade of the strong, loving husband was cracking in front of my eyes, revealing a serial cheat and philanderer. My instincts about him had been correct.

'We need to talk alone, Vicky. Why don't you go and pack your bag, Tom, then you can discuss this at home with your wife.' He needed to be out of the way in order for me to twist the knife completely, without interruptions.

Vicky nodded, before agreeing firmly. 'Go away, Tom, I can't even look at you now. Leave me to talk with Claire on my own.'

He started to reply as she shook her head and he slowly

stood. With a quick glance over his shoulder at me, he disappeared, leaving us alone at last.

CHAPTER THIRTY-NINE

Vicky wiped her eyes with her hand before asking, 'Why did you do it, Claire?'

'I wanted to get you back for those years of abuse you doled out in school.' I wasn't going to sugar-coat it.

'You could have been honest with me. I don't understand how you could have said nothing for years. How could you have an affair with Tom while pretending to be my friend?' She began to cry again and I fought to suppress the urge to shout at her.

'Stop crying, Vicky, for goodness' sake!' I snapped. 'You were a complete bitch in school, you and those friends of yours.'

She paled further at those words, but stopped crying as if on command. Convinced she'd simply used the tears to elicit sympathy, I hurried on. 'You made my life a complete misery. And then when you were called out by Mr Shaw, you, Elodie and the others turned the entire year against me. No one spoke to me for weeks. I had to go into school every day completely isolated. You butchered my hair and you planned the nightmare at the Belfast Gardens with George McClure.' Words which had been pent up for years came tumbling out of me.

Her head dropped onto her hands, and she could no longer maintain eye contact.

'I'm sorry.' That was all she said. Nothing else. No explanation, no excuses. I waited as the silence between us grew.

'That's it?' I was incredulous. After thirty years, she couldn't offer even one word in her defence?

I stared, astonished, until she raised her eyes. She repeated it. 'I'm sorry.'

'Well that feeble attempt at an apology is not good enough, Vicky. A leopard doesn't change its spots. You were one of the original mean girls, there's no way you could become this paragon of virtue; doctor, wife, friend.' I knew my voice was becoming high-pitched, though I was incapable of preventing it. My shaking hands belied my weakness, so I used both of them to lift the glass and swallowed another swig of the gin in an effort to get myself under control.

She sighed before speaking. 'You're right, I was awful and there's no justification. I got involved with Elodie and the others, and believe me when I say they were as mean to each other as they were to everyone else. It was survival of the fittest, and I became as bad as them, or they would have dropped me. When you're a teenager, the most important thing in life is to be popular and accepted. I didn't know any different.'

She'd got that correct: the most important things were to be popular and accepted. I had been neither. To claim she knew no different infuriated me. Age was no excuse for wrongdoing. It seemed she expected me to feel sorry for her. Echoes of the snip of the scissors banged in my head, along with the blinding image of her triumphant face in the Belfast Gardens. She tried again to revert to my affair with Tom, but I was having none of it.

Cutting her off, I retorted sharply, 'I don't care at all about Tom. In fact there's nothing he enjoyed more than messaging me when I was with you.' I dredged up the most damaging and unforgivable things I could think of. I'd rehearsed them for so long, yet now the time had come, I could barely remember the grand pronouncements I had practised. All I could think about was hurting her as much as she had hurt me.

'And what about you? Does Will know? Or should I ring him now and tell him?' Her voice was raised and my heart seemed to stop. She had flipped completely from penitent to vindictive.

'Don't you dare!' I hissed with as much malice as I could muster. 'Leave Will out of this. I will tell him.'

'Oh, so you have this big showdown with me, then tell Will in your own way, in your own time? I don't think so!' She was riled now, eyes flashing at me, and I caught sight of the vicious teen she had buried under the imitation of impeccable Vicky. Scrabbling in her handbag, she made a great show of searching for her phone, but stopped short with my next words.

'Tom made the first move, Vicky. Do you remember the night at the Melville Hotel last year for Annie's charity dance? He chased after me, and I suspected before tonight he'd done it before. He's a cheat and liar. Will's a good man who doesn't deserve to be told in anger.'

Her face was strained, as she set the bag down with a sigh. 'You're right. He is a cheat. The first time I found out was just after I had Flora, and there's been other women since then. Possibly even more I don't know about.'

'Why did you stay with him?' I was curious, and as much as I was loath to admit it, I unexpectedly felt a little sorry for her.

'I love him.' She licked her lips. 'I assumed he'd never do it with one of my friends. Because no matter what you think, that's what you've become, Claire.' She looked at her hands and said, 'I'm so ashamed of my behaviour at school and for how much I hurt you. And others. I realised by sixth form how vile

Elodie and the others were, so when school finished, I dropped them completely. I haven't seen or heard from them in years. That's why I didn't go to the reunion. I was frightened to face them and everyone else. I've tried to make up for my dreadful behaviour over the years, even though there's a part of me that knows I can't. And you have no idea how much I regret it all.'

She'd said it. I felt an overwhelming relief as I dropped back in the chair, overcome with weariness. I'd got the apology I had demanded and desired. And surprisingly it all seemed so trivial, so inconsequential now I had heard the words.

All that remained was the stark reality I had cheated on my husband and I was going to have to profess all to him.

'I don't understand why you said nothing for all these years. Why now?' Her face was drawn and she was wringing her hands.

How could I tell her I didn't understand, myself, why I'd done it? I'd never given reprisal much thought until the night at the hotel, and then it spiralled so rapidly. I'd got caught up in the catharsis of dishing out some of the pain she had caused me. For years I'd secretly been thrilled Tori from the popular clique had chosen me to be her friend, and it had been enough. And then I'd been unable to resist Tom's advances, and some twisted plan had formed for the ultimate betrayal.

Maybe like Laura always said, there was a kind of menopausal madness which exacerbated bad behaviour. And made the most irrational things seem rational for a time.

It didn't make sense to me, so how could I explain it to her? Or anyone else.

Mutely I shook my head. 'I don't know,' I replied bluntly.

'Were you never really my friend?'

'No,' I lied. 'It was always a means to an end.'

She stood up and said so quietly I barely heard it, 'I considered you one of my best friends, Claire, even if you never considered me one.' She snatched her bag and I saw her reaching for her phone, probably to ring her husband. I was completely alone with only my guilt for company.

I'd done what I wanted, I'd destroyed the image of her picture-perfect marriage, only to discover it was far from perfect without my meddling. The veneer of their ideal life had cracked open and spewed its secrets. And now I had my own confession to make, but it would wait until tomorrow.

Why did I not feel triumphant?

Why did I want to curl up in a ball and rewind time to the first night at Laura's, when I was introduced to Vicky. I should have admitted straight away I was Clare Hefton and demanded an apology about her role in my past. I should never have allowed this friendship to form or retribution to have preoccupied me.

Hot tears splashed down my cheeks as I made my way back to the empty bedroom, my grand plan collapsing around me. I'd cheated on a man who loved and accepted me despite my many flaws and faults, to try and seek vengeance on someone who had concealed their spiteful past.

I'd been a fool.

And now I had to confess all to my husband and would have to face the consequences, no matter how difficult.

CHAPTER FORTY

I slept little after the confrontation with Vicky, instead I sat for hours on the cold balcony of my hotel room, draining a bottle of white wine I'd ordered from room service. I'd torn the duvet from the bed and wrapped myself in it, glaring morosely at the shadowed grounds while listening to the burbling river flowing nearby. A crescent moon illuminated the gardens, and I'd surreptitiously watched as a couple wound their way across the grass, moulded together, ignorant of my stare. Envy pierced me at their happiness as they vanished from sight and I reflected on my life.

From my earliest memories of our fractured family, to meeting Will and having my girls. From the cramped terraced home of my childhood, to the beautiful detached home I now lived in.

From being rejected by my peers, to becoming an integral part of a solid friendship group.

Everything had come full circle.

For now I was about to fracture my own family and face rejection from my peers again. And for what reason? Because I had lost my mind and surrendered to my primitive quest for justice. Belatedly I deduced there was a real possibility Will would be unable to forgive me and I could lose everything.

Only now I ascertained my decisions over the past year had been questionable and I couldn't fathom why I'd made them, or why I'd capitulated to the desire to destroy everything I held dear. Ultimately I may never know, and would have to put it down to my year of living recklessly.

In the end, shattered by my ruminations, I dragged the duvet indoors, where I coiled into the foetal position on top of the bed and shut my eyes. Before I fell asleep, I was comforted by the knowledge finally it was finished. And maybe, just maybe, Will could move past this and we could face the future together.

When I woke next morning, it was already check-out time, and I had a vice-like pain in my head. I'd eaten nothing except toast yesterday morning, and then polished off the double gin and a bottle of wine. What an idiot. Nausea swelled as I stood up and I had to wait for it to subside before I could shower. I needed to scrub my skin clean of the past day, although I knew the stains of it would linger long.

When I had showered and dressed, I packed my case. I had no further need of the secret phone, and didn't have the inclination to look at the photos one last time. I would cut up the sim card and smash the phone at some point. Briefly I surveyed the room. Tom had cleared out before I'd returned yesterday and I'd had no communication from him since. My other phone had been on silent throughout and now I read the messages I'd missed.

I scanned the excess of mundane messages from my family and friends. Vicky hadn't been online and had therefore not yet updated the Book Club about her discoveries. I was certain her version of the past would be at odds with mine. I had to presume she would not divulge that we'd known each other a lifetime ago.

Really, what did it matter?

I'd made my choices no matter how ill-judged, and whatever happened as a result of them, would happen. The Book Club would doubtless be confounded at my duplicitousness, astounded at my deceit and Kate would cry and wail at the unfairness of it all.

Dejectedly I tucked the phone into my handbag, and with a last glance around the room, wheeled my case to the lift and hit the button for the ground floor. Checking out of the hotel and the drive home passed too quickly, not helped by my headache and sickness. A nightmare of my own making.

I pulled up in front of the house to find Will had installed light-up reindeers in the front garden, along with two miniature trees either side of the front door. A fresh berry wreath hung from it, its lights welcoming in the gloom. He had done it to surprise me, as he knew my abhorrence of short, dark winter days.

My legs felt like lead as I slowly climbed out of the car and headed for the door, leaving my case in the boot. When I stepped into the hall, I inhaled the festive scent of orange and pine from the candles he had lit for my return. Tears choked me as I called feebly for him, hearing his hello from the kitchen. I trudged in and he frowned when he saw me, asking anxiously what was wrong.

'I need to tell you something, Will, please come into the living room with me.'

Intuitively I knew he wanted to embrace me, however I couldn't allow it. If I didn't confess straight away, I would lose my nerve and it would unquestionably make it worse for both of us. I rested on the edge of an armchair, motioning for him to sit on the sofa opposite me. His amiable face was a study in worry, and as his frightened brown eyes stared bewilderedly at me, I hesitantly started my admission.

His face changed from warm and loving to incredulous, then horrified. The face which had looked at me with only love and affection for nearly thirty years visibly shut down, crumpling in misery. And worst of all, his eyes filled with tears as the enormity of my deceit was laid bare. I had never hated myself as much as I did then, inflicting the worst pain on the person who had cherished and accepted me for more than half my life.

And then shade crossed his face, and I could see he found it unforgivable, this great treachery. No matter my reasons or my attempts at validation, I had crossed the boundary and he was incapable of absolving me of my crime.

Standing up, he said in a broken voice, 'You're not the person I thought you were, Claire. I thought you loved me, but I was wrong. Love isn't revenge and destruction of everything you hold dear. Love isn't vengeance, it's forgiveness. I gave you everything and you've thrown it in my face. I don't want you to say another word or to come after me.'

Curtly he turned and I heard his hurried footsteps in the hallway, fading as he went into the bedroom. At first I sat there, wallowing in self-pity, and then it dawned on me what it meant.

He was leaving me.

Quickly I sprang up from the chair, before rushing into our bedroom. He was flinging clothes into the ancient overnight bag which lay in the bottom of his wardrobe. He refused to look at me, or to answer my increasingly frantic demands he talk to me. Furiously he zipped it up, before moving up close to me.

'Get out of my way, Claire.' His harsh tone was alien to me, barely controlled rage radiating from him, saturating the air.

I shook my head, refusing, reaching out to grasp him. Pleading I loved him, he couldn't leave, we could work through it together.

His eyes remained fixed on my face, and he was impervious to my hysterical cries as he shook me off.

'Don't you understand why I had to do it?' I bawled wretchedly. 'She bullied me, tortured me daily for years.' His eyes were blank and I understood too late the hollowness of my words.

For there was no excuse I could make which could justify what I had done.

Shakily I dropped my hands and stepped aside to let him by. As he passed me, he asked sharply, 'Are you going to tell the girls or will I?'

'I will,' I managed and he nodded once, before leaving the room. I stood motionless as I heard the front door slam behind him and the sound of his car engine revving. I had no idea where he was going, or what he was going to do. Sinking to my knees, I roared and railed against the unfairness of life and my own lunacy.

Any time I had considered his reaction, I was convinced he would forgive me, like he had always done. Such was my delusion, I had never expected him to leave me. I had anticipated hurt and even anger, but never inflexible fury. I had to hope it was simply the heat of the moment and he would be back. Would allow me to make amends. Ultimately he would forgive me.

However his harsh tone and detached face had chilled me to the bone.

I don't know how long I lay on the bedroom floor, disbelieving, exhausted. After a time I rose and crept onto our bed. My mind was completely empty. I couldn't figure out what I should do. I kept praying he would return so I could make him accept my apology. Then I realised with mounting horror I hadn't actually said sorry to him. It had seemed so glaringly obvious to me I profoundly regretted everything, I'd forgotten to say the words.

What kind of person was I?

Self-loathing, my old companion, swept through me. No wonder my husband had left me. And once I'd confided in my daughters, they would categorically desert me too.

With immense effort, I managed to refrain from going straight into the kitchen and downing a bottle of gin. Despondently I went outside to the car and seized my handbag which was lying on the passenger seat. I tramped into the house and searched through it for my phone.

It was answered on the third ring.

'Mum, I've done something dreadful.'

The mollifying tones of my mum calmed me a little, and I was able to say those appalling words. *I've been cheating on Will and now he knows.*

'Oh, Clare,' she said, disappointment and disapproval palpable from miles away. 'What on earth were you thinking?'

'It's a long story,' I babbled. 'Vicky is Tori from school. I decided it would be a great way to get her back for everything.'

'I can't make any sense of this,' she said. 'Are you okay to drive here or will I come over?'

'I'm okay to drive, I'll come over now.'

I hung up, went through into the kitchen and poured a large glass of water, feeling marginally less panic-stricken. I'd go and see Mum and she'd make it all better.

First though I needed to send Will a message.

I am so sorry. I know I've done a dreadful thing. Please, please forgive me. I love you

Staring at the phone, I willed him to reply as the message

remained unread. And then as I was closing the front door behind me, my phone buzzed. My heart lifted for the tiniest moment until I read the message. It wasn't from Will, it was on the Book Club chat.

Claire what the hell have you done?

CHAPTER FORTY-ONE

I sat in Mum's sitting room, clasping the mug of steaming coffee and tried to compose myself. The small room felt even tinier as it was crammed with mismatching furniture and floor-to-ceiling knick-knacks. I'd confessed all, and explained my reasons. I could tell Mum was stunned by my behaviour. My excuses were feeble at best, nonsensical at worst. I'd expected her to understand and forgive me, but it was apparent she was struggling.

I was a disappointment to my family. I could tell by the hurt expression in her eyes, the way she found it hard to look at me.

'I'm sorry,' I tried again.

'Sorry you did it, or sorry for yourself?' she asked directly. Trust Mum.

'Both, if I'm honest.'

'How could you have ever supposed this would be appropriate? It went on for over a year!' She shook her head, astonishment clear. 'Why did you feel justified in cheating on Will? To exact some sort of warped retaliation for things which happened years ago? Sometimes I don't understand you at all. Will has given you a beautiful home, two gorgeous girls, you want for nothing. So different to when you were growing up.' She shook her head sadly.

'With a drunk for a father.' The bitterness shot out.

'We did our best in the circumstances,' she retorted quickly.

I rolled my eyes and kept talking, deflecting from my behaviour by reminding her of my dad's. 'Oh, I know. We had little money, just enough to spend on beer.'

'Your dad went through a lot, Clare. Could it be time to forgive him?'

I was astounded. 'Forgive him for being a wifebeater? Forgive him for spending what money we had on the drink? I don't think so.' I was furious with her, with him, with the sad existence we had lived. Her cries, his shouts and the slamming of doors suddenly engulfed me. Those cries and thumps and shouts woke me in a panic at night, quivering and in a cold sweat.

It was unforgivable. He was unforgivable.

Sighing deeply, she looked out of the window at her lush garden, recalling that bleak time with difficulty. She sat in silence for a few minutes, then seemingly made a decision and looked directly at me. Her voice was quiet, a little unsteady.

'Those were dark days, right in the middle of The Troubles. Bombs, shootings, fear and death roamed these streets. All it needed was to be in the wrong place at the wrong time and your life could change in the blink of an eye.' Her lip trembled as she paused.

'Dad accepted a job with a company which did building work for the security forces. It was better pay which came with a price. A target on his back. One day, he was waiting with two other workmen for the minibus to collect them to take them to their next job. He nipped into the newsagents for a sneaky packet of cigarettes. As he paid for them at the till, he heard gunfire.' She was upset now, eyes glistening with tears. 'He hid in the shop until the shooting stopped, then went outside. His two workmates were dead on the footpath. If he hadn't gone into the shop for the cigarettes, he would have been shot as well.'

She looked defeated at the memory, and I recognised her pain as raw as if it had been yesterday, not decades ago.

'He couldn't forgive himself. He felt he was a coward. Survivor's guilt, they call it now. It plagued him, the image of those men lying there. Him hiding in the shop. He came to believe it would have been better if he'd run out and been shot too. He lived, when so many others didn't. What did he have to complain about? Soon the only respite he got from his nightmares was drinking to forget. He would come home; I would fight with him and he'd lash out. Over and over until he drank himself into oblivion one last time.'

My insides wrenched at the tale. I never knew any of this because I had never asked. Selfishly, I had no interest in why a man would become a pale shadow of himself. Of the trauma he had witnessed and lived through. Of a guilt so great he could see no other way out.

'I loved him so much, Clare, and we had been so happy until then. One sunny June day changed everything, and he withdrew to a place I couldn't reach. I tried to help him, but I couldn't. Nothing could. The booze took the edge off it for him.'

Stiffly she got up and went over to the wooden display cabinet, overcrowded with her ornaments, and opened the middle drawer. Stooping down, she reached in and brought out an old-fashioned photo album in purple, green and brown. A throwback to the seventies. She placed it gently on my knee with the simple instruction to open it.

Nervous for some unknown reason, I did and on the first page was a wedding photo of a young couple running through a shower of confetti. Their grins were wide and they held hands firmly. My parents. How in love they looked. Without speaking,

I turned the pages, photo after photo of them together, happiness personified. Then one after the other with first one little girl, then a second. Both with the striking green eyes like their father. My father. In every photo we were smiling; on the beach, in a swimming pool with armbands on, gathering bluebells in a wood. I remembered none of it. I had erased the good memories and retained only the bad.

At the back I found a dry, ancient newspaper article dated June 19th 1985:

WORKMEN GUNNED DOWN ON THE STREET

I skim-read the article with mounting horror. Read the vivid account of the day which had changed my father's life, our lives, forever. His name was barely mentioned at the end, a minor footnote in history.

> A third workman was inside the shop at the time and it saved his life.

'Why did you never tell me this before now?' I wiped the tears away, reluctant to set the photo album down.

'It was so long ago. I tried to protect you from it, you were only children. Maybe you would have understood him better if I had told you.' A beat, as if to say it was unimportant now. 'You do what you think is right at the time. Hindsight is a wonderful thing.'

How true that was.

The door to the sitting room opened and Phil stuck his head around it. Immediately he took in the scene, tear-stained faces and the photo album.

'I wondered if you wanted another cup of coffee?' he asked gently.

I shook my head, as did Mum.

'I've told Clare about Martin. It was time.' She looked fondly at my stepfather. He stepped into the room, went over to Mum and placed his large hand on her small shoulder.

'Are you okay?' His words were for her.

She reached up for his hand, then said, 'Phil worked with your dad. He was the foreman in the company. If you have any more questions, he'll try and answer them. Won't you?'

Phil nodded, his face a mass of worry lines and concern.

I finished my coffee and hugged them both before leaving. While I had no questions for now, they would certainly come over time.

What do you do when your entire history hasn't been what you supposed it was? When you knew a fraction of the story, but not all of it?

Without giving it any consideration, I drove to the cemetery my dad had been buried in. I'd never visited his grave, not even once since he died so many years ago. When I reached the car park, I parked and sat lost in my thoughts for a time. I had no idea where his plot was, and shame weighed me down.

Luckily there was a groundsman tidying up, and I asked if he knew where my father's grave might be. He pointed to the end of a row and I walked along the ancient path, reading the headstones until I found his.

A simple headstone marked the plot, which was spotless and well-tended. A fresh winter wreath lay on the green stone chips; red berries, holly and ivy. Someone had placed it there recently. It was under a wide old tree, beside a wall and the serenity of the churchyard calmed me. I read the headstone, the words blurring.

MARTIN HEFTON
Beloved son, husband, father
1st January 1950 – 29th April 1998

He had been forty-eight when he died. What a waste. What a tragedy.

Great sobs built up in me as I remembered his smile, the sound of our laughter as he had given us piggybacks in the garden, chased us into the waves on Portrush strand. Memories I had refused to recall, that I had rigorously and thoughtlessly repressed. I wept for the lost years and the great misfortune of this small country, where it seemed nearly every family had been touched by the violence of the past.

And I wept for the hideous disaster I had made of my once gilded life. When I had allowed my obsession to consume me and destroy not only my marriage, but also another marriage and our friendships.

CHAPTER FORTY-TWO

The following day I had the harrowing experience of telling my daughters Will had left me because I was having an affair with his friend. The ferocity of their outrage had stunned me. When I had tried to defend my illogical reasoning, they had yelled their disgust and mortification in my face. Cruel and hurtful words which stabbed the core of me.

They were shrill, whirling banshees, but I deserved it. A deadly silence had descended as they packed more of their belongings into bags and instructed me not to contact them. I pleaded and begged for forgiveness, as they threw their belongings into the boot of the car and drove off, faces tear-stained and haggard with emotion. I wailed on the doorstep like someone demented, oblivious to the cutting wind and hailstones like pellets. The pain in my heart was crushing.

Completely spent, I'd staggered inside, locked the doors, pulled all the blinds and drunk myself into a stupor. The hangover had lasted two full days and into the mix came a raging Kate and a furious Annie. I'd consumed at least another bottle and a half of wine before they arrived, and was living on bags of crisps and microwave meals. My brain was befuddled and sleep deprived, and I'd taken to listening to sad songs on repeat, wallowing in the past and the abject bleakness of my future. There seemed to be no light at the end of this vast, gloomy tunnel.

Unwilling to answer the door, I had crouched out of sight in the conservatory. They rang the doorbell insistently, while Kate screeched through the letter box that they knew I was inside and wouldn't leave until I opened the door. I'd not showered since the hotel and was wearing the same clothes I'd been in for days, when I flung the door wide open.

It was plain they were shocked by my appearance as Kate's mouth formed a round O and Annie stammered they wanted to hear my side of the story. Abruptly I stepped aside and waved them indoors. No point in freezing to death on the doorstep for what I assumed would be a fleeting visit. Before I shut the door, I was amazed to see the weather had changed, and a thick layer of frost coated the world. One of Will's reindeer had fallen over and the Christmas trees he'd lovingly decorated for my homecoming now had sparkling tips. The fields in the valley below were dusted with white and the clear blue sky taunted me. The air was crisp and cool and I sucked it eagerly into my lungs, easing the tension. In times gone by, I would have adored this winter wonderland. Now it swamped me with jagged loss.

I slammed the front door with a bang, and turned to find them speaking animatedly together in the hallway. I had no intention of offering them a coffee or a seat, so crossed my arms and leaned as casually as possible against the door.

'Well, what do you want to know?' I asked defiantly.

Annie's glare was calm and direct, while Kate's intense desire to unravel the whole despicable tale spilled over. She was practically bouncing up and down in her trainers, eyes alert with barely restrained hunger for every scandalous detail. 'Why did you do it?' she asked tremulously. Honest to goodness, if she cried I'd push her out of the door and down the steps.

'What have you heard?' I replied, interested to find out exactly how one sided Vicky's story had been. I stared at them both, these friends of mine who thought they had known my every secret, had shared every feeling. How wrong they had been.

'You and Tom have been having an affair and you've broken Vicky's heart!' Kate exclaimed, chin jutting aggressively.

Not even trying to stop from rolling my eyes, I looked at Annie and raised my eyebrows.

'We're here so you can tell us your side of the story, Claire. I don't believe for one minute you've done this for no reason.' At least Annie was showing a modicum of wit.

'And if I tell you my side, what then?' I said tiredly. 'You only know a small bit of it. Did Vicky tell you we knew each other from school?'

Obviously confused, they shook their heads. So I gave them the potted version of how our lives had been in the good old days. How Tori/Vicky hadn't recognised Hefty Lump and somehow the bully and the victim had become friends. Years later, I had sought my revenge. My words were empty, my justifications clumsy, and I stumbled over them.

And ultimately I could tell they didn't fully believe me. They supposed I was embellishing, that it was unthinkable Vicky could have been a bully. For they were acquainted with only one side of the caring, altruistic doctor, having never witnessed or been on the receiving end of the arrogant, malicious teenager. Abruptly I stopped, and waited for the inevitable outcry.

'What a debacle, Claire! I'm sorry, I can't believe it,' said Annie at last, sadly shaking her head. 'Even if what you say is true, you've still been having an affair with Tom. With our friend's husband. It seems like you've used all of us, lied to us for a long time.' Her disappointment was evident. 'What about Will and the girls? Did you think of them at all? I don't understand you or why you would do it.'

Kate nodded vigorously. 'I don't either. No matter what you say, you've broken the girl code.'

I snorted at the incongruous image of a middle-aged woman preaching about girl code. They looked at me like I'd lost my mind, so I opened the door and told them to get lost. Or words to that effect. I was too weary to describe the exact events which had defined my school life, and the legacy of trauma they had wrought.

Annie came to a halt beside me and said in a very serious and ever so sombre tone, 'Go and sober up, Claire. Accept you've done something terrible and ruined our friendship.'

Before I could stop myself, I sneered, 'It takes two to tango, Annie. Tom cheated on Vicky. Have you lectured him yet on his lack of morals?'

I knew by the stiffening of her shoulders she hadn't. Nor could she answer me. So I slammed the door with such force I thought it might split down the middle. Then I roared with incompetent rage at the injustice of it all. They didn't believe me. No one believed me. And they all blamed me, irrespective of Tom's role. Hurt and despair struck me, like a physical blow. I told myself it was no less than I had expected. I had known they would choose Vicky, like all those years ago, when the school had taken the side of her and her friends.

I returned to the conservatory, flicked on Netflix and poured another glass of wine.

The days merged into one, as each grey morning crawled into the black of night. I rarely opened the curtains, living on alcohol and food from the freezer, languishing with regret. My house became my refuge, my mind numb, my heavy limbs lethargic.

It was almost Christmas and apart from my mum and most surprisingly Liz, I'd had no contact from anyone. Mum rang me daily and encouraged me to stay with her and Phil for a time, worried I might do something stupid. I mollified her with reassurances I was coping, and confirmed I'd spend Christmas Day with them. Liz messaged me regularly, asking if I wanted her to visit, offering company. Her kindness was unexpected and meant all the more after our precarious history. Their unwavering support stopped me from sinking into a deep depression in those early days.

Apart from them, my phone was stubbornly mute. There was nothing from Will, my daughters or the Book Club. I'd been removed from the WhatsApp group. There had been radio silence from Tom and Vicky as well. No doubt they were whispering sweet nothings into each other's ears, or perhaps renewing their wedding vows. I'd never taken Vicky for a fool, but if she stayed with him after this, that's exactly what she was.

I messaged Will and the girls daily, begging their forgiveness. They never responded. I wished they would miraculously reappear on the doorstep and we could rebuild our lives. Helpless, hopeless wishing which tormented me. I suspected Will had moved in with his parents. Sadly I lacked the courage to go and find out. The thought of seeing the animosity and revulsion in their eyes stopped me. I could have driven to the girls' digs, but again my nerve failed me, terrified they would refuse to answer the door.

Surely they would come home for Christmas, for it seemed impossible they wouldn't. After a few days, I had to face the unpalatable fact they were not going to simply reappear and resume our lives as though nothing had happened.

At some point I ran out of alcohol and basics, so risked

driving into the neighbouring town to buy more. I avoided the village, scared I would see Vicky or Tom, reeling at the prospect. I showered quickly and changed my clothes for the first time in days. As I pushed the trolley around the supermarket, hair still wet, my nerve endings jangled as tinny Christmas music played deafeningly throughout the shop, and over-excited children ran like headless chickens up and down the aisles. I detested Christmas now and sobbed in the sweet aisle as I remembered I hadn't bought Eva and Poppy any treats for their stockings. The sinking realisation, even if I had, they wouldn't be opening them beside the tree and they'd be somewhere else with someone else and I'd be alone.

I'd wiped my streaming eyes and wheeled the trolley to the self-service till, which refused to serve me until some young girl with long talons and a puckered mouth confirmed I was over twenty-five. Her contemptuous look at the three bottles of gin and six bottles of wine made my cheeks hot with indignation and shame.

'I'm having a Christmas party,' I lied, and her sniff of disdain was audible.

My shoulders slumped with embarrassment as I scurried out of the shop, head down, hoping not to bump into anyone I recognised. Relief swept through me when I reached the solitude of the car and I hastily unloaded the bags into the boot. I'd have to shop elsewhere for a while, fearful of the shop assistant and her withering gaze.

Spontaneously I drove the long route home, into the hills and along the coast road. When I reached a curve in the road, I slowed down, searching for a white car parked in front of my in-law's house. As anticipated, Will's car was out in front, though there was no sign of life. I sped up, tears blinding me, having confirmed where he was, glad he was with people who loved him. I had to suppress the urge to swing around, and drive up and down outside until he burst from the house and I caught a glimpse of him.

When I arrived home, I heated the tasteless chicken curry I had bought and washed it down with wine.

I was surviving, but only just.

CHAPTER FORTY-THREE

A day or two later, I lolled dejectedly on the conservatory sofa when the doorbell rang. The last thing I wanted was to speak to anyone or get another lecture on my loose morals. I wanted to flounder alone in my misery. So I let it ring, and swallowed another huge gulp of my gin. They were persistent, and it rang again and again, until I had to answer it.

Laura stood there, wearing an uncertain smile and holding a bottle of Pinot in front of her.

'I thought you could do with a friend,' she commented, pushing past me and heading straight for the kitchen.

'Do you really want to be friends with an adulterer? What will all your nice friends think?' I asked bitterly. Misery does not love company.

'Oh, boohoo, Claire. Toughen up and quit whingeing.'

She surprised me, this straight-talking Laura. What happened to the mealy-mouthed, downtrodden widow I knew so well?

'Find me a wine glass and pour me a big one please.' She plonked the bottle down on the granite worktop with a clunk, deposited her coat on a nearby chair and raised her eyebrows at me.

Mulishly I did as I was told and also topped up my gin while I was at it. Wordlessly, she followed me into the conservatory, though the light was dimming and the shadows stretching outside. I should have switched on a lamp, but preferred the dark these days. Mysteriously my fear of the dark had vanished along with my family.

'Are you okay?' she asked, taking a mouthful of her wine, looking at me over the rim of her glass.

'Great thanks. My kids hate me, my husband's left me and I've lost all my friends. Oh, and I'm also at risk of losing my job. So life couldn't be better.'

'Why are you going to lose your job?' She ignored the rest.

'Long story,' I replied. 'Look, why are you here? Haven't you heard I'm to be shunned?' I was as blunt as I could be, no space in my soul for politeness at the minute.

'Claire, I have no idea why you did what you did, but I'm not going to judge you for it.' She studied the wine in her glass, swirling it around. Seemingly having reached a decision, she continued. 'I want to tell you something I haven't told anyone before.'

I indicated she should go on.

'I told James I was leaving him the night before he died.'

I was shocked, for I had no idea she had even been considering it. How had it come to this? She had never hinted at a rift so great she wanted to end her marriage. I opened my mouth to speak until she raised a hand to stop me.

'Please, I need to tell you this in my own way. I was desperately unhappy in my marriage for a long time. James was difficult in the extreme and for the last year or so, he'd become so controlling it seemed I was going to suffocate. He put a tracker on my phone and lied about our finances.' Her eyes had taken on a faraway look and I noticed she was grasping the stem of the glass so firmly her knuckles were white. 'There's more, but I can't relive it. I'm still recovering.' She fell silent, and I could tell by the haunted expression in her eyes she was replaying what had happened.

'Why didn't you tell me?' It burst out of me, even though she'd asked me not to interrupt.

'I was humiliated. I told no one. You never know what's going on behind closed doors, do you?' I shook my head and she went on. 'I didn't even recognise it myself for a long time, then it dawned on me one day. Coercive control. A toxic relationship.'

She held my gaze before saying, 'And now the reason I'm not in a position to judge you, Claire. I was sleeping with Sam when James was alive.'

'That's it?' I replied without thinking. 'You're comparing your set-up with mine? You had a control freak of a husband and found a saint. I have a saint and slept repeatedly with my friend's husband. It went on for over a year, Laura. I don't deserve your understanding or your kindness.' My voice shook with the effort of admitting it.

Suddenly it was vitally important someone understood my reasons, when everyone else had recoiled at my actions. 'You said you had no idea why I did it. She bullied me at school. Vicky, or Tori as she styled herself then, was part of an exclusive group of bullies and I was an easy target as I was unattractive and shy. When we moved here, I recognised her straight away. However she didn't know me as I had changed so much from school. I despised her initially, but bizarrely we became part of the same group of friends. Then the dinner dance at the Melville Hotel last year. Do you remember? Vicky and I both wore red dresses. She looked as fantastic as ever, and I felt a pale imitation beside her and it all came flooding back. I went out to the foyer to get some air, and

Tom appeared from nowhere on his mobile.' Even now, the memory of the look he gave me made my insides melt. 'It started as a flirtation, nothing more. Well, you know exactly how it ended. She's playing the victim, leaving me to pick up the pieces.'

Laura said nothing for so long I began to worry she too believed I'd fabricated it all. Then she said, 'I believe you, Claire, though it's hard to think of Vicky as a bully. Do we ever really know anyone?' She shook her head as if to shake off the truth. 'I'm truly sorry you had to put up with that. I do wish you'd felt able to confide in me.'

Now I shook my head, for if I had, would she have believed me? I'd never know.

A comfortable quiet stretched between us as we sipped our drinks, broken only when Laura said, 'Vicky seemed to have it all, didn't she. Looks. Brains. Money. Tom.' I smiled in agreement. 'It was another thing we couldn't admit to. We pretended we confided in each other, but it was smoke and mirrors. I hid my appalling secret and you hid yours.'

We sat in a silence for a time, until I offered to replenish our drinks.

'Top it up. Sam will come for me whenever I ring him.' She held the glass up until it was full.

'You seem different, Laura,' I commented, retaking my seat and tucking my feet up beneath me.

'I am different. Do you notice how I'm no longer preoccupied with Robbie?' The side of her mouth lifted ruefully. 'James was riddled with jealousy about his son. Couldn't for the life of him understand why I missed him so much when he was in Scotland. Hated him for it, I think. Jealousy is at the root of so much unhappiness, isn't it?'

'Yes it really is. It's pathetic, isn't it? My reason for destroying everything?' I urgently needed someone, anyone, to believe me about Vicky. To validate what I'd done and my reasons for it.

'Claire, I'm going to say this as a friend. I believe you about Vicky and your past, and I'm incredibly sorry about what you went through. I have to be honest, I don't think I'll ever understand why you chose to do what you did, as it's hurt Will so badly. You need to stop drinking and start on the road to recovery.' She said it firmly while maintaining eye contact, until I looked away. 'Your girls are furious with you, but they love you and they'll come round.'

'How do you know? They think I'm the worst mother ever.' I almost shouted, heartache consuming me.

'Because Robbie and Eva are in a relationship.' She smiled grimly at me, and I could tell she regretted that she was the one divulging this piece of information, and not my daughter. 'She's been at our house quite a bit over the past week. And I mean Sam's house, not the one in the village. That's why I've not been round here until today. I've been staying with Sam and supporting Eva.'

I started to weep then, for that was certainly what Eva had wanted to tell me. I'd been so engrossed in my own life I'd failed her. And she'd never confided in me her childhood friend was now someone important to her. She'd relied on Laura to guide her through this difficult week.

Laura leaned forward to take hold of my hand, before squeezing it reassuringly. 'She loves you, Claire. Children find it almost impossible to acknowledge their parents are people in their own right and not simply Mum and Dad. You need to pull yourself together, or Eva and Poppy won't rush to see you again. Isn't it time to forgive yourself as well as everyone else?'

I disregarded that particular gem of wisdom for the time being. Tears leaked from my eyes. Perhaps I was less unlovable than I had supposed. I held her hand tightly. It was hard to believe I had dodged such physical expressions of friendship a few short weeks ago. Now they felt like a lifeline to redemption. Suddenly comprehension hit me full whack in the face.

Laura knew the secret me, the one I had painstakingly hidden behind my façade, and she had not discarded me like Annie and Kate. She saw me for who I really was and stayed anyway.

'Please tell Will I'm sorry and I love him.' I whispered it as she nodded.

'What are you going to do for Christmas?' she asked then. 'You can't stay here on your own.'

So the girls weren't going to forgive me before Christmas. With a start, I remembered it was the day after tomorrow. I'd stopped going into the living room with the tree, the gaudily wrapped presents nestling under it mocked me ceaselessly.

'I'll go to Mum and Phil's. Will you take the girls' presents for me and please ask them to at least reply to my messages so I know they are safe?'

'Yes I will. I need you to promise me you're going to stop drinking and start eating properly. And, Claire, you need to see the GP. From everything you've been saying, it sounds like you need proper help, not a bottle of gin.'

Her words cut through my stupor and made perfect sense. She was right. I needed professional help and as much I was self-medicating with alcohol, it was a perilous road with only one possible outcome.

'Menopausal madness.' We said it at the same time and gave a small laugh. Some sort of madness anyway.

She persuaded me to shower while she cooked me some delicious concoction from the contents of my cupboards. She then poured me a large glass of tonic with plenty of ice. Unexpectedly I discovered I was famished and devoured her concoction hungrily. It would take more than a hot meal and a shower to make me whole again, but knowing I had a true friend to help me went a long way towards restoring my faith in friendship and the future.

All I needed was for Will, Eva and Poppy to forgive me and allow themselves to trust me again.

It seemed like an unachievable dream.

CHAPTER FORTY-FOUR

My family continued to vent their anger towards me by mostly ignoring me. I'd messaged Will and the girls on Christmas Day, and received short texts from Eva and Poppy. Other than those, my phone remained unbearably silent. No ping from a message. No ring from a call. My broken heart was crushed further that freezing December morning when I sat alone in my beautiful house and sobbed over the unopened and unwanted gifts piled under the tree. Laura had taken the girls' presents with her, leaving the over-the-top gifts I'd ordered for Will unclaimed.

I had a subdued Christmas dinner with Mum and Phil, drinking Shloer while eyeballing the wine. Liz, Pete and Max had popped in for a quick visit and I began to process the true meaning of family, as no judgement was passed on me, nor condemnation voiced. Liz had taken me aside and I readied myself for a torrent of abuse.

Instead she surprised me by pulling me roughly into a hug and whispered, 'Clare, you're a complete eejit, but I sort of understand. Wish I could have seen that bitch Tori's face when you told her who you were.' It was small crumbs of comfort, and my shoulders had sagged with both relief at her words and disbelief at her empathy. While not condoning my behaviour, she wasn't spitting nails with horror and outrage either.

I unlocked my front door after our turkey and ham and called out in the vain hope I would get a reply. Only the echoes of Christmas past greeted me as I succumbed and opened a bottle of wine.

The following day I surrendered to the unshakeable urge to go for a drive, ignoring the torrential rain which had rolled in over the hills on Boxing Day morning. The road climbed high above Belfast and I drove into Cave Hill country park. Rain-laden clouds spread above me, so close it seemed I could reach out and touch them. The car park was empty, no one despairing enough to leave the warmth and dryness to venture out. I was soaked through by the time I had walked to Napoleon's Nose, my hair drenched, my hands freezing.

I stood a few metres from the edge, surveying the city, which lazed about far below me, colourless as far as the eye could see. My mind raced about uncontrollably, but the relief was profound when I realised I had no desire to step over the edge. Wearily I lifted my eyes to the heavens and let the rain teem over me, mingling with futile tears. Eva and Poppy had saved me once; I couldn't let my own girls suffer any further as a result of my selfishness. I trudged back to the car and drove home, determined not to drink to ease the burden of my pain.

At the beginning of January the girls agreed to visit me. They remained perplexed by my behaviour, and I had no enthusiasm to once again attempt to explain or justify what I'd done. It was a new beginning as we steered our way through our burgeoning adult relationship. I was no longer merely Mum. I became a fallible person who had made an irresponsible, stupid mistake. Their anger had softened into something more malleable, and I knew by their sidelong looks, they shared a willingness to mend our relationship.

I desperately wanted to ask Eva about Robbie. However I bit my tongue, for fear her face would close down and she would retreat. Hopefully in time, she would confide in me.

Will sent the occasional message requesting I leave the house while he came by to collect more clothes and things he needed. I always replied immediately, my heart in my mouth, nervous he would follow it with something ghastly. Like he wanted a divorce. Each time he was due, I would drive off and park close to where I knew he would pass on his way to the house. A speeding glimpse was all I got, never enough, always yearning for more. When his car passed me on the return trip, I would dejectedly drive home. There I sobbed at bare drawers and empty hangers. His toiletries now sat on a shelf in his parents' home, his clothes filled their drawers and all I was left with was faint hints of him.

I'd made an appointment at the start of January with my doctor, who had prescribed medication and counselling for my shambolically muddled mind. It was difficult not to blur the edges of my misery with drink, but my resolve outweighed the desire. As my mental health improved I felt the occasional spark of optimism I would survive. I would not blame the past year on hormones, or anxiety, or menopausal mayhem, though it was possible they had played some small part.

Imelda my boss had contacted me the week after the festive holidays to inform me I could resume work after a written warning. They had been unable to confirm Eric's theory, nor prove I had been using vacant houses for illicit assignations. I was astonished at how grateful I was for the opportunity, and as I set foot inside the estate agents after my enforced absence, I resolved to make amends for my previous apathy and idleness at my job. For it was a lifeline when I could no longer face long days of isolation at home. I increased my hours to work Monday through to Thursday. Each Friday I volunteered at a woman's refuge – up to then I had simply donated my barely worn clothes to them.

Laura kept in touch with me regularly. She was spending most of her time at Sam's, flitting in and out of the village and her empty house on the street. Her confession about wanting to leave James had initially taken me by surprise, however when I mulled it over, I understood everyone has mysteries they keep locked within the confines of their hearts and minds. One cool day in late January we walked along the long sandy beach we had strolled on with Kate in the autumn. The brisk sea breeze buffeted us as we dandered along in companionable silence.

After we had taken a seat at the same picnic table, she confided Vicky and Tom were no longer the flawless couple they had depicted, and she was finding this betrayal worse than all the others. With their children at university, there was no buffer at home and it seemed they too were navigating a way through the damage. Whether it was reparable remained to be seen.

Sadly the Book Club lay in tatters, as it transpired Kate and Annie were firmly in Vicky's camp. It bothered me less than everything else, as I'd known all along female friendship was fickle. Nevertheless when I walked past the village café one morning and saw the four of them sitting at our usual table, laughing together, I felt an unaccustomed twinge of something sharp in my stomach. I tried to convince myself I didn't need their friendship, it had all been fake. Head down, I scuttled past, the hurt and the loss almost flooring me. I had prepared myself for it, but the reality of my bad choice was a harder and lonelier road than I had ever supposed.

One Saturday in late January I had returned to the car having been to the village butcher. As I clicked my seatbelt into place, I noticed Tom's car pull in a few spaces down from me. We were separated by a four-wheel drive, and my pulse quickened with anxiety. Vicky stepped out of the passenger door and hurried towards the shops. It was evident neither of them had spotted me.

It was the first time I had seen Tom since the Averie and I deliberated about what I should do. I could crouch down and hide, hoping he wouldn't see me. Or I could face him. Giving myself no time to change my mind, I got out of the car and rushed over. I opened the passenger door and slipped into the seat Vicky had just vacated. The seat I was intimately familiar with. Tom's head swung around and he stared at me in disbelief.

'What the hell, Claire. What are you doing there? Get out!' Barely restrained annoyance.

'Hi, Tom,' I said. 'Long time no see.' My heart beat wildly, though I was eerily calm. His handsome face twisted in anger, a muscle twitching in his cheek. 'I wanted to apologise.' The words came easily and I continued quickly, afraid Vicky would return. 'I'm sorry if I hurt you. For using you. It was wrong of me.'

He shook his head, hands clenching and unclenching on the steering wheel. 'You need to get out, Claire. Vicky will be furious if she sees you here.'

'I don't really care if she is.' It was suddenly true. 'Anyway, I wanted to thank you for a lot of fun and the good times.' I recalled his thousand watt smile shining only on me, and how when this had all started, he made me laugh and added intrigue to my sometimes dull life.

'Please,' he said, voice breaking a little. 'Please leave before she comes back.' The tension had drained from his face, replaced with something gentler. A hint of remorse, or wistfulness.

I shrugged and reached for the door handle. As I pulled it, he muttered, 'I'm sorry too. Take care of yourself, Claire.'

I smiled quickly, surprised to find the words were sincere, and exited the car with as much dignity as I could muster. I didn't know why it had been important to say it, I'd certainly not given much thought to it in the intervening weeks. However I was glad I had done it.

For I was sorry. Sorry I'd used him as a weapon. Sorry I'd got involved with him. And sorry I'd once felt more for him than I'd ever expected. For that had not been my intention.

By early February I hadn't spoken to Will for nearly two months. I would text him daily and although I never received an answer, I could see he had read them. I had stopped begging for forgiveness, instead telling him about my day, my volunteering, silly stories from work. In his typical generous fashion, he had continued to pay the bills and allowed me to use my credit card as before. I had lost my passion for overspending on new clothes, make-up and the like. I retained my gym membership and bought fresh food I cooked from scratch and over time lost my scrawny, unhealthy pallor.

One evening I got an email from Airbnb to remind me it was nearly time for our trip to Crofters Cottage for Valentine's Day. I'd totally forgotten we'd booked it the last weekend we'd snuggled together there. Memories rolled unremittingly over me as I recalled our stay, when I had been embroiled in my deceptions and Will had unknowingly protected me from the worst excesses of my mind.

Spontaneously I decided to go on my own, the notion of a couple of nights away with the ocean outside the window enticing me. I could go after my morning at the woman's refuge, eat pub grub in the Stile and Donkey and walk by the restless ocean. Filled with positivity I planned my weekend with precision and debated for a time whether to include it in my daily texts to my unresponsive husband. Eventually I decided against it. I couldn't bear to reopen old wounds, for I wanted to protect him now rather than him protect me.

With help from the counsellor the GP referred me to, I began to understand I had taken Will and his love for granted, and I had sapped his good nature for everything I could. While once I had found it endearing, in the end it had become intolerable, and I had subconsciously fought against it. For he had placed me on a pedestal and I couldn't live up to his expectations. Rather, I had taken a wrecking ball to it.

On the Friday of Valentine's weekend, I drove along the now familiar coastal route, past the Stile and Donkey and yet again missed the concealed driveway. Cursing while smiling a little, I turned the car at the same point in the road and found it easily on the return.

The weather was stormy, wind whistled through the trees and stripes of grey were splashed across the sky. I got out of the car and inhaled the tangy air avidly. Tubs of early spring colour welcomed me at the door and I used the app to unlock it. I flung it open and the overpowering feeling of sorrow and loss swept through me as I entered the living area to find it unchanged. I wondered if I had been rash returning here alone. Then I caught sight of the sea through the front window and watched it, fascinated.

You'll be okay, I reassured myself.

You made your bed, now you've got to lie in it, the devil on my shoulder whispered.

I carried the cool box with my food into the kitchen, depositing it into the fridge, a bottle of white wine stuck carelessly into the door. I had reduced my drinking to a healthy level, unable and unwilling to abstain completely. Once I retrieved my case from the car, I shut it with a bang.

Reluctant to miss any more of the dying daylight, I went

straight outside for a walk. Only me, the beach and the gulls. Spontaneously I took a photo of the cottage and sent it to Will. Then I switched my phone off, incapable of watching the screen remain blank with the absence of reply.

I walked the length of the coastal path, along the harbour to the lighthouse. Rain fell untiringly now, and I breathed deeply while releasing my stress with each exhalation. Small boats tossed and turned angrily, and waves broke around the lighthouse as ripples sped across the bay. I strolled back towards the cottage and picked my way along the sand, dodging waves and seaweed.

The outside light shone dimly through the murk and I firmly closed the door behind me. I shrugged off my wet coat and stepped into the shower. I planned to have an early dinner at the Stile and Donkey and as I stood beneath the water, I reminded myself of all the good things in my life.

My daughters. Mum and Phil. My renewed relationship with Liz. Laura.

I had so much to be thankful for and I couldn't allow the negatives to drag me down.

Briskly I dried off, dressed in jeans and a sweatshirt, and went into the living room. There I futilely searched for my car keys, having forgotten where I'd set them. As I emptied the contents of my handbag onto the table, I was startled to hear wheels crunching over the stones on the driveway and the sweep of lights briefly illuminated the kitchenette window. Frightened, I stood uncertainly behind the table. I couldn't remember if I'd locked the door and my heart raced as I heard footsteps outside.

Before I could move, the door opened and cold air rushed in.

I'd forgotten how tall he was, and he was much thinner than before, but with the same gentle eyes, which were guarded now.

His look was reserved and I dug my nails into my palms, unable to speak.

Then Will smiled tentatively and calm flooded over me as it became clear.

He had forgiven the unforgivable.

Perhaps redemption was possible after all.

THE END

ALSO BY ALISON IRVING

Casual Cruelties

ACKNOWLEDGEMENTS

My thanks to Betsy, Fred and the Bloodhound team for their patience and continued faith in my work. A special thanks to Clare Law, Abbie Rutherford and Tara Lyons for their wisdom and advice which makes my writing better.

Thanks to Andy for his unfailing encouragement and support, and for always being there for me.

Thanks also to Alex and Jamie for being generally pretty awesome.

Mum, thank you for your never-ending encouragement and support. Dad, I wish you were here to share this.

The Troubles in Northern Ireland were a dark period in our history, when many families, including my own, lost loved ones. Every day I am grateful our small island has moved beyond those days, but I wanted to acknowledge the legacy of hurt left in the hearts of those who lived through them, and were affected by them.

Finally, this book explores the long-lasting consequences of school bullying, but it is not the exclusive domain of childhood or adolescence. For anyone who is experiencing bullying, there is help and support available:

nationalbullyinghelpline.co.uk
anti-bullyingalliance.org.uk
Samaritans.org

A NOTE FROM THE PUBLISHER

Thank you for reading this book. If you enjoyed it please do consider leaving a review on Amazon to help others find it too.

We hate typos. All of our books have been rigorously edited and proofread, but sometimes mistakes do slip through. If you have spotted a typo, please do let us know and we can get it amended within hours.

info@bloodhoundbooks.com

Printed in Great Britain
by Amazon

46383008R00169